FILE FOR RECORD

PHOEBE ATWOOD TAYLOR
WRITING AS ALICE TILTON

FILE
FOR
RECORD

A Leonidas Witherall Mystery

A Foul Play Press Book

THE COUNTRYMAN PRESS
Woodstock, Vermont

This edition is published in 1987 by Foul Play Press,
a division of The Countryman Press,
Woodstock, Vermont 05091.

ISBN 0-88150-101-8

Printed in the United States of America
By Capital City Press, Inc., Montpelier, Vt.

FILE FOR RECORD

Mr. LEONIDAS WITHERALL ignored the brown crusty crumbs that dripped off his gray tweed suit as he sat down at his study desk and plucked from a pigeonhole a sheet of notepaper on which was engraved in red letters: Forty Birch Hill Road, Dalton Center, Massachusetts. Like a Texas Ranger drawing his trusty Colt, he picked up a pen and determinedly dipped it into the tiny hollow silver bust of Shakespeare that served for an inkwell.

For more years than he cared to remember, people had been telling him how he resembled that inkwell, how he was the spitting image of the Bard himself. Leonidas now grimly hoped, as he poised his pen over the notepaper, that the kinship was more than skin deep. To do full justice to the bizarre narrative he had to write would require all the skill of Shakespeare, with added pinches of Dick Tracy, Baron Munchausen, and Houdini!

His pen bore down.

R. H. Haymaker, Esq.,
R. H. Haymaker and Company,
Main Street, Dalton, Mass.

DEAR SIR:

Leonidas paused. A letter sent directly to Haymaker's store would instantly involve that pretty elevator girl, since she was the only employee whom he could mention as having spoken to, and the only one who actually knew his errand. On the other hand, she was the last person to know more, and to expose her to any concerted pumping would be grossly unfair. Perhaps, after all, he ought to telephone Haymaker—except that pent-up, wrathful irritation poured forth over a phone always fell so short, and so flat. And sounded so unutterably foolish, to boot!

He surveyed the long loaf of French bread propped against the desk, took out a fresh sheet of paper, and made a new start.

R. H. Haymaker, Esq.,
101 Olde Forge Road,
Dalton Hills, Mass.

DEAR HAYMAKER—

Leonidas paused again. To the average crow, 101 Olde Forge Road was a scant mile from Birch Hill. Perhaps he should hike over and tell his story. But a vision of the slightly pompous Haymaker with his white

8

moustache quivering and his eyes bulging at the recital caused Leonidas to dismiss the thought as highly impractical. While Haymaker probably wouldn't even listen to more than the first few sentences, he'd at least read a letter through to the bitter end. Haymaker was a sucker for the written word. Throughout the directors' meeting that forenoon, Haymaker had urged people to put things in writing.

Snapping on the fluorescent desk light, Leonidas pondered. Should he start with the loaf of French bread, as his only tangible evidence of what had happened, or should he end with it, in proper chronological sequence? He decided it would be fruitless to confuse the issue by beginning with the end. Two hundred consecutive years in the drygoods business provoked a certain stilted and literal quality in a family's mode of thought. Their minds ran to yards, cards, bales, and scales. Generations of Haymakers had always sold the very best drygoods to the very best people, and they took both the process and themselves very seriously.

"Dear Haymaker," Leonidas murmured thoughtfully as he swung his pince-nez on their broad black ribbon, "I am at a loss to understand why your new director should be subjected to such a bizarre experience in his natural and—considering this afternoon's sudden downpour—completely justifiable attempt to track down and retrieve a forgotten umbrella from your Lost and Found Department—dear me, *that* will never do! It carps."

He put on his pince-nez, dipped his pen into Shakespeare again, and started to write.

DEAR HAYMAKER—

Following my first directors' meeting, I lunched with our mutual friend, Admiral Coe-Chester.

That was in the nature of a character reference, he thought. Coe-Chester was notoriously fussy about his luncheon companions.

Emerging into a violent shower, I recalled having left my umbrella, an aged but serviceable implement with a crooked briar handle and a knotted leather strap, either at the meeting or in the store. I therefore rushed across Main Street and dove into your emporium. After successfully infiltrating through a massed attack of several hundred women on a few pairs of all-silk stockings, I asked an elevator girl where I might find a misplaced umb—

In a gesture of irritation, Leonidas crumpled up the sheet of notepaper and tossed it into the leather wastebasket. You couldn't coldbloodedly boil the story down like that. You had to picture the setting of Haymaker's ground floor with its modernistic showcases and indirect lights, with ordinarily sane Dalton women battling like drenched fishwives over those silk stockings, with harassed Haymaker salesgirls and floormen trying to still the bedlam and keep the casualties—

both among the women and the stockings—to a minimum. You had to describe the red-headed elevator girl, who managed in spite of a military uniform with a Sam Browne belt to look as unclothed as Little Egypt.

"I have mislaid an umbrella," Leonidas had informed her politely. "Could you possibly tell me where—"

"Lost and Found, sixth floor. You sure need it," she added, eyeing his soaked coat. "What a rain! Cats and dogs."

Leonidas agreed, started to comment on the deafening din of the stocking warriors, and broke off as a brisk, pleasant-looking woman wriggled through the milling throng, approached the elevator and also asked where she might find a lost umbrella. Her white hair was tied up in a blue bandanna, and she wore tartan-plaid slacks and a belted, fur-collared trench coat. Mentally, Leonidas checked her off as the first middle-aged woman he'd ever seen who looked well in slacks. They half smiled at each other in that vaguely polite fashion of two people in a large elevator, and then the woman looked sharply at him. Leonidas, thoroughly accustomed to being told he looked like Shakespeare—more than one Shakespeare lover had pulled his beard, prodded him in the midriff, and asked if he were real —turned and studied the framed store guide and sales announcements on the elevator's grillwork. Ordinarily he rather enjoyed the chitchat that accompanied what his friends referred to as "The Dawn of Shakespeare" interlude. But after the directors' meeting and Coe-

11

Chester's rather distressing tidings, he didn't feel conversationally inclined. He wanted to retrieve his umbrella, hurry home, and get to work on the problem Coe-Chester had brought up.

They rode to the sixth floor in silence, except for the muted humming of the elevator girl, who slammed the doors after them and swooped back to the ground floor as if she were loath to miss a single minute of the silk-stocking war.

A sign with an arrow had pointed the way to the Lost and Found, and Leonidas slowly followed the woman past empty offices filled with battered golden-oak furniture which contrasted oddly with the rest of the store's sleek chrome and glass-mirrored modernity —and particularly with the red leather and solid mahogany of the directors' room on the floor above.

The Lost and Found Department turned out to be a bare counter in front of a golden-oak wall that was blank except for a glass-knobbed door. There was no clerk or attendant, nor any bell with which to summon one.

After a few minutes of silence, the woman, who had been staring at the glass-knobbed door, turned to him.

"I suspect," she said, "that everyone on this floor has been called down to help handle that stocking crowd. I'm in a simply terrific rush—I've got a cake to frost. Don't you suppose that the found things are behind that door? And couldn't we just open it and get our umbrellas ourselves? I assume you're after one, too, aren't you? It's the sort of day that makes you remember lost umbrellas. Anyway, couldn't we get 'em ourselves, or d'you think we'd better waste time finding someone?"

Before Leonidas could answer, she had lifted up the hinged counter and was turning the doorknob.

"Oh, damn!" she said. "It's locked. And I'm in such a hurry!"

"I'll ring for the elevator," Leonidas said, "and ask the girl to have someone sent up."

As he turned away, the woman started to say something, but when he paused inquiringly, she had waved him on.

"Never mind. It wasn't important. But *do* tell them to hurry, won't you?"

How long, Leonidas wondered as he stared at Shakespeare, had he actually spent pushing that elevator button? Certainly five minutes. Probably ten. Perhaps even longer. All he knew was that even now he could feel a slight soreness in his thumb where the button had left its imprint.

When it had become apparent that neither the redheaded elevator girl nor any of the others intended to pay the slightest whit of attention to the buzzer, Leonidas wearily turned back to the Lost and Found. It had been his intention first to explain the general situation to the woman, and then to walk up a flight and talk with R. H. Haymaker, himself. What was the use of having been made a director, he remembered think-

13

ing, if you couldn't get your mislaid umbrella back
with some degree of celerity? Next time Haymaker
confronted him with a demand for suggested improve-
ments, he could speak up with authority and announce
that the Lost and Found was far from peak efficiency.
It hadn't before occurred to him what power he now
wielded in this store. With a flick of his finger, he, the
owner of Meredith's Academy for Boys, could virtually
renovate R. H. Haymaker's Lost and Found!

"Regretfully, all the elevators seem to be on stri—"
Leonidas stopped short, whipped on his pince-nez,
and closely scrutinized the limited area of the Lost and
Found. Either the woman had crept into the golden
oak, or else she had melted into thin air.

At all events, she was gone!

Certainly, Leonidas thought, she couldn't have taken
any of the elevators. Had she walked down the stairs,
having given up her umbrella expedition as a bad job?
She couldn't have, he promptly told himself. In order
to reach the staircase, she had no alternative but to pass
by the elevators. And she hadn't. And surely she
couldn't have departed by way of the locked door!

While he stood there, peering around, he had become aware of a slight rustling sound beyond the
golden-oak partition.

"Er—did you," he raised his voice, "get in? Did you
manage to unlock the door?"

He lifted up the hinged counter, stepped forward,
and tried the knob.

The door was open, and he walked through.

And that, no matter how you chose to look at it, was that!

How could you properly describe the rest to Haymaker when you, yourself, didn't know what had happened, except for the lump on the side of your head?

Leonidas rubbed it pensively as he leaned back in his desk chair. With the passage of time it had lost some of its duck-egg aspect, but without doubt several days would pass before the bas-relief remnant would subside into a mere black-and-blue spot.

But like the loaf of French bread, the lump didn't prove anything. Any extraneous object might have been responsible, from a bedpost to a baseball to a brickbat. Haymaker would point that out. Haymaker would never concede that a lump like that could possibly come from his Lost and Found Department. Haymaker would argue, and with perfect reason, that a crusty loaf of French bread could be purchased at half the grocery stores in Dalton.

Obviously someone had biffed him as he passed through that magically unlocked golden-oak door. Who had biffed him and what he had been biffed with were matters of conjecture. It seemed reasonable to assume that the woman in the tartan slacks would hardly bother to waste the time to knock out a perfect stranger, particularly if she really were in a hurry to frost a cake. And she looked, Leonidas felt, like the sort of woman who well might have a cake to frost. She didn't in the

15

least look like a woman who made a practice of biffing her fellow men as they walked through golden-oak doorways in department stores.

How long *had* he been out?

Leonidas pursed his lips and considered. He had left the club and Coe-Chester around half past three. It was perhaps four o'clock when he went through that door. It was now quarter to six. He had been home perhaps fifteen minutes, and he had spent perhaps fifteen more in walking home. That meant that he had been unconscious from four o'clock until five, or thereabouts. That had been no sissy biff. His head still throbbed, although not as badly as it had when his eyes first opened, when it seemed that a thousand gremlins were thrusting tiny daggers into his eyeballs.

Besides the throbbing and the daggers, he recalled the sound to which he'd regained consciousness. Cloppety-clop, cloppety-clop, cloppety-clop. The un-mistakable sound of a horse's hooves, although with his head pounding and his eyes prickling, it had taken a bit of figuring to recognize the clops. And even more to realize that he was in a hamper. A large, wicker basketlike hamper. In something driven by a horse. A wagon, obviously. It seemed so simple, now, and yet Leonidas remembered with what difficulty he had men-tally hitched a wagon to the horse. That he should be in the vehicle bewildered him, he recalled, more than finding himself curled up like a shrimp in a wicker hamper full of crumbs.

The cloppety-clop had slowed down to a clop-clop, then to a clop, and then stopped entirely.

Leonidas alibied his hesitancy at that point by assuring himself gravely that he couldn't have been more than two-thirds or at the most three-fourths conscious. Clearly he should not have remained there, shrimplike, wondering what to say. But at the time the problem had appeared almost unsurmountable. Just what *did* one say? How *should* one address a person who had apparently thrust one into a hamper?

The sentence he'd finally decided on was no ringing tribute to his wit or to his intellectual agility.

"I beg your pardon, but would you be good enough to let me out?"

He felt as if he were shouting, but the words had materialized with a faintly muffled and indistinct quality, as if he'd been talking into a feather pillow.

He'd repeated it several times before he managed to achieve any volume. Then he'd pulled himself together, given a mighty shove, and popped out of the hamper like a jack-in-the-box.

He was in a small delivery wagon—surrounded by dozens of long loaves of French bread!

Fresh French bread, warm from the oven. He sniffed hungrily as he looked over the tailboard at the woods visible on either side of the tarred road. Birch trees, bare maples, oaks with tired, withered brown leaves —all of it a far cry from the golden oak he'd entered!

The driver's seat was empty, the reins hooked care-

17

lessly over a nail. The horse, a weary gray animal, craned his neck and whinnied, but whether the sound indicated surprise at his presence or whether it was merely a friendly greeting, Leonidas couldn't tell.

He couldn't tell, either, what impulse prompted him to pick up a loaf of the bread after he jumped out of the wagon. But he had. And while he brushed the crumbs off his suit, someone whistled. At once the horse, fired with sudden energy, started cloppety-clopping off up the road and around the corner, and out of sight.

Leonidas knew that he should have followed, that he should have located the driver, that he should then and there have delved to the root of the situation. But his head had started pounding again, and the gremlins returned to torture his eyeballs. Clutching his bread, he'd sat down on a wet log until the pain abated.

During those few painful moments, he recognized the wooded section as Dalton Hills, and realized that the wagon had been stopping at the foot of someone's service drive. Whoever had been carting him from Haymaker's Lost and Found all the way to Dalton Hills couldn't, he decided, have considered it a very remarkable expedition, if the person casually took time out along the way to deliver French bread! And how utterly absurd someone's orders must have sounded— providing the driver of the bread wagon *was* acting on orders.

18

"Oh, just dump Witherall in a crumby hamper, and drop him off with a loaf, will you?"

When his head had cleared, he'd tucked the bread under his arm and tramped home along the damp streets whose surfaces were plastered with oak leaves. Not until he turned up the path to his front door had the incredibleness of it all hit him with full force. To seek out a mislaid umbrella in the Lost and Found Department of Dalton's best and oldest department store—and to emerge, after an hour-long period of involuntary unconsciousness, on a rainswept road in Dalton Hills, in a wicker hamper surrounded by loaves of bread!

Who could have biffed him, anyway? Not the elevator girl. Not that woman—but where had she disappeared to? And who was she, anyway? He'd never seen her around in Dalton before, but of course the magnet of a silk-stocking sale might draw customers from Carnavon or Pomfret or Framfield, or any of the surrounding towns. Obviously he must have been biffed by someone on the apparently vacant sixth floor. Some hidden employee, perhaps? Could it mean that Haymaker's was already tiring of its new director, that this surreptitious biffing was the Haymaker method of indicating that he'd better resign forthwith? Perhaps biffing new directors was an old Haymaker custom, like ducking the coxswain of a winning crew.

Leonidas sighed and swung his pince-nez. He

19

couldn't phone the story to Haymaker. He hadn't the skill to write it properly. He'd therefore have to tell it, in person. To Haymaker himself, and to no one else. While the police might be considered his most logical confidants, they were the last people on earth whom Leonidas intended to tell. For the Dalton police were bears for publicity, and a story like his would provide them with a field day. And that would never do. Haymaker had talked very seriously at the directors' meeting about the good name and prestige of the store, and of the strenuous efforts being made to keep all the customers happy and contented in the face of most unhappy shortages, limitations, ersatzes, and just plain lacks. His experiences with the Lost and Found would not, Leonidas felt, inspire customer confidence and good will!

He would fortify himself with a small brandy and a hot bath, put on his best gray suit, have a bite of dinner, and then sally forth to Olde Forge Road.

"Bread!" he said aloud. "Why *bread?*"

Haymaker would ask that, too. Why should you end up with bread in a wagon, if you set out after an umbrella in a store?

Leonidas shrugged, turned off his study light, and went upstairs.

He had one foot in the tub when his front door chimes sounded.

Tossing a dressing gown over his shoulders, he went to the speaking tube at the head of the stairs.

"Yes?" The monosyllable was curter than he'd intended it to be.

"It's Mrs.—" He didn't catch the name that echoed hollowly back.

"Yes?" He was neither in the mood nor the costume, Leonidas thought irritably, to cope with a lady brush salesman, or a lady canvasser.

"I'm a friend of Cassie Price's," the voice went on breathlessly. "I've just run out of gas on the corner—"

He would not, Leonidas told himself firmly, nobly jump into the breach and offer to lend her a pint. Not even if she were Cassie's dearest friend!

"I'm on my way to the Victory Swop," the woman continued. "May I leave—"

What she wanted to leave jumbled into an unintelligible word, apparently Russian in its origin.

"Er—I didn't understand that," Leonidas said. And privately decided if it was a dog or a child, he was going to continue not understanding until she gave up and went away.

"Lady Baltimore." At least, that was the way it sounded on the second-floor landing. "May I leave it in your house while I go get my lawnmower gas tin? It's in a box, and it won't be any trouble, or in your way. But of course if you'd rather I didn't—" She was beginning to sound faintly annoyed.

"Oh, by all means leave it," Leonidas said politely. After all, if it—whatever "it" was—could be encased in a box, it could hardly be either a dog or a child.

"Unfortunately I'm taking a bath—perhaps you'll open the door when I click, and—er—leave it in the hall?"

He pressed a button, the door was shoved open, and a hand deposited a large white box on the blue figured Kabistan rug. Then the door was slammed shut.

Leonidas returned to his tub. For a Bostonian suburb usually described by news magazines as "Smug, stodgy, Buick-and-beachwagon-in-every-garage Dalton," he personally found the place far from stodgy. Or dull. Where else could you spend an afternoon as he had? Where else would strange women leave strange boxes named Lady Baltimore in your hallway while they rushed off to rob an innocent lawnmower of its rightful gas?

He had frankly feared that time might lie heavy on his hands when Meredith's Academy, which he'd inherited from his friend Marcus Meredith, had been turned into a naval communications establishment. But what he missed in the to-do of running the Academy was amply compensated for by all the other jobs he'd been acquiring, one by one. As Daltonians went to war, or to Washington, delegation after delegation called on him, and in the name of patriotism flung at him another post. He was now a director of the Golf Club, a director of the Dalton National Bank, the warden of Oakhill Sector A-1, vice president of the Community Chest, a director of Evans and Caswell, and of Haymaker's. Sometimes the extent of his activities appalled him.

But for all that had happened afterward, he thought with pride, he'd acquitted himself quite well at his first board meeting at Haymaker's. He'd swung his pince-nez and looked wise, and he'd never have had to say a word if Haymaker hadn't pointedly and directly asked him for suggestions. It had been a stroke of genius on his part, bringing up the accounting like that. He'd spoken with quiet dignity, like an ambassador in the movies.

"The accounts are all right, I suppose, and all that sort of thing?"

Everyone seemed quite pleased with him for mentioning the matter. Haymaker had scrawled vigorously on his memorandum pad and promised him an accounting practically at once. He'd coined a most useful phrase, Leonidas decided, one which he would employ at every directors' meeting where someone skidded around the thin ice of his ignorance on nonacademic topics.

The back door chimes rang as he stepped out of the tub. Someone rattled the door impatiently.

"Oil! Oil!"

Leonidas hurriedly pushed up the window and peered down into the darkness.

"My dear fellow, I was never gladder to see anyone!" he said with sincerity. "Shove in the round catch in the center of the cellar door knob, and go right down. The coupons are on the ledge by the tank. Grab

23

a bottle of beer on your way out. Grab two. I didn't expect you for a week."

Practically before he had the window down, the front door chimes rang again.

"Yes." Leonidas spoke without enthusiasm into the tube.

"Is Mr. Haymaker there?" a man's voice demanded.

"Mr. *Hay*maker? *R. H.* Haymaker?" Leonidas sounded as startled as he felt.

"Yes. Is he here? I'm after him."

"Frankly," Leonidas said, "so am I. But he's not here. Er—who's calling, please?"

There was no answer, and as he repeated the question, he heard the sound of a car being driven rapidly away from the front of the house.

"Never," he said to himself as he picked up his bath towel, "a dull or stodgy moment! Now *why* should that person have thought that Haymaker might be *here*, I wonder? Haymaker never called on me here in his life! Perhaps it's that lump on my head, but I'm definitely at a loss to understand any angle of this Haymaker situation!"

And it had to be solved before he could tackle that problem of Coe-Chester's, which he'd faithfully promised to look into at once!

He dressed rapidly, and as he gave his tie a final pat, his ears caught the woop-woop-woop of the Oakhill siren, which always sounded to him rather like a man giving a bad imitation of a sickly bullfrog. Holding his breath, he counted the woops and the pauses between them. Unless someone had flubbed the signals again, this was the wardens' Red-urgent call!

He leapt down the stairs four at a time, and grabbed up his tin hat, knapsack and whistle from the hall table. Then he rushed back upstairs, snapped off the bathroom light, and on the return trip missed putting both feet through the woman's white box by something less than an eighth of an inch. A moment later he had rolled his bicycle from the rack and was pedaling furiously toward his post. It was the Red-urgent, all right. The street lights had gone out.

He slowed down at the corner of Birch Hill and Oakhill long enough to blow his whistle violently at the Haverstraws, who were slightly deaf, and then he proceeded to the ridge from which he presumably had a bird's-eye view of his entire sector.

Almost at once the blue headlight of a bicycle, wavering from the exertions of a none too competent rider, appeared, drew nearer, and Leonidas heard the precise and faintly petulant voice of Henry S. C. Compton, his village warden.

"Witherall—I say, Witherall, are you there? I don't understand this at all, Witherall! It wasn't on *my* schedule."

"Perhaps," Leonidas suggested with a touch of irony, "it is—er—on someone else's schedule."

"I can't think whose!" Compton returned. "*I* wasn't told a thing about it! Not a thing! Be sure you make out the new report, Witherall—you have your new rubber stamp, haven't you? Remember, the report must be made out and in my hands within three hours after the All Clear. I'd prefer to have it sooner. I want headquarters to know that we're right on our toes up here!"

"M'yes, indeed." As Compton pedaled away, Leonidas found himself wishing that the man wouldn't worry so about reports. Nothing worthy of a report ever occurred on Oakhill A-1. And Compton had been very annoyed when Leonidas once obligingly tried to create a reportable incident by describing a slight brush between a skunk of A-1 and a Scottie that belonged to Warburton over on Oakhill A-2.

Leonidas absently watched the searchlights, noted that Elm Hill's had been moved to a better position, and wondered again why anyone should have expected to find R. H. Haymaker at his house. Could he— Leonidas's eyes narrowed—could he have been involved in something? Could that empty sixth floor have been due to a holdup, say? Could someone afterward have remembered him, the way people always did, as "The Man with a Beard"? If anything untoward had taken place, he was going to find himself in a most awkward position, not knowing for an hour what *had* taken place! He could be accused of all the crimes in the book, and be utterly unable to defend himself. Perhaps he'd better write his story down, after all, and have it ready in case of any emergency.

Haymaker had brought up at the directors' meeting the problem of keeping employees in the face of higher-paying war jobs. He'd mentioned having to bring back elderly saleswomen who'd been on the store's retired list for years, and he'd commented sadly on having to relax Haymaker's usual standards in hiring new clerks. Could someone of that elderly group have cracked under the strain of working again, perhaps even have gone berserk and caused some bizarre incident? Or had one of the dubious new employees taken it into his head to rob the store? Whatever might have happened, it still couldn't satisfactorily explain why he, personally, had come to in a hamper in a wagon, being delivered with someone's daily bread!

The siren went woooooooooop, in mournful triumph, the street lights flashed back, and Leonidas thoughtfully mounted his bicycle and started home. Without doubt that nervous little Mrs. Arlington had been at the Report Center again, and given, as usual, the wrong code word.

He stopped by the Haverstraws, blew his whistle until their living room light went on, and then hurried home.

He'd better write his story at once, he thought as he entered his study and snapped on the light.

Then he took a step backward toward the hall, and involuntarily put a hand out against the door jamb to steady himself.

There would be no need to write Haymaker anything.

For Haymaker was lying there before him on the rug, in front of his own study desk.

And Haymaker was dead. There was no doubt or

27

question about that. He had been stabbed by a sword whose handle and hilt were visible against the man's white shirt front.

Leonidas's head suddenly began to throb and pound as it had when he'd emerged from the bread wagon that afternoon. He heard the chimes of his front door dimly, as if they were miles away, and he realized vaguely that someone was entering the hall. Probably in his haste he'd forgotten to close the door tightly.

"Mr. Witherall! Oh, Mr. Witherall!"

The sound of his name being called out somehow magically cleared Leonidas's head. He swung around, and then whipped on his pince-nez.

The woman approaching him was the white-haired woman of the elevator, of the Lost and Found!

"It was good of you to let me leave my—" she stopped as her eyes, automatically turning toward the lighted room, caught sight of the figure on the rug. "Merciful heavens! That's Ross Haymaker!"

"M'yes," Leonidas said. "I know."

"That sword! He—he's been murdered!"

"M'yes," Leonidas said again. "I know."

"Will you tell me," the woman demanded coldly, "why you chose to kill him with my great-great-grandfather's samurai sword?"

CHAPTER 2

LEONIDAS deftly caught his pince-nez in mid-air as they practically bounced from his nose.

"And just exactly where," the woman went on, "did *you* get it?"

"Madam," Leonidas said courteously, "allow me to assure you that I did not kill Mr. Haymaker, that I found him here just two minutes before you—er—arrived, and that I neither have, nor ever in this wide world had, the faintest connection of any sort whatsoever with your great-great-grandfather's infernal samurai sword!"

"If you didn't," the woman returned, "*who* did?"

"If that samurai sword is one of your family heirlooms," Leonidas countered, "perhaps you are better able to answer that question than I."

"But I left it on my porch this afternoon!" she said. "Right beside the little fir tree in the tub! And look at it *now!*"

"I left my study," Leonidas said, "quite empty." He made a little gesture toward the floor. "And look at *it* now! Er—d'you mind telling me who you are?"

"Why, I *told* you when I left the cake!"

"Cake?" Leonidas looked at the white box by the front door. "You left *that*, and it's a *cake?*"

"Certainly. A Lady Baltimore cake. I told you so. I said I was Constance Lately, a friend of Cassie Price's, and that I was on my way to the Victory Swop when my car ran out of gas, and I didn't dare leave the cake in the car for fear it might get stolen before I could go filch the lawnmower's gas, so I could leave it here! I told you all that. I howled it into your speaking tube at the top of my lungs!"

"M'yes," Leonidas said, "I suppose you may have, but many of the details were blurred in transit. Er— you are really *quite* sure that's your sword?"

"I could pick that particular sword handle out of the ruins of Tokyo!" she said. "After all, it's hung on one wall or another of every house I've ever lived in, all my life. Some shogun gave it to my great-great-grandfather while he was helping Perry open up Japan. We used to display it with great pride, but after Pearl Harbor I packed it away out of sight. Yesterday I dug it out. I decided to see if anyone would swop anything for it, and if there weren't any offers, I'd give it for scrap. Someone told Arthur Case, and he phoned and said he'd like to see the thing. That's why, when I went downtown this afternoon, I left it on the porch. So that he could look at it if he came while I was away. I put it beside the little fir—Mr. Witherall, I simply can *not* stand here and talk about little potted firs with poor

Ross Haymaker lying there! Something has got to be *done!*"

"It is my intention to summon the police," Leonidas said. But before he could add, "as soon as you've told me where you disappeared to this afternoon," Mrs. Lately gave an anguished little cry.

"Oh, *dear!*"

She sounded so completely miserable that Leonidas put on his pince-nez and looked at her sympathetically.

"Er—were you," he inquired, "a particular friend of Mr. Haymaker's?"

"A particular fr—you haven't lived in Dalton very long, have you, Mr. Witherall?" she asked cryptically.

"Eight years."

"Oh, you barely know the streets, then!" Mrs. Lately said. "*I* was born here!"

"Er—I'm sure," Leonidas said, "that I've never seen you around, have I, until today?"

Mrs. Lately smiled. "My mother was a Dalton. One of the Daltons they named the place for—don't you know me, really? Haven't you even *heard* of me? Didn't Cassie write you that I was coming back to live in Aunt Kate's old house? When I left Cassie in San Francisco, her parting words were that she was writing you about me, and that I must look up Bill Shakespeare the minute I arrived. I've had you on my mind for weeks!"

"Cassie's last letter," Leonidas said, "was a very heavily censored epistle from Australia, where she was involved with the Red Cross. Possibly you were the censored part. And now I must phone for the police as soon as—"

"Wait, please!" Mrs. Lately said. "This is going to be a little complicated for me, and since the Dalton police don't seem to have changed much in thirty years, I'd like to straighten out a few things before they get here. You see—oh, this is *so* silly, having to dig this up again! But when I left Dalton thirty years ago, I ran away from Ross Haymaker!"

"Er—you ran away from him?"

"Yes, and I'd just been married to him, too. It really," Mrs. Lately said, "created rather a stir at the time. Bill Lately was Ross's best man, and I hadn't seen him before the wedding—he'd been in South America, and his boat was late. The minute I saw him in the church, I knew I was making a fatal mistake, and —well, Bill and I just ran away from the reception. Never regretted it for a moment, either. I hadn't seen Ross from that day till I came back. He was charming and so was I, but naturally there was a certain undercurrent. You see my point, Shakespeare—you really *do* look like him, don't you?"

"M'yes." Leonidas spoke almost absently. He had just caught sight of a paper protruding from Haymaker's coat pocket. A sheet of white notepaper with a familiar red-lettered heading. His own notepaper!

"If you hadn't been so distant in that elevator this afternoon," she went on, "I'd have commented on the

32

resemblance then, and told you who I was. Shakespeare, Cassie said if ever I got into trouble, I should come to you. She said you were very handy with problems— don't you *see* what'll happen if Ross is found with *my* sword in him?"

"M'yes," Leonidas said again.

"So before we call in the police, can't we somehow find out when he was killed, just so *I* might know where *I* was at the time? I've been rushing around all evening. And it's against the law, isn't it?"

"Murder? Definitely," Leonidas said. "The authorities resent it deeply."

"No, no, I mean stealing gas from lawnmowers! If they ask me where I was when Ross was killed, and I say that I was stealing gas from lawnmowers, that's not," Mrs. Lately said, "going to sound well!"

Leonidas agreed.

"And then there's Dunphy, that fat lieutenant at police headquarters," Mrs. Lately said. "The same Dunphy that Ross sent after Bill and me thirty years ago. You see, in my excitement I forgot to leave behind one of those classic 'I'm-deserting-you' notes, and for a while Ross simply thought I'd been kidnaped. We explained things to Dunphy when he caught up with us at the station, but thirty years haven't mitigated Dunphy's opinion of me in the slightest. And my brother—oh, I can't even dare contemplate what brother'll say! Bill Shakespeare, can't you *guess* when this might have happened?"

33

"Within the last hour and a half." Leonidas had been busily guessing for some minutes.

Mrs. Lately sighed. "No one on earth," she said despairingly, "could *ever* prove where I've been in the last hour and a half! I can only tell Dunphy I was snitching that gas, and ducking into bushes so wardens wouldn't spot me out in the blackout! You know I left the cake here, but you never actually *saw* me, and the fact that I was here at all is slightly awful. Bill, in stories people always know the time of a murder by looking at people's watches. They stop, or something. Could we—uh—could you look, perhaps?"

"The stopped-watch theory," Leonidas said, "is to a great extent a fictional device, and of dubious accuracy. A watch might not have been running anyway, or it might be stopped at any convenient time. I'm quite sure this must have taken place during the blackout while I was away from the house. You'll note that someone has taken the trouble to draw my study's blackout curtains. Someone, furthermore, has thrust into Haymaker's coat pocket a letter I started to write him, and which I later tossed into the wastebasket. While I fail to see what anyone may have gained by that action, I nevertheless doubt if anyone would paw through my wastebasket while I was home. However—"

He stepped into the study and carefully drew the coat sleeve back from Haymaker's left wrist.

A moment later he returned to the hall, and Mrs.

Lately looked at him in alarm as he hurried past her and carefully closed the half-open front door.

"Bill Shakespeare, what's the matter?" She followed him into the living room, where he jerked down the Venetian blinds and pulled the long drapes across the windows. "What's the *matter*?"

"While you," Leonidas said, "may with some justification feel that the long tentacles of fate have entwined themselves around you, and that the stout Dunphy all but has a noose draped around your neck, I have come to the reluctant conclusion that the noose was intended for me. Haymaker's watch was stopped at four-thirty!"

"At *four*-thirty?"

"No one on earth," Leonidas quoted her own words back at her, "could ever prove where *I* was at four-thirty this afternoon. Er—my particular bête noire in the police department is Sergeant O'Malley, who was called back from the retired list last year. I was returning from Pomfret with an overexuberant Meredith's Academy baseball team—it's too long a story to go into now, but nothing in the nature of a reconciliation has ever taken place between the sergeant and myself. He follows me like a dog about the streets of Dalton, wistfully hoping I'll disobey some antique law for which he can run me in. He is a master of obsolete laws, the baseball team and I found out."

"I know O'Malley," Mrs. Lately said reminiscently. "I once threw a green tomato at him."

35

"The baseball team," Leonidas said, "preferred the overripe variety. O'Malley is going to look at Haymaker's watch and ask me where I was at four-thirty. I can only honestly say I don't know. Then he will look at that letter in Haymaker's pocket and ask why I was writing Haymaker. And just the thought of trying to explain this afternoon to O'Malley congeals me." He leaned against the arm of a red leather chair. "Er—*you* wouldn't happen to know where I was at four-thirty, would you?"

Mrs. Lately drew a long breath and sat down on the sofa before the empty fireplace. "I don't know," she said in a small voice, "where *I* was!"

A light dawned in Leonidas's eyes. "Did you," he asked eagerly, "by any chance come to in a bread wagon, with a lot of crusty French bread?"

"It was a laundry. At least, an alley back of it. I was in a sort of canvas hampery thing on wheels, with a lot of dirty linen strewn over me! Oh, I'm so glad to be able to tell someone about this!" she said. "I thought I'd have to go to the grave with the episode locked in my bosom! If it had happened in any other store but Haymaker's, I'd have rushed back and raised the roof and six riots, but of course I *couldn't* face Ross! I simply couldn't. Not with a story like *that*!"

"Er—what happened?" Leonidas asked interestedly.

Mrs. Lately shrugged. "I don't know! After you left to get someone, I heard a noise behind that golden-oak door. Then I saw the handle slowly turning—it was

36

the eeriest thing! I called out and asked if anyone were there, and no one answered. I suppose a more cautious person would have called you, but I just lifted up the counter and of all things, that door was unlocked! I opened it and went in, and that's all I know."

"Someone biffed you?"

"They certainly did, and I have a horrid lump to prove it. Oh, I never should have gone into Haymaker's in the first place! The only reason I did was that I'd got caught in that downpour without an umbrella, or a single cent, and the bank was closed, and I couldn't bring myself to buy another umbrella—I have ten at home I've bought for sudden storms. I yearned to borrow cab fare from you, but you were so distantly engrossed with your own thoughts, I didn't dare speak up in the elevator."

"Er—hadn't you really lost an umbrella at all?" Leonidas inquired.

"No, I was just going to ask for a black umbrella with a funny handle and take what was offered—d'you mean *you* were biffed, too?"

Leonidas briefly told her his story, and at its conclusion they were both silent.

"What," Mrs. Lately said at last, "does it all *mean?*"

"I have not," Leonidas said truthfully, "the remotest idea. But I feel sure Haymaker was not killed at four-thirty. I'm certain he was killed here while I was at my post. I can only regretfully conclude that whoever killed him also happened to know it would be next to impossible for me to explain my whereabouts at four-thirty with any degree of satisfaction."

"But the police, or the medical examiner—*some*one can actually tell the exact time, can't they?"

"Ultimately," Leonidas said. "But in the interim, we have before us a long and probably very tedious interval with Dunphy and O'Malley, and rather an—er—extensive assortment of headlines. How did you get home from the laundry alley?"

"I walked. I felt dazed, and I didn't really want to walk, but after I got started, I felt all right again. Besides, I was in a rush to frost that damned cake. Losing that coffee is a bit of a tragedy, too!"

"Coffee?" Mrs. Lately, Leonidas thought, had Cassie Price's mental habit of leaping beyond you like a rabbit.

"There was a well-founded rumor that Mrs. Pell would swop a pound of coffee for a genuine prewar Lady Baltimore cake, and everyone I know has spent the day hopefully using up all their sugar making one," Mrs. Lately explained. "For this Victory Swop thing tonight, you know. I wanted to get there first. I had some notion of sitting on the steps of Lyceum Hall with my cake in hand, ready to pounce on her. See here, you don't honestly think this is a *plot*, do you?"

"I fail to see," Leonidas said, "how it can very well be anything else. Was the sword still on your porch when you arrived home?"

"I never looked to see. I was so angry about being

biffed and not being able to *do* anything about it. My only consolation was thinking of the headlines I missed by being so restrained. I thought 'em up while I frosted. 'Errant Bride Who Deserted Haymaker Three Decades Ago Claims Foul Play in Lost and Found.' 'Widow of Ex-Husband's Best Man Comes To in Laundry Hamper. Constance (Pink) Lately says Mind Utter Blank.' Look, I understand why I couldn't tell anyone, but why didn't you go straight to Ross, or to the police?"

"That half-written letter in Haymaker's pocket is my explanatory effort," Leonidas told her. "As a Haymaker director, I naturally never considered the police."

"You're a director? Then you must know Ross well!"

"On the contrariwise, I know him very slightly. But as one of the few Daltonians left home from the war, I'm in great demand. In fact," he added, "if I'm involved with a murder, it's going to play hob with a lot of directorates and boards."

"What *are* we going to do? We ought to do something, Bill Shakespeare, right away! You know, I really feel sorrier about this than you may suspect. I always liked Ross. I'd probably have been very happy with him if Bill hadn't appeared on the scene. I think this is a simply frightful thing—and I only wish I could delude myself into thinking Dalton's forgotten me and won't dig up my youth. What'll we *do?*"

"Just solve it ourselves, and then summon the police," Leonidas ignored her startled exclamation. "If I'd not come directly home from post A-1, if—say—I'd gone to the Victory Swop, I never should have known Haymaker was here, because I shouldn't have found him. It's possible I might not have returned from the Victory Swop till quite late. I might not have found him till three or four o'clock this morning."

"But you can't—"

"Therefore," Leonidas blandly continued, "I think you and I will go to the Victory Swop, establish ourselves as being there, and then we'll just set to work and solve this. Then we can, at some later time, present the police with both a murder and a solution. There will be no need to bring up your past, or to jeopardize my directorial future."

"But we can't! *We* can't solve a *mur*der!"

"Oh, I rather think we can. I've done it before, as Cassie may have told you."

"But we have no clues!"

"We have a magnificent clue," Leonidas returned. "We are quite sure that whoever biffed us on the sixth floor is very probably involved."

"And how d'you expect to find out who that was?" Mrs. Lately demanded with asperity. "Why, it might be *any*one!"

"It's amazing," Leonidas said lightly, "how things work out. Great oaks, and all. First I want to phone Haymaker's house and find out when he came home from the store, and, if possible, what time he left there this afternoon. He has a very chatty maid. I've spoken with her before."

40

Mrs. Lately followed him out to the hall telephone and eyed him dubiously while he carried on a lengthy conversation with Haymaker's maid.

"He never came home from the store at all," Leonidas reported when he finally set down the receiver. "He phoned around four that he was leaving the office and going to the club, that he wouldn't be home for dinner, and that he might be quite late."

"Why are you so happy about it? What does that prove?"

"It proves definitely that the person who biffed us is the person who killed Haymaker," Leonidas said. "Who else would be able to make that subtle connection of stopping his watch at exactly four-thirty? That was really a brilliant touch. Safely halfway during the period when I might be expected to be in a comatose state, you see, and yet allowing Haymaker a good theoretical half hour to get here from the store. Hm. My house was picked for the scene of the crime, a time was picked which would leave me at an utter loss —indeed, Mrs. Lately, I'm beginning to think that someone dislikes me nearly as much as he dislikes Haymaker!"

"I point out to you that someone bears me no particular love!" she said. "After all, it's my sword!"

"Ah, the sword," Leonidas said. "That's something we should settle right now. D'you live very near Haymaker on Olde Forge Road?"

"Really, it's the next house. When I decided to take

41

over Aunt Kate's, I frankly didn't know he lived there. My good brother was frightfully shocked. But as far as actual distance goes, I'm at least four hundred yards away on the corner."

"A rambling white house? M'yes, I know it. Suppose, now," Leonidas said, "that someone is waiting for Haymaker to come home—we'll assume it's after four, and he's already coped with us on the sixth floor. Now, he knows that Haymaker walks home—"

"How d'you know he does?" Mrs. Lately interrupted.

"He told every last director about his patriotic walks to and from work," Leonidas said, "and I'm sure he tells everyone. Yes, your corner would be an excellent spot to wait for and intercept Haymaker, either in a car, or on foot. You left the sword on end, did you not?"

"Why, yes. I stuck the point down between two boards so Arthur would see it standing there. I'd forgotten I did that—how did you guess?"

"It wouldn't be noticed otherwise. M'yes, if someone was waiting for Haymaker on your corner, he'd be inclined to see your sword sticking up. If he had murder in mind, he was probably opportunist enough to go get it, without being observed. And if, to boot, he'd just thrust you into a laundry hamper, he might feel that taking your weapon was rather a smart gesture. M'yes, indeed!"

Mrs. Lately looked at him and shook her head.

"How can you stand there, making assumptions left

42

and right," she said, "dreaming all this up out of whole cloth when you haven't an ounce of proof or evidence or anything else! It's sheer fantasy!"

"Dear lady, we haven't the time to waste in laborious pondering," Leonidas returned. "We are not Oscar Wilde, taking half a day to insert one lone comma, and half a day to remove it! Before we get to work, it's only logical for us to pluck from thin air as many shreds as we can. We know that our villain was on Haymaker's sixth floor around four, we know he was on your corner some time after—"

"Wait!" she interrupted. "While you're gaily making assumptions, you're leaving out important details! If he went to my corner from the sixth floor, then *who* took us away from there in our respective hampers?"

"To prove my theory about that," Leonidas said, "may possibly require getting into Haymaker's later."

"By getting in," Mrs. Lately's voice brimmed with suspicion, "d'you mean *break*ing in?"

"Just getting in," Leonidas said blandly. "I've no intention of smashing in a plate-glass window, I assure you. I rather think that after biffing us, our villain thrust us into the nearest large receptacles he could find, and that later, somehow, some perfectly legitimate person, whose duty it was, removed them, and us. If it should transpire, for example, that the employees' restaurant is on the sixth floor, I could understand why both a laundry hamper and a breadbasket might be there in close conjunction. We shall endeavor

43

to find out. Now," he added, "we must get started—dear me, *what* can I swop?"

"Shakespeare!"

"I've been cleaned out," Leonidas said, "of copper, tin, brass, nickel, iron, steel, and rubber. It narrows one down—ah, I have it! Cousin George's Dahlia Cup!"

"Bill Shakespeare," Mrs. Lately said, "are you really serious in this *mad*—this in*sane*—this—this—"

"If you mean, do I intend to find out who murdered Ross Haymaker," Leonidas said, "certainly I do! I should feel a similar obligation toward anyone who had the misfortune to meet murder on my premises, even if he were not in a sense my employer, and even if I were not in a sense involved. First, however, we must go to the Victory Swop. That Dahlia Cup will be ideal. It's small and portable, yet solid silver. It was the Pompom First for 1920, as I recall, and Cousin George—"

"We *can't!*"

"We've *got* to go to the Victory Swop," Leonidas said, "to establish the fact that I'm not home—I thought we covered that rather carefully. We can leave, don't you see, bearing our swops. And at intervals return. There is nothing like a large public gathering to establish an alibi. Particularly one with a patriotic aura. Hm. I need several other small items—why, Mrs. Lately, you seem discouraged!"

He looked at her solicitously as she sat down on a footstool by the hall table.

"I will not move," she said defiantly, "until you've explained things more—how could anyone take those hampers away with us in 'em and not know we were in 'em?"

"If you pushed hampers around for a living," Leonidas said, "I doubt if you'd inquire too much into their contents. I dare say some stalwart Haymaker porter rolled us on to the freight elevators. We descended, and were rolled elsewhere. I wonder what anyone would give for a few volumes of Haseltine?"

"But if we'd sensibly gone to the police, or Ross, or someone, our villain would have been in a terrible hole!"

"Ah, but we didn't. Very possibly someone suspected we wouldn't. And even if we had, we couldn't accuse anyone. Did you ever read the adventures of Lieutenant Haseltine?"

"My sons did. They still do—look, how can we find out about motives?"

"We may assume," Leonidas said, "that someone will benefit by Haymaker's death. In due course, we'll try to find out who inherits the Haymaker store, the Haymaker money, and the various Haymaker properties and enterprises."

"How?"

"We will delve, hither and yon. And now, if you're satisfied, shall we make ready to go? We have much to do—first to the Victory Swop. Then to Haymaker's—

45

probably the nightwatchman can tell us who pushes hampers, and we can seek the person out. And I'd like to learn which oil driver called here—he may have seen someone lurking around. Hm. I wonder if Haymaker's lawyer might possibly be mesmerized into telling us his chief beneficiaries! And *how* I wonder who actually called here asking for Haymaker! Was he checking up on my presence, or did he hope, by mentioning Haymaker's name, to learn if I'd seen him? I should have looked into him then!"

"*What* oil driver?" Mrs. Lately said. "*Who* called here? It's the first I've heard of them!"

"They were bath interruptors. Then, of course, there was the blackout. I'll have to find out just how bona fide that was—"

At the sudden sound of the front door chimes, both of them jumped.

"We'll ignore it," Leonidas whispered. "My first public appearance after manning post A-1 is going to be at the Victory Swop with you!"

Someone pounded on the door.

"Witherall! Oh, Witherall! Witherall, it's Henry Compton!"

Mrs. Lately rose from the footstool and clutched at Leonidas's arm.

"My brother!" she breathed the words in his ear. "He *must*n't find out about Ross and that sword!"

"Witherall!" Compton yelled, and then banged

46

again at the door. "I want your report for the record!"

"And if I know my dear brother," Mrs. Lately murmured, "he'll get in if he has to pound your door down! Bill, he must *not* get in!"

Leonidas put a finger to his lips, tiptoed over to the speaking tube by the foot of the stairs, and pushed back the round metal lid.

Compton was talking with someone who was apparently on the sidewalk.

"Oh, he must be here! I think his lights are on—I can see a crack under the door. Have you made out your report, Beeding?"

Leonidas could just hear the dull rumble of Major Beeding's voice without catching any of his words.

"Fine, fine!" Compton said heartily. "Capitol! Leaves only Witherall. He's very careless about his reports. I have to be after him every time. No excuse for his being so careless!"

"My dear brother," Mrs. Lately whispered, "hasn't changed a bit in thirty years!"

The chimes skipped a few notes under Compton's impatient thumb, the door was banged and the knob rattled, and Compton continued to shout.

Finally, at the end of ten minutes, he departed.

Mrs. Lately drew a long breath. "Not until I heard brother's voice," she said, "did I fully realize my alternative. I think you're stark mad, Bill Shakespeare, but let's get on to the Victory Swop and embark on this

47

mad expedition before Henry comes back—because he *will* come back, you know! Probably with a battering ram under his arm."

"M'yes," Leonidas said, "I have a horrid feeling that he means to pursue me for that report—and I certainly don't intend to take time out at this point and pen him a few lines about Haymaker's being stabbed in my study with his—er—family sword. Er—while you did mention a brother, I must admit I—er—"

"He's equally loath," Mrs. Lately said, "to acknowledge me as his sister. But I know what you mean. He affects me the same way. Mother, too. She spent a dutiful two weeks with Henry every year, and then rushed back to me and the five noisy Lately boys like a lifer let out of Sing Sing. Go get your Dahlia Cup and the Haseltines before Henry returns!"

"At once." But halfway up the stairs, Leonidas paused. "Er—did you say *five* Lately boys?"

"Yes. When the fifth one went into the Marines, I decided to come back to Aunt Kate's. I thought I'd rattle less. Will you hurry? And don't put on any lights! They'd draw Henry like a moth."

Five minutes later, while Leonidas groped for the Dahlia Cup in an upper-hall storage closet, Mrs. Lately silently appeared behind him.

"Bill," she said breathlessly, "there's someone in the cellar!"

"The *cel*lar?" As his fingers closed over the handle of the Dahlia Cup, Leonidas had a sudden vision of a

48

careless oil man leaving the door open. "Oh, dear me!"

"Sssh! Come down and listen—oh, Bill, if it's Henry Compton!"

"Let us," Leonidas's fervent whisper was almost a prayer, "hope not!"

"What'll we do if it is?"

Leonidas gripped the silver cup and said nothing. It would distress him to be forced to take severe measures with Mrs. Lately's own brother, but if the worst occurred, he had a laundry hamper, himself!

He should have checked up on that cellar door, he told himself firmly as he tiptoed after her down the stairs. He should have given some attention to the problem of how Haymaker and his murderer might have gained entrance. He should not have taken it for granted that he'd probably left the front door ajar when he rushed off to post A-1.

"Listen! Hear that?"

Leonidas heard a sound, but it didn't come from the cellar, and he relievedly said so.

"It's from the front. The front steps. I think Henry's returned," he whispered in her ear, "but thank heaven, he is not in the cellar! I wonder if—wait here while I take a look!"

He tiptoed upstairs to the west bedroom and craned his neck.

A moment later, he was back at her side.

"Your brother," he said grimly, "is *camped* on my top step. Complete with tin hat and arm band!"

49

"But, Bill, he's not the noise I heard first! I just heard it again, and it *is* down cellar! I'm absolutely sure of it!"

Leonidas closed his eyes and strained his ears.

"There!" Mrs. Lately nudged him. "Then—did you hear it *then*? I tell you, it's from the *ce*llar!"

Leonidas shook his head. "Back door," he said. "Not cellar. Hm. D'you suppose your good brother brought a friend to help lay siege?"

"It came from the cellar!"

"Back door. Follow me into the kitchen, and I'll prove it to you. I'll have to snap out the hall light," Leonidas whispered, "because I'm sure the kitchen shades aren't pulled down. Grab hold of my coat, and don't let your elbow hit against anything that might knock over and bang—"

Mrs. Lately giggled as they proceeded into the kitchen.

"Sssh!" Leonidas said severely.

"I can't *help* it, this is *so* silly!"

"Sssh!" Leonidas tiptoed across the linoleum floor to the kitchen sink, then climbed up on the ledge and peered out the kitchen window.

Certainly there was a figure looming on his back steps!

"*I* hear, now," Mrs. Lately whispered. "Who is it, Bill? Where is he?"

She climbed briskly up on the ledge beside him, and Leonidas pointed.

A match flared suddenly to a cigarette tip, a face was lighted up, and the pair on the ledge just barely managed to choke back startled exclamations.

"O'Malley!" Mrs. Lately whispered. "It's O'Malley!"

Another match flared, and another face appeared.

"Dunphy!" Leonidas said.

CHAPTER 3

"WHAT IN the wide *world* would make *that* pair choose *this* time," Mrs. Lately murmured irritably, "to cluster around *your* back door? W*hy*—"

"Sssh!" Leonidas whispered. "There are more!"

"More? There can't be!"

Leonidas pointed. "See?"

A moment later, two more cigarette tips glowing in the back driveway materialized into two more cops.

"What are they saying?" Mrs. Lately demanded in an urgent whisper. "D'you suppose they know about Ross? If we could only *hear* them!"

"Shush!" Leonidas reached up and slid open the segmented ventilator set into the upper part of the kitchen window.

"So Haverstraw still thinks his prowler was after coming this way?" Dunphy's question to the newcomers floated into the kitchen with a gust of sharp October air.

"Yeah, he's sure. He says the fellow run out of his cellar when he went down to get some wood, and he come over towards this way."

"Then," Dunphy said philosophically, "we might as well be waiting here out of the wind as anywheres else, I'm after thinking. You two boys go take yourselves another prowl around, and me and O'Malley'll be keeping a sharp lookout from these steps here."

Leonidas closed the ventilator and quietly climbed down from the ledge.

"What'll we do now?" Mrs. Lately asked as she followed suit. "How can we get *out?*"

Leonidas led her back to the front hall before answering.

"I care almost less about our getting out," he said, "than about the possibility of their getting in! Frankly, I wouldn't put it past those two to sneak in and make themselves cozy in the kitchen!"

"But with Henry at the front door, and with them at the back, we're—we're surrounded, or encircled, or immobilized, or something, aren't we?"

"To a high command," Leonidas said, "we would be ostensibly bottled. But we have an excellent avenue of escape in the garage door. Unless, of course, someone has taken it into his head to wait there for a street car. Now, I have the Dahlia Cup, and a Haseltine book in either pocket of my trench coat. Let us gather up—er— Lady Baltimore, and see if we can't manage to slip out. I rather think that we can."

"But is it safe?"

"Er—fully as safe," Leonidas assured her, "as remaining here. We can't be found here now. I'm afraid

53

we've already burned all our bridges, Mrs. Lately."

"Under the circumstances, I don't think you need to be so formal," she said. "My friends call me Pink."

"Give me Lady Baltimore, Pink," Leonidas said. "The box is a bit bulky, and I know the stairs to the cellar better than you do. Is your car at the corner of Birch Hill and Walnut Hill? Fine. We'll make for it."

"But there's less than a gallon of gas!" she warned him.

"If there's enough to remove us from the vicinity of your brother," Leonidas said, "that will be more than ample. Now *do* be very careful going down, Pink. We can't put on a light. The turn is at the sixth or seventh stair and watch for the last step. It has a deceptively short rise. Ready?"

She giggled softly as he opened the door and they started down.

"I keep thinking of those idiotically blood-curdling adventures of Lieutenant Haseltine," she whispered. "I *feel* like something out of Haseltine, all of a sudden —did you ever listen to the radio version that begins with thunder and bugles and a man yelping 'HASEL-tine to the RES-cue!'?"

"M'yes, indeed, I know it well." Under happier conditions and on a less precarious flight of stairs, Leonidas reflected, he would break down and confess that among his friends, this very house was known as "The House that Haseltine Built."

"These are *easy* stairs, Bill!"

54

"I'm down." Leonidas started across the linoleum floor, and then stopped as he heard the sudden muted thud of Pink falling.

He groped out, found his carpenter's bench, put the cakebox on it, and then hurriedly tiptoed back to her.

"Are you hurt?" he whispered solicitously.

"I *fell* on something!"

"You haven't sprained an ankle!" Leonidas almost forgot to keep his voice down.

"No, no! I fell on a mink coat."

Leonidas found himself blinking.

"On a *what?*"

"On a mink coat," Pink whispered. "M-i-n-k c-o-a-t." She spelled it out. "Now, help me up!"

"Never," Leonidas said, "did I ever keep a mink coat in my cellar!"

"Perhaps you never did, but there's one here now. It's a coat, and it's mink. Feel it."

Leonidas reached out a hand. It *was* a coat, and it was certainly fur.

"*Mink?*" he asked uncertainly.

"My dear man, there are some things I can tell in the dark, and a mink coat is one of 'em! Help me up. I'm caught in the sleeve, and I'm sitting on your beastly Dahlia Cup."

"*Who* left it here?" Leonidas asked blankly.

"I did, I dropped it—oh, you mean the coat? *I* don't know," Pink said. "I certainly shouldn't leave it on your cellar floor if it were mine!"

"It's perfectly extraordinary!" Leonidas had to remember to lower his voice again. "Amazing! Presumably the only person who came down here was an oil
man— I know all three of the drivers by sight, and I
know they don't wear mink coats! Their usual costume
is dungarees and visored caps and zippered coats with
'Quarl's Quality Oil' tattooed on the back—what did
you say?"

"I said, at long last I've found what I've been wanting," Pink told him. "I've stumbled on a clue. A tangible clue!"

"You—" Leonidas broke off as something, somewhere in the corner, made a series of gurgling sounds,
then gave a thwarted rattle, and then abruptly sub-
sided.

"Bill!" Pink scrambled to her feet and clutched
his arm. "What was *that?*"

"That," Leonidas said sadly, "was my oil burner, going out from lack of fuel. It's a sound I've regretfully
learned to recognize."

"But you said your oil man came!"

"Evidently I erred," Leonidas said, "in assuming that
the person who yelled 'oil' was an oil man. Dear me,
how I yearn to flip on the lights and search this place.
I wonder if it would be safe to grope."

"Grope?"

"While it's admittedly a repulsive thought, someone must belong to this coat," Leonidas pointed out,

56

"and as you suggested, it's nothing one would ordinarily leave behin—"

"Want the lights to go on?"

The voice that interrupted him did not belong to
Pink!

Although Leonidas instantly grasped the fact, it took
him several seconds to digest it thoroughly. Beside
him, he could feel Pink stiffen, like a cat arching her
back.

"Er—I beg your pardon?" Leonidas asked politely
in the general direction of the voice.

"I said, d'you want the lights to go on?"

It was a clear, young-sounding contralto voice, and
it belonged to someone over near the oil burner.

"Er—the lights?" Leonidas said.

"Stop playing for time! If you make a move toward
me, I'll flip on the lights—or didn't you know the cops
were outside?"

A ghastly vision of the inevitable chain of events
appeared suddenly to Leonidas. Scene after scene
flicked rapidly through his mind.

Lights. Onrush of police. Instant advent of Henry
S. C. Compton from the front steps. Must make out
post A-1's report, at once, without fail, immediately!
Rubber stamp in desk drawer in study. Can't keep
Compton out of study. Can't keep anyone else out,
either. My God, that's Ross Haymaker! Great-great-
grandfather's samurai sword! Did youse know this man

57

was here, huh? Whyn't you call headquarters, huh? Where was you after being at four-thirty, Mr. Witherall, huh? Huh? In a hamper, huh!

"My finger's on the light switch," the contralto voice went on inexorably.

"Take it *off!*" Pink sounded as though she, too, had been seeing visions.

"Exactly. Er—remove it," Leonidas said. "Remove it at once. Er—just what do you wish?"

"I want my coat!"

"I don't blame you," Pink said promptly. "Anyone would. I covet it, myself. Come get it—oh, come on! We have absolutely no intention of making a single move that might bring those silly fat cops down on us!"

By her hesitancy, it was evident that the girl mistrusted them deeply.

"Come, come!" Pink said impatiently. "I'd take it to the door and leave it there for you, except that I don't know where the door is! Get your coat and run along —we're in just as much of a hurry to leave as you are!"

"M'yes, indeed," Leonidas added. "Er—by the way, how'd you happen to be here?"

"I came for my coat!"

"Are you the prowler they're after?" Pink inquired.

"Wh-what makes you think I am? No! No, of course not!"

Of course she was, Leonidas thought!

"Well, I can't dangle this coat toward you much longer, my arm's breaking in two," Pink said. "If you

58

don't grab it pretty quick, I shall be tempted to call the police, myself!"

The girl darted from the corner and snatched it from Pink's hand.

"If you follow me, I'll scream!" She ran toward the door, opened it, and fled.

"While that got rid of her," Leonidas said thoughtfully, "I'm not at all sure we should have permitted such a hasty exit—I gather, however, that you have some inkling of her identity?"

"I haven't the faintest idea who she is!"

"But—"

"I simply did my best," Pink said, "to be pleasant, and give her the coat, and get her out—but I'll know her again, Bill! She's about five feet four—her arm was on a level with mine when she grabbed the coat. And of course she's blonde."

"How'd you know that?" Leonidas demanded.

"Why, by her perfume! It's for blondes. It has a number. Four-fifty-one," Pink said. "My son Pogo spent all last winter pursuing a blonde child who reeked of it. I can tell this girl again by that. Easily."

"We can hardly—er—sniff our way through the younger sets of Dalton and vicinity," Leonidas said, "in an effort to establish her identity. Frankly, I'm disappointed. I shouldn't have permitted her to get away if I hadn't felt from your attitude that you knew her, or at least guessed who she was."

"I'm sorry," Pink said contritely. "My only desire

59

was to have her get away from that light switch and out of the cellar. If Henry Compton were *your* brother, you'd understand better why I wanted her out of the way before she caused any commotion! But don't be unhappy about her, Bill. Few blondes in Dalton these days wear mink coats so casually that they leave 'em in cellars. Someone at the Victory Swop will recognize her description. If they don't, a few phone calls will solve her. Besides, I think she was telling the truth. I believe her. I think she really did come here for her coat."

"I'm sure she did," Leonidas said. "What perplexes me is when she left it and why she left it, and how she happened to leave it. And, if she was Haverstraw's prowler, what was she doing over in their cellar when her coat was here? And what could she have been doing here in the first place?"

"Oh, dear, I never once thought of all those ramifications!" Pink said. "I only thought of Henry Compton's face—Bill, I saw an oil woman the other day! Perhaps she was an oil *woman!*"

"In," Leonidas said, "a mink coat?"

"Well," Pink said defensively, "I'm only trying to think of helpful things! If this were a book, she'd turn out to be a ward of Ross Haymaker's, and he would have lost all her money in the stock market, or frittered it away in riotous living or something. And it would turn out in the last chapter that she killed him for revenge. Only she didn't sound to me like any very sinister character, Bill. I think she was really a lot more afraid of us than we were of her."

"I have heard that same statement," Leonidas remarked, "applied to rats, skunks, and numerous poisonous reptiles."

Pink sighed. "I still think she simply came for her coat. She had such an *honest* voice!"

"One of Lieutenant Haseltine's greatest peacetime problems," Leonidas said, "is Vincent Rumleigh, whose honest voice is constantly extracting valuable securities from widows and orphans of means. Let us, however, look on the brighter side. If she got away without causing any trouble or fanfare, the coast must be clear. Have you still got my Dahlia Cup? Good."

After retrieving Lady Baltimore from the carpenter's bench, he guided Pink across the cellar to the door leading into his garage.

"Now a step down," he said, "and now out this other door here—dear me, how well that girl must have known this layout, to have darted out as efficiently as she did! Carefully, please—we'll cross the driveway to the lilac clump, and then circle around the house."

They had barely reached the bushes when a scrunch of gravel behind them caused Leonidas to turn his head quickly.

A man had just stepped out of the doorway through which they had just emerged!

"Bill—look!"

Almost before the words were out of Pink's mouth,

the man had sprinted down the driveway and out of sight.

"Bill, did you see *that?*" Pink said breathlessly. "Bill, there was someone *else* in there with us, all the time! Bill, I'll wager *he* was the Haverstraw's prowler—don't *you* think he was?"

"Er—he's certainly someone's prowler," Leonidas said.

"*He's* the one O'Malley and Dunphy were after! I told you," Pink said triumphantly, "that girl had an honest voice! I *knew* she just came for her coat—what d'you suppose he was after?"

"Galoshes, possibly. The only thing that is clear to me," Leonidas said, "is that my cellar is being used as a universal assembly base. How glad I am that I snapped the spring lock at the head of the hall stairs! Come along, Pink, if we don't get to the Victory Swop soon, we won't establish anything. What time is it, ten?"

"Five past eight," Pink told him. "I just looked at my watch. But I know what you mean. It *seems* later, doesn't it?"

After they circled the house, Leonidas stopped cautiously just beyond his garden.

"The coast is clear." Pink craned her neck and looked back. "We can go out on the sidewalk, Bill. Brother's gone, and there wasn't a soul out back, either. Well, now we can get the beachwagon and hurry along to Lyceum Hall."

"I have," Leonidas said, "a certain disinclination to be seen on the Birch Hill sidewalk right now. While you get the car, I'll remain here with Lady Baltimore. Slow down as you go by, and I'll hop on."

Pink hurried away, and Leonidas stepped back into the shadow of some evergreens.

It was all very well for Pink to be so casual about the girl in the mink coat, he thought. And while he could see where the girl might be easily identified from Pink's point of view, he personally had grave doubts about it.

Indeed, he was entertaining grave doubts about all the plans he had so glibly brewed—it seemed like several years ago, although a glance at his own watch proved it was only half an hour. Back there in the hall, everything from the solution of the hamper problem to finding out about Haymaker's will had appeared so very sane and simple. But out here in the cold, clear October air, Leonidas could only view his prospective tasks as incredibly formidable. To put the affair on a cash basis—that was a term he'd picked up at the directors' meeting—he wouldn't give two cents for his chances of finding out who called for Haymaker, or who the fake oil man was, or the girl in the mink coat. Or anything else.

And once again his conscience began to smite him about Admiral Coe-Chester's problem, which he had so faithfully promised to look into. After all, he still had some obligations to Meredith's Academy, even if it belonged now to the Navy, and swarmed with a lot of grown men who forever seemed to be pacing stiffly about the duckboards bearing guns.

Leonidas shook his head. He'd have to cope with Haymaker first. Coe-Chester would understand. Probably, in his heart, Coe-Chester never really thought that he could help, anyway.

He sighed as he shifted Lady Baltimore from under his right arm to under his left. If only he could shift the perspective of this murder with equal ease, and tackle it from the other side, and figure out who this enemy of his could be! For certainly murdering a man in one's study was not the work of any close, well-meaning friend!

"Enemies, enemies!" he murmured thoughtfully. "Dear me, where could I have made any enemies lately?"

An even, martial scrunching along the gravel sidewalk caused Leonidas to give up his fruitless enemy hunt and duck back.

But it was only Major Beeding marching smartly along, whistling to his invisible dog.

Beeding, it occurred suddenly to Leonidas, was his man. Beeding knew all about Haymaker's. Beeding not only was on the board, but he also managed the store. Beeding would know in an instant who pushed hampers, and why the sixth floor had been empty that afternoon. Beeding was the ideal person of whom to ask questions.

Leonidas opened his mouth to call out, and then he found himself hesitating.

Was Beeding also the sort of person to whom you could explain the presence, in your study, of a corpse? Particularly Haymaker's corpse?

"Now, I rather wonder!" Leonidas said.

The hearty, tweedy Beeding, a comparative newcomer to the neighborhood, had lavishly renovated the old Manson house, played a great deal of golf with Henry S. C. Compton, and drove a fantastically streamlined green roadster with a lot of chromium pipes protruding from its hood and fenders. That was all that Leonidas really knew about the man, except that he loved to talk about his former Army life, and discussed Army methods and Army routine at the drop of a hat. He'd talked at length to the directors about the necessity of upholding authority and discipline and morale among the employees during these trying times, and his voice, tirelessly booming through pages and pages of statistics, had come very near lulling Leonidas to sleep.

"I think not. No."

Leonidas made the decision with a certain amount of reluctance, and nearly changed his mind as he watched Beeding march off down the hill.

But while Beeding knew all the answers, he told himself firmly that almost any other Haymaker employee would know them, too. The red-headed elevator girl, for example. She was probably quite accustomed to answering odd and miscellaneous questions without troubling herself much as to the reasons why they were asked.

The sound that he'd been waiting for, that of a car starting, came at last to his ears. Leonidas took a fresh grip on Lady Baltimore and made ready to hurry out to Pink's beachwagon when it approached.

But the beachwagon whizzed past him at such a clip that he was caught flat-footed.

He hadn't even time to shout, or to move his hand from the cakebox, and wave.

As he looked after the car in bewilderment, he heard the horn toot jerkily. Then the brake lights flashed on, and then the beachwagon started to back up.

The horn tooted again, twice. Not real toots, but rather urgent little yaps, rather as if someone's elbow had accidentally hit against the horn button.

Ordinarily Leonidas would have thought nothing of them, but coupled with the beachwagon's speeding by and then backing up, they were enough to put him on guard.

Instead of rushing out on the sidewalk with Lady Baltimore, he continued to wait by the evergreens.

A moment later he was devoutly thanking heaven for Pink's quick wit.

For Henry Compton, still wearing his tin hat, emerged from the front seat, ran up the steps of Number Forty, and jabbed his finger at the doorbell like someone spearing a wild boar.

"I keep telling you, Henry," Leonidas heard Pink's voice ring out as if she were announcing a train, "he is *not* home! He's at the Victory Swop! He *told* me he was going to the Victory Swop!"

"If he knew he was going to the Victory Swop," Compton returned, "then *why* didn't he make out that report for the record before he left? I very definitely reminded him! I told him the reports had to be filed within three hours, and he said he would! He is the most careless, irresponsible—"

Still fussing, Compton returned to the beachwagon, and Pink drove off.

Obviously, Leonidas thought, she had been waylaid by her brother, and was taking him as a passenger through no fault of her own. But had she enough gasoline to come back? Would she send someone after him? He could always walk over and take the bus, but if Pink had been quick enough to keep him and Compton apart, very probably she would figure out some way to get him later. He decided to wait.

Beeding strolled back up the hill, whistling and calling to the still invisible dog. He spent rather a long time out in front of Number Forty, and Leonidas wistfully hoped that the dog hadn't discovered his new tulip bed. Every other dog in the neighborhood had enjoyed a good dig at those new bulbs, and they were beginning to show signs of wear and tear.

Leonidas made up his mind to give Pink fifteen minutes. Then he'd cut across lots to the bus. That was

67

one advantage of manning post A-1. He had learned every nook and cranny of Birch Hill, and could slip about it at night like a cat. Topography and directorates were apparently the two new fields being opened to him by the war.

The dim tap-tap of feminine heels along the street's tarred surface caused him to peek out between two branches to see if the newcomer might possibly be Pink, already run out of gas.

Beeding heard the sound, too, and was staring interestedly down the hill.

Then, to Leonidas's unfeigned amazement, Beeding turned on his heel and ducked into the woods across from Number Forty!

The tap-tap came nearer, slowed almost to a stop, as if someone were pausing to look at something, and then speeded up again.

Leonidas cautiously leaned forward.

A girl, wearing the slacks and loose, light-colored gabardine coat that were rapidly becoming the standard uniform of female Dalton, was walking jauntily up the flagstones to his front door. She looked first at the street number, and then rang the bell.

There was something very familiar about her, and Leonidas racked his brains to think who she might be. The new grocery girl? She was taller. The drugstore girl? She was fatter. Not a telegraph girl. They rode bicycles. He couldn't seem to visualize her behind any counter, or in any sort of motion.

68

She turned, and something in the pert swing of hei shoulders and the toss of her head placed her at once.

She was that red-headed elevator girl from R. H. Haymaker's!

Simultaneously with Leonidas's flash of recollection, Major Beeding burst out of the bushes and started across the street.

The girl heard the noise, saw him, and darted quickly down the steps.

"Jinx!" Beeding boomed. "Jinx! Is that you? Jinx!"

The girl ran like a deer across the lawn, and Beeding, showing surprising agility for a man of his height and girth, raced after her.

"Jinx! Stop! Halt! Come here! Halt at once, I say!"

Leonidas found himself feeling very annoyed by Beeding's brusque, crack-of-a-whip orders. After all, the girl was no buck private A.W.O.L. She had every right to ring his doorbell if the fancy struck her.

He particularly disliked the way Beeding grabbed at her, too. Beeding had no business chasing elevator girls over other people's lawns!

Setting Lady Baltimore down carefully by the evergreens, Leonidas stepped over to his perennial bed and picked up a thick bamboo plant stake.

Then, affixing his pince-nez, he strode over to the garden path toward which the girl was trying to dodge.

She got by Beeding, started up the path, and as Beeding followed her, Leonidas's foot went out.

A few moments later, Beeding was writhing helplessly on the ground, and his cries were sufficiently agonized to cause Leonidas a brief stab of remorse.

Then, reflecting that the fellow deserved it, he picked up Lady Baltimore and walked over toward the girl, who had stopped running at the noise of Beeding's headlong tumble.

"Wha—"

"Sssh!"

Leonidas took her firmly by the arm and plunged into the maze of Birch Hill.

Some seven minutes later, he paused by the summer-house of the Hassett's garden, next to the Golf Club.

"There," he said, as he rested Lady Baltimore against the rustic rail, "I doubt if Beeding will bother you here, and the Hassets are in Florida."

"Say, for crying out loud, Mr. Witherall, what'd you *do* to him?"

"I had some slight experience," Leonidas said, "with the junior commandos at Meredith's Academy last spring. Our Spanish teacher had been a guerrilla in the Civil War, and we learned to wreak—er—considerable havoc. Frankly, I caused rather more havoc than I intended, but unless something went very wrong indeed, Beeding's injuries should only amount to a few twisted tendons. At least, that's what Roderigo prophesied for that particular stake action. Tell me, just what was the underlying significance of Major Beeding's peremptory boorishness?"

"How's that again, Mr. Witherall?"

"Er—why was Beeding chasing you?"

"Oh," Jinx said casually, "it's my damned morale."

"Your—er—what?"

"Morale. It's the elevator girls' night to go to drill and sing and all. At the Y. It's supposed to lift up our morale, and I should ought to be there waving a wand right now."

"I fear," Leonidas said honestly, "that I don't entirely understand."

"Why, it's classes. You sing—oh, like 'Old Mac-Donald had a Farm,' and do a lot of exercises with wands. Then they march your feet off you. Beeding says it'll take us out of ourselves, like."

"It frankly takes me out of myself," Leonidas said, "just listening to it. Er—I still don't grasp why Beeding was chasing you."

"Why, if you don't go for your morale," Jinx explained, "Beeding gives you demerits. What it boils down to is he docks you, though it don't sound that way. Well, Beeding knows it's my morale night, see, and he knows I should ought to be there waving wands. I been ducking him for half an hour, the old wolf! If you hadn't of loused him up, he'd of caught me, and bang—another bagful of demerits for Jinx, and probably him trying to date me up besides. That was pretty white of you, Mr. Witherall!"

"May I ask," Leonidas said, "how you know me, and my name?"

"I thought I seen you somewheres before when you

71

got into the elevator this afternoon," Jinx said. "You reminded me of someone and I kept wondering who. It was somebody I seen in pictures."

"Shakespeare, possibly?" Leonidas suggested.

"Shakespeare? Gee, no!" Jinx laughed. "Monty Woolley! Then when I come down after leaving you on the sixth floor, Mae—she's Car Two—she said you was the new director, Mr. Witherall. She was the one took you up to the directors' meeting. Listen, do you think Beeding really knew it was me? I kept turning my face away from him so he didn't really get to see me, and I can always say it was my sister. I got a sister," Jinx said righteously, "and if *you* said it was my sister, see, I'd be okay. Beeding can't give my sister any demerits."

"This demerit system," Leonidas said, "is something Beeding neglected to go into, today, and I think I may assure you that it will be subjected to some extensive revisions at the earliest possible moment. Now—"

"But you'll say I'm my sister, won't you?" Jinx interrupted.

"M'yes, indeed, if you wish. Now tell me," Leonidas said, "did you—er—intend to call on me?"

"Gee, that's something else you'll have to go to bat for me on," Jinx said. "Because it wasn't my fault I missed Turk, and I'd of got to you sooner only on account of he didn't turn up, and then Beeding got in the way and I had to keep ducking him—will you explain all that?"

"I rather wish," Leonidas said, "that you'd explain it all to me, first."

"Well, gee, I don't know just where to start," Jinx said. "You remember I took you and that woman up to the sixth floor?"

"Vividly!"

"Then I came down—honest, those women were a howl, fighting over those stockings! Me and Mae, we nearly died! Mae laughed so hard she broke the catch on her Sam Browne belt, and while I was helping her take it off, the seventh floor buzzed. It was Mae's trip, but she was so weak from laughing, I went up instead, and it was Mr. Haymaker—what did you say, Mr. Witherall?"

"Go on," Leonidas said, "quickly!"

"Well, I took him down, and he gave me this note to give to Turk, see?"

"To whom?"

"Turk—don't you know Turk? He drives for Mr. Haymaker. There's always been one of Turk's family working for the Haymakers. Oh, you must know him. You must've seen him around. He's about twenty-five, and tall, and dark—he's fullback for the Dalton Demons!"

"I haven't seen an able-bodied man of twenty-five around," Leonidas said, "in months."

"Turk's record keeps him out of the Army—everything else, too," Jinx said. "The minute anyone takes a gander at Turk's fingerprints, they send him home.

73

Well, Mr. Haymaker gave me this note for Turk, see, but Turk never came. So when I got home, I called his mother, but she said Turk's going crazy on some other job Mr. Haymaker gave him, and she doesn't know where he is. So you'll explain to Mr. Haymaker why you got it so late, won't you?"

"Why I got *what* so late?"

"The note, of course!" Jinx drew an envelope from the pocket of her gabardine coat and held it out. "You see, after I called Turk's mother, I looked at the envelope, and it said on it Turk was to deliver this in person to Mr. Witherall of Forty Birch Hill Road—"

"I'm sure you'll forgive me," Leonidas said, "if I seem to snatch that from you—"

"Want a light? I've got a little flashlight in my pocket," Jinx said. "I'll snap it on so you can read—say, listen, Mr. Witherall! Did you hear like a noise in the woods back there?"

"If I heard—er—like a symphony orchestra, with Toscanini conducting," Leonidas said, "it would not deter me from reading the contents of this note from Haymaker—where is your light? Put it on!"

"Wait now, Mr. Witherall—it's voices, hear? Listen! If that should be Major Beeding coming after us," Jinx said, "then you can't stop here to read any notes!"

"Beeding," Leonidas said, "is probably home rubbing himself with arnica. Even if he isn't, I'm sure that no one could possibly have followed us through those woo—"

74

"Listen, Mr. Witherall! Those voices are getting nearer!" Jinx said anxiously. "Hear? And see—flashlights! Somebody's hunting something, and I bet you it's Beeding hunting me!"

Leonidas turned, listened, then hurriedly put the note in his coat pocket, picked up Lady Baltimore, and took Jinx by the arm.

"Isn't that Beeding's voice?" she demanded.

"No," Leonidas said, "that is Lieutenant Dunphy and some of his cohorts—come along, my child! You and I are leaving!"

He led her past the Hassett's empty house with its vast porte-cochere, past a tennis court and the bleak remnants of a rose garden, and was about to step on to the sidewalk when he saw two figures marching along by the street lights some ten yards away.

Leonidas could never figure out later whether he nearly pulled Jinx's arm off in the next few split seconds, or whether she came nearer to pulling off his.

But before the two marching figures came abreast of the Hassett's driveway entrance, Leonidas and Jinx were both flat down on the ground, with Lady Baltimore nestling between them.

"Beeding!" Jinx said in Leonidas's ear.

Leonidas, contemplating the tin hat of Henry Compton, hardly heard her.

CHAPTER 4

"HOLD IT! Here's Hassett's drive," Compton said. "That's where Dunphy said to wait for them—you know, Beeding, you're absolutely right. We absolutely must maintain order during alarms and blackouts. I saw Haverstraw at the swop, and he told me about this prowler in his cellar. Said his wife was in such a completely nervous state he had to take her out of the house!"

Beeding clucked his tongue sympathetically.

"I'd only gone to the swop to locate Witherall, so when Haverstraw told me about the prowler," Compton continued, "I decided to come right back and look into the situation. If that prowler was roaming about during the blackout, Witherall should have seen him and put him on his report!"

"Hasn't Witherall made out his report *yet?*" Beeding asked in a shocked voice.

"No. I don't know," Compton said, "what I'm going to do about him! Now, as I was telling you, I saw a man running along Birch Hill Road just a few minutes before I met my sister—she drove me to the

76

swop," he added parenthetically. "Fellow in a turtle-neck sweater. And I saw him again a few minutes before I met you, running along Maple Road. Now I think he's the man we want, don't you?"

"Well," Beeding sounded as judicial as if he were delivering a Supreme Court opinion, "of course it might just be someone out running. Keeping fit, and all that."

"I thought of that right away, but I don't know anyone who runs around here," Compton said, "do you? Except that Foss boy, but he always ran mornings, and he's a bombardier now, anyway. If I hadn't seen this fellow twice, I shouldn't think much about him. But under the circumstances, I feel it's only wise to have a look around. Lucky Dunphy and O'Malley and their men were still in this vicinity. Very efficient, our police."

Leonidas, restraining with difficulty a small, derisive snort, saw Jinx stuff the corner of her coat collar into her mouth. Compton's remark had apparently struck her as being irresistibly funny.

"Good idea of Dunphy's, to comb these woods," Compton went on. "Seemed to have their eye on Hassett's here, too. They knew it was a vacant house. You know, Beeding, I think we'll have to ask to have one of the auxiliary police taken off traffic duty and posted up here—though there'd never be any need for him if fellows like Witherall were only on their toes! I must say, I wish all my wardens were like you!"

77

"Well, of course I've been in the service," Beeding said. "That makes a great difference. I understand the necessity of reports."

"Witherall's supposed to be very bright," Compton said, and then paused as if he expected the statement to be challenged. "Just what do you think of him, Beeding?"

"Oh, the man gets around a lot," Beeding said. "He knows the best people. He's *in* a lot of things."

"It's strange, isn't it?" Compton said. "I don't understand it, either. For example, men like you and me, who've been in the town a long while—well, frankly, I expected that *you'd* be put on the bank board. I never for a minute considered the possibility of their selecting Witherall. Not when they could pick a man of your experience!"

"I never gave the matter a thought." Beeding's tone was elaborately casual. "But I will say, I thought they'd give you the golf club, after all the work you've put in on the Greens Committee. I don't know where the club would be, if you hadn't had the foresight to lay in all that fertilizer, and get the new sprinklers!"

Leonidas bit his lip.

It was slowly dawning on him that the jobs thrust on him, which secretly amused him, and which he'd accepted only in an effort to be helpful, really meant a tremendous lot to these two!

The smile faded from his face.

Was it possible that the person who killed Haymaker, this same person who so obviously intended Leonidas himself to be involved, might be some good, honest Dalton citizen whom he'd unintentionally done out of one directorate or another?

Jealousy was an angle that he should not have overlooked, he thought to himself. But it had never before occurred to him that anyone might possibly be jealous of him for acquiring these new posts!

"Trouble with Witherall," Compton said, "he will not take these things seriously! Why, he's almost flippant about reports! I'm told that he pulled Meredith's out of the red—they say the school was in a very bad financial condition when old Meredith left it to him. And he must make money somehow. He does himself very well, and that house of his must have cost him a pretty penny—if you *like* those modern, flat-topped things! But the thing I don't like about the man, he always seems to be laughing at you with a straight face. Did you ever hear, Beeding, that he worked for the government?"

"The government? No!"

"Well, it's hearsay, of course, but my wife said someone said—it was at the Red Cross, and they were rolling bandages," Compton said, as though the virtue of bandage rolling somehow canceled the taint of gossip. "Anyway, someone said that Witherall said that he was writing for the government."

Leonidas frowned, and then suddenly recalled a casual comment he'd made the previous week at some-

79

one's cocktail party. But when he lightly said he wrote for the government, he had meant that the royalties derived from the adventures of the excellent Lieutenant Haseltine went for the most part toward the payment of his taxes!

"My wife," Compton said, "wondered if he could be in some sort of secret service. You know he's a great friend of Admiral Coe-Chester's."

"Is he, really?"

"Witherall's about the only person Coe-Chester ever goes to see," Compton said. "I wonder where Dunphy and O'Malley went with their men? I was sure I heard them in the woods when we stopped here."

"I thought I did, too. I wish they'd hurry. I've got to go home," Beeding said with considerable feeling, "and do something about this shoulder of mine!"

"Just what *did* happen?" Compton inquired. "I gathered when I met you and the police that you'd been mixed up with this prowler, but did he hold you up and try to rob you, or what?"

"I was simply walking along Birch Hill Road—walking along, whistling and minding my own business," Beeding began righteously.

Jinx poked Leonidas.

"And then," Beeding continued, "someone jumped me. No amateur, either. The fellow was an expert at dirty gangster stuff. Something must have frightened him away, because he didn't take my watch, or wallet. Just trussed me up somehow with a stake and my belt."

"Your *own* belt?" Compton sounded as if that somehow were a very significant and sinister fact.

"My own belt. If O'Malley and Dunphy hadn't come by—their prowl car had a flat, and they were hunting for a house where someone was home so they could call the garage for a spare," Beeding said. "Well, if they hadn't come along, I'd probably have broken my arm getting loose. I'm just barely able to move my shoulder, now. Of course it was unquestionably the work of Haverstraw's prowler. Dunphy thinks he may have something to do with that flat tire, too. Said he wasn't at all sure that someone hadn't deliberately let the air out."

"It's bad business, all of it," Compton said. "We can't have that sort of thing going on up here on Birch Hill and Oakhill. This district rarely ever has a prowler, and I don't think anyone was attacked here before, ever! I only hope it makes Witherall understand the necessity for making out reports. If Witherall had been on his toes, he'd have spotted this fellow, and if he'd made out his report at once, then we could probably have looked into the matter before the fellow even got into Haverstraw's cellar—where can those cops be? They certainly should have finished combing the woods by now!"

"Let's cut back and find them," Beeding suggested.

"After all, if you saw this fellow running in plain sight out on the street, perhaps they'd better take a look around on the streets—"

Leonidas and Jinx lay very still while Compton and Beeding strolled up the driveway past them.

"Did you hear what he said!" Jinx whispered indignantly as the sound of their footsteps died away beyond the porte-cochere. "The dirty liar! Just walking along, minding his own business! How'd he dare tell him a lie like that, Mr. Witherall?"

"If he was found by the police," Leonidas raised himself up and looked cautiously up the driveway, "yowling as he was yowling when you and I left, he had to have some explanatory story. I dare say that Dunphy at once suggested to him that it was the work of a prowler, and probably Beeding agreed with hearty and immediate relief. The fact that he didn't mention you proves that he does not choose to make public that episode, or his part in it. Now I wonder who that fellow in the turtle-neck sweater could be!"

The timing would seem to indicate that it might be the same person who had rushed out of his own cellar, if Compton had seen him just before he saw Pink, and since Pink had started for her beachwagon after the fellow had dashed away.

"They'll have themselves a time finding him, if you ask me," Jinx said. "All the boys where I live in Dalton Lower Falls, they all wear turtle-neck sweaters. All the Dalton Demon teams do, too."

"Indeed!" Leonidas said. "And I believe you said, did you not, that Haymaker's Ganymede, that—er—Turk was a Dalton Demon?"

"That's right. Turk wears one all the time," Jinx said. "Well, Mr. Witherall, what do we do now?"

"Haymaker's note," Leonidas got to his feet, "is and has been burning a hole in my coat pocket. But I don't wish to pause and expose myself under any street light while I leisurely peruse it. Nor do I think your flashlight would be quite safe. Let us edge our way along to the corner bus stop and trust that we can get a bus downtown before the police or Beeding or Compton catch up with us—you can transfer to the Dalton Lower Falls bus, can't you?" he asked as he picked up Lady Baltimore.

"Sure," Jinx said as they started off, keeping well in the shadow of Hassett's arborvitae hedge. "Only—well, do you mind if I just sort of string along with you for a while? Because if I'm with you, see, and delivering a note for Mr. Haymaker besides, then Beeding can't say a thing to me. You see, I sort of think he's sore enough so as even if he didn't tell that guy or the cops anything about me, he'll phone to the morale class and check up on me. And when he finds out I'm not there, see, there'll be hell to pay tomorrow. Particularly," she added shrewdly, "if that shoulder's still hurting him."

"It's only fair to warn you that—er—stringing along with me," Leonidas said, "may just conceivably lead

83

you into far more trying problems. Far more trying than the last few minutes."

"Gee, it's been a lot of fun—you know what it makes me think of?" Jinx said. "It's just like the adventures of Haseltine on the radio. That's my favorite radio program."

"Is it, indeed!" Leonidas said. "Mind that wire by the flower bed! You know Haymaker—er—do you like him?"

"Oh, he's a nice old guy," Jinx said. "He scares the pants off Mae and Gerty and the other girls, but I get along with him fine. I kid him along, and he likes it. My mother worked for him, see, and my grandmother ran the first elevator they had in the old store. People used to come from as far as Pomfret and Carnavon to see Haymaker's lady elevator man."

"I see. Jinx, you can be of undoubted assistance to me, and I should like to have you. But I feel that you should know what you're getting into. May I caution you," Leonidas said as they skirted the tennis court of the house next to the Hassett's, "not to cry out with alarm, or make any unusual sounds, as the news I have to tell you is neither pretty nor good."

"Shoot," Jinx said briefly.

He told her the story as they made their way on toward the corner, and when he concluded, she expressed her feelings in a voice choked with anger and indignation.

"That's the limit! That's terrible! Nobody had any

call to harm a man like Mr. Haymaker—listen, Mr. Witherall, I bet that he knew! I bet that's why he wrote you that note! He guessed he was in some sort of danger, see, and maybe he knew you worked for the government, like that guy said."

"But I don't," Leonidas told her. "I write for myself—since you expressed some admiration for Lieutenant Haseltine, I may as well confess that he is some of my handiwork."

"Well, gee, what do you know!" Jinx said delightedly. "What happened to Caprice?"

"To—er—whom?"

"Caprice. She was the red-headed telephone girl used to help Haseltine all the time," Jinx said. "I always loved her on account of she had red hair like mine—oh-oh! Hold it!—there's a prowl car right smack on the corner, under the light. See?" she pointed, and then giggled. "Gee, look at 'em, will you? In conference, yet!"

Dunphy, O'Malley, and their two satellite cops were standing like a cluster of statues by the side of a light-blue sedan whose rear wheel leaned disconsolately against the granite curbing.

"Gee, don't they look worried! You'd think they none of 'em ever seen a flat before?" Jinx said. "Well, what do we do now, Mr. Witherall?"

"I rather feel that they will be here," Leonidas said, "for some time. M'yes. And Beeding and Compton will very shortly track them down, too. Appar-

85

ently without the stimulus of that pair, they've lost all
official interest in the prowler—I wonder, in passing,
if they ever really cared much, or if they merely
jumped at the chance to spend an evening in the open,
away from the somewhat fetid atmosphere of headquarters! Suppose, Jinx, we wait for the bus at the
corner of Elm Hill Road."

They turned and retraced their steps past the Hassett's.

Near the end of the block, Leonidas stopped,
sighed, and set Lady Baltimore down at the foot of a
maple tree.

"What's wrong now?" Jinx demanded.

"Beeding and Compton. They're on the corner opposite the bus stop. I can see the street light glinting
down on Compton's tin hat."

"What're they doing there, for Pete's sake?"

Leonidas shrugged. "This," he said wearily, "is fast
becoming what one might sum up as a balk. We
could well waste the entire night running back and
forth between one corner and the other. I suppose we
had best cut across the golf course. I have a definite
aversion toward venturing again through the woods
back to Birch Hill Road. Altogether too much hap-
pens there."

"But if we cross the street," Jinx said, "won't those
two spot us?"

"I'm sure they will. It's a problem," Leonidas said,
"which is momentarily baffling me."

86

"Haseltine once disguised himself as a tree, and crossed an open field that way," Jinx suggested.

"The fallacy of Haseltine," Leonidas said, "is that fiction is occasionally much stranger than fact. Besides, Haseltine was not required to carry a Lady Baltimore cake."

"Is *that* what's in that box?" Jinx demanded. "A cake? Well, gee, why don't you just leave it here?"

"I've carried it so long," Leonidas said, "it is virtually a part of me. Er—it's a swop. It belongs—dear me, what's that?"

He put on his pince-nez and stared across the street.

Something that looked like a caravan, outlined with tiny blue lights, was winding down the side road from the golf club. A cornet blared out a few bars of the Marine Hymn, a bugle promptly drowned it out with a lusty rendition of Reveille, and was in turn overwhelmed by a loud and prolonged drumming.

"Sounds to me," Jinx remarked, "like Dalton Lower Falls the night that the Demons beat the Pomfret Panthers!"

"If this is any organized festivity," Leonidas said, "I really should know about— I wonder, now, d'you suppose this could possibly be the Junk Parade?"

"The what?"

"Someone phoned me about it last week. And now that I think of it, I promised to attend," Leonidas said. "I believe the object was to collect all the large

87

pieces of scrap that had recently been unearthed about the club and its grounds, load it on to wagons, and cart it by some devious route to the scrap-collection center. Stops were to be made at the home of any member, or anyone else who had contributions too unwieldy to be coped with individually, and I believe the lure was that if one contributed one's boiler or iron fences, one got a free ride."

"Say, those are Pfahl's brewery wagons!" Jinx said. "The ones with the black horses!"

"M'yes. When I was informed about all this, it was explained to me that since everyone in Dalton had an unfulfilled yearning to ride behind those horses, the scrap turnout should be stupendous. It's not a particularly dignified venture," Leonidas said as the cornet and bugle fought it out, "but it's providing the excuse for a party, and it may prove of some value in the war effort."

"Gee, wouldn't I give my shirt!" Jinx said longingly.

"Er—for what?"

"A ride. I always loved those horses!"

"Jinx," Leonidas said, "why didn't I think of that myself, at once? Come!" He picked up Lady Baltimore. "Hurry. We'll catch them at the turn, and hop on!"

Five minutes later, he and Jinx peered out from behind their hiding place, a discarded water tank on the last wagon, at Beeding and Compton on the corner.

"Their expressions," Leonidas said as the wagon rumbled past, "suggest that they find this whole performance pretty vulgar and common. But if this parade serves no other purpose than to remove us from the hill, I shall consider it a highlight of the social season," he had to raise his voice as the bugle blared. "Fully on a par with Madame Creighton's famous anniversary dinners. The—"

Leonidas gave up entirely as Jinx started to beat the water tank with a long-handled iron dipper which she'd picked up from the bottom of the wagon.

Halfway down the hill, Leonidas took his hands from his ears and pulled at her arm.

"Jinx! Your flashlight, please! I can't wait any longer to read that note!"

While the wagon rumbled, and the cornet praised God and passed the ammunition, Leonidas scanned the lines written in Haymaker's old-fashioned Spencerian script.

DEAR WITHERALL,

I am deeply grateful for your suggestion and can only congratulate you on your amazing perspicacity. It is my hope to catch you at the club, which I heard you give as your destination, but if I should miss you there, I shall give myself the pleasure of calling at your house as soon as possible.

Faithfully yours,

R. H. HAYMAKER.

Leonidas reread the note, folded it carefully, and put it back in his pocket.

"Did he know he was in danger?" Jinx demanded. "Did he guess something was wrong?"

"He guessed something was wrong," Leonidas said. "But exactly what—dear me, is this caravan turning west? We don't want to go west, Jinx. Hop off!"

Jinx, still gripping the long-handled dipper, obediently hopped off and turned to help him with the cakebox.

"Where *are* we going, anyway?" she asked. "What did he say, Mr. Witherall?"

"To the Victory Swop," Leonidas said absently. "*My* perspicacity—now what in the world did Haymaker mean by that? A less perspicacious director never sat at that mahogany table! *My* suggestion— why, the only time I opened my mouth was when he directly asked me a point-blank question, and I quakingly countered with a question about accounts! They were the only things that came to my mind! Haymaker couldn't mean the accounts!"

"I don't know what you're talking about," Jinx said, "but if all you talked about was accounts, then why shouldn't Mr. Haymaker mean accounts?"

"But Jinx!" Leonidas sounded as bewildered as he felt. "Don't you see, I wasn't serious? *I* know nothing about accounts! I only mentioned them because I had to mention something! If I'd thought of cauliflower,

I'd have mentioned cauliflower. On the other hand, he said he'd send me a statement— Jinx, d'you suppose it's possible that Haymaker, in preparing some sort of accounting or statement for me, actually found some discrepancy?"

"Search me," Jinx said. "But gee, Haseltine's always saying if anybody ever gets killed, it's for love, or money. And Mr. Haymaker was sort of old for love. What I mean to say is, if he got killed, it was probably on account of money."

"If I thought," Leonidas said, "that my impromptu question caused Haymaker to discover that funds had actually been misappropriated, and that his discovery touched off some chain of events culminating in his murder, I should feel far, far worse about all this than I do now. Oh, if I could find out who called for him at my house! If only I'd gone downstairs to see that oil man! If—"

He broke off as he recognized the driver of the beachwagon that swerved around the corner.

Clutching Lady Baltimore, he ran out into the street in an effort to stop Pink before she sped away up the hill.

But the beachwagon rattled on out of sight.

"Someone you know?" Jinx asked.

"Mrs. Lately. Pink. The woman in the elevator with me this afternoon. I'm beginning to suspect that fate never intends us to meet—"

Another car drew up to the curb in front of them, and a genial-looking man thrust his head out the window.

"Saw you hail that beachwagon, brother. You two want a lift?"

"Thank you, we're on our way," Leonidas said, "to the Victory Swop. If that's your destination, or in the vicinity of your destination, we'd be only too happy to be—er—lifted."

"Thought that's where you were bound when I saw your daughter's dipper. Get right in, friends. I'll take you to the door. My front seat," the genial man added proudly, "is one big swop, but maybe you can squeeze in the back there."

They squeezed in, and the car bounced off with a tinny clatter.

"Just don't let that gocart hit against the lamp, sister," the man yelled. "And keep an eye on that crock. It's full of sauerkraut!"

Jinx, balancing the gocart with one foot, and holding on the crock's top with the other, vainly tried to get Leonidas's attention above the din. But Leonidas seemed oblivious to her efforts, to the assorted clatter, even to the sauerkraut that spilled on his shoe.

At last the car bounced to a stop.

"Well, well, here we are!" the genial man said. "Right at the door, brother!"

"I'm deeply grateful," Leonidas said. "Perhaps

you'll permit me to assist you with—er—my, my! Did we come all the way with—er—all this?"

"That's okay, brother. I'll take it in. Wouldn't trust anyone with my swops—see you later, brother!"

"Say, Mr. Witherall," Jinx said. "I think—"

"Come along," Leonidas said. "Quickly, before our friend changes his mind about our helping him. I'm glad to be here! I want—"

"But listen, Mr. Witherall—"

"This way, Jinx. There's the entrance. I want to see everyone," Leonidas said, "and if you possibly can, I want you to assure everyone that I've been here since the swop opened, and for all you know, opened the very doors to the first swopper!"

"But Mr. Witherall!" Jinx protested as they entered the hall. "Look—this isn't Lyceum Hall!"

Leonidas put on his pince-nez and stared around at the vast, barnlike auditorium, filled with people talking at the top of their lungs.

"Isn't Lyceum Hall?" he said. "But my dear child, it's certainly a hall, and it's certainly a swop! Of course it's Lyceum Hall!"

"I kept trying to tell you on the way!" Jinx said. "This is a hall, all right, and it seems to be a swop, too. Only it's not in Dalton Center, Mr. Witherall! This is Pomfret!"

Leonidas stared at her, and then stared around at the people.

93

He couldn't see a single familiar face!

"D'you mean," Leonidas began.

Jinx nodded.

"I tried to tell you," she said. "It's the wrong swop!"

Leonidas sighed and took a fresh grip on Lady Baltimore.

"Let us," he said, "be gone at once. If it costs a king's ransom, we are taking a cab back to the right, or Lyceum Hall, swop! Because a glimmer, a very faint glimmer, has come to me. I am beginning to perceive a slight rift in the clouds. I've got to put in a brief appearance at the right swop, and then—"

"Witherall! My dear fellow!"

Leonidas found himself practically embraced by a tall bald man in a dinner jacket, with a gigantic white button in his lapel that proclaimed him to be master of ceremonies.

To the best of his knowledge and belief, Leonidas had never laid eyes on the bald man before in his life, but that fact was not preventing the bald man from greeting him like a dear and long-lost cousin who had just admitted to owning five white sidewall tires in good condition.

"By George, Witherall, I was getting pretty worried! Haymaker promised he'd be sure to send someone over from Dalton if he couldn't make it himself—come along, come right this way!"

Gripping Leonidas by the arm, he turned and

started to plough through the milling throng toward the front of the hall.

"Coming through, please, coming through!" he bellowed. "Coming through!"

With his other hand fully occupied in maintaining Lady Baltimore on an even keel, Leonidas couldn't break the man's grip. There was nothing to do but permit himself to be tugged bodily along. Like a football, he thought, being taken for a reluctant touchdown.

Jinx pulled at Leonidas's belt.

"Hey, Mr. Witherall! Hey, who is he? What's the big idea?"

"Put your hand over the box lid. Lady B's getting crushed," Leonidas said. "Frankly, I don't know!"

"There!" Panting a little, the bald man came to a halt at the foot of the raised platform. "Quite a crowd, isn't it? Oh, this young lady with you? I forgot, Haymaker said he'd try to get one. Sorry I couldn't be at the meeting today—got your breath?"

"M'yes," Leonidas said, "but—"

"Good. Up with you, then, up with you!" Herding Jinx and Leonidas in front of him, the bald man propelled them up the short flight of steps to the platform and insinuated them into two tarnished gilt chairs near the center of the stage. "You wait right here, now, while I speak to the orchestra and get the microphone turned on. Don't get carried away, and start swopping. I don't want to lose you. Either of

95

you," he added with a gallant bow toward Jinx. "I'll be right back."

Leonidas automatically looked toward either end of the stage. But it was a platform, pure and simple, and you left it as you got to it, by the short flight of stairs. Surveying the crowds jammed between them and all available exits, he decided that their chances of being trampled to death far outweighed any possibility of escape.

His sentiments were echoed by Jinx.

"If you want to know what I think," she said, "I think we're stuck! Say, Mr. Witherall, what goes on? Who *is* this guy?"

"He referred to Haymaker," Leonidas said, "and spoke of the meeting today—could he be a Haymaker director whom I haven't met?"

"I know all the directors," Jinx said, "but I never seen him before! You're the only new one. But he has a sort of familiar look. I know his face, but I can't place his head. I guess if I seen him, it was with a hat on. Maybe he's a customer—say, what do you think he wants us to do?"

"For all I know, we may be asked to swing from the chandeliers, or give a brisk tumbling exhibition," Leonidas said. "Or—er—render a few vocal numbers. We are obviously going to be a center of attraction. We're being stared at as if people expected us to produce top hats full of rabbits, at the very least. I—"

"All set!" the bald man returned, beaming. "Now,

I'll just introduce you, Witherall, and you give 'em the talk, and then the—"

"Which talk?" Leonidas interrupted firmly. "I have several, you know."

"Why, the little bond talk. Then the young lady can wind it up with a song or two. All right, everybody, all right!" he advanced to the microphone. "One, two, three, four! Woof-woof, testing!" he said roguishly. "All right, everybody, now!"

While he quieted the hall, Jinx turned anxiously to Leonidas.

"Gee, can you?"

"Give them a little bond talk? My dear child," Leonidas said, "I can give them a great big bond talk! But—er—can you give them a few songs?"

Jinx grinned. "They call me," she said, "the Dinah Shore of Lower Falls!"

Twenty minutes later, the bald man shook their hands warmly.

"By George," he said, "I must admit I didn't know you could do that sort of thing, Witherall! Why, that was practically a fireside chat! And the little girl's a corker! What did you say her name was?"

"Er—Jinx," Leonidas said. "Er—just Jinx. Now, we must be getting along. Perhaps you'd clear the way for us to—er—expedite matters?"

"Oh, you can't go! Stay and meet the folks, and give 'em another turn later!"

"Regretfully," Leonidas said, "we're expected over

at the Dalton Center swop. We're rather late, as it is."

"Too bad," the bald man said. "Pomfret loved you! But if you've got another turn to do over there, of course, I suppose you'll have to be running along. Tell Haymaker I'm sorry he couldn't make it himself, but that you two went over like a steam roller. Tell him I don't think we made any mistake when we asked *you* to be a director—oh, officer!" he called down to a policeman standing in front of the platform. "Oh, Jimmy! Yoo-hoo, Jimmy! Clear a path for these good people, will you?"

"That's most considerate of you," Leonidas said as the bald man shepherded them down the steps and off the platform. "M'yes, indeed. Most considerate. We are really—er—pressed for time."

"Meet the pride of Pomfret's police force," the bald man said heartily. "Officer Rocco. Jimmy, get them out of here, will you? They're in a terrible hurry!"

"Surest thing you know," Jimmy said. "Just you follow me, folks!"

"Oh, by the way, tell Haymaker I'll see him tomorrow," the bald man said. "Tell him I'd be the lawyer of his dreams if I only had your gift! Oh, what I could have done to juries if I could pour out words like you do! *What* a lawyer *you'd* have made, Witherall! But I suppose that the bar's loss was education's gain, ha ha! Oh, and one more thing. Tell Haymaker that now he can die any time he wants to, and everything'll be all right!"

Leonidas stopped and put on his pince-nez.

"I beg your pardon," he said politely, "but I'm afraid I didn't quite catch your—er—last message for Haymaker!"

"Just tell him he can die happy, because I laid his new will away in his vault box this afternoon. Okay, Jimmy, take 'em away! Run 'em out!"

CHAPTER 5

"RUN 'EM OUT!" the bald man continued. "Hurry up, hurry up! And let's all give 'em a great big hand as they run out, folks! Come on, everybody, a great big hand for these good people!"

He gave Leonidas a hearty push that all but sent him reeling toward the path that the policeman was opening up through the crowd.

It was fate, Leonidas decided as he regained his balance, nothing but fate that after being obstructed and thwarted in his own home, on his own sidewalk, and in his own neighborhood, everyone now eagerly wished to hurry him out and away from the one man whom he had from the first desired to seek out and talk with!

And while he himself was very largely responsible for this exuberantly hasty exit, he was not going to allow himself to be separated at this point from R. H. Haymaker's lawyer. True, it would necessitate his backing water practically to the extent of creating a tidal wave, but this was no time, he felt, to be squeamish about inconsistency.

"Anything the matter, Witherall?" the bald man wanted to know.

Leonidas turned around and smiled his most winning smile.

"My swop!" he said.

"Your swop?"

"M'yes." Leonidas pointed to the white cardboard box. "I forgot to swop my swop," he said. "So did Jinx. And we can't possibly leave with the same swops we brought! Jinx! Oh, Jinx, where's your dipper?"

Jinx, already starting through the crowd, finally heard him and came back.

"What's she want for the dipper?" the bald man demanded. "If we've got it in the hall, it's hers, all right! And what's in your box, Witherall?"

"Jinx," Leonidas said, "wants a—a tea strainer." It pleased him to think that the first object to enter his mind had been both small and portable. "And I am open to offers on the finest Lady Baltimore cake you ever saw!"

He felt a few misgivings as he took off the lid, but Lady Baltimore had stood up incredibly well, considering the ground she'd covered.

In the ensuing babble of offers, of which the bald man promptly took charge, Leonidas put on his pince-nez and looked a little worriedly at Jinx.

"Dear child," he spoke loudly enough so that the bald man could hear, "d'you *feel* all right?"

"Say, I never felt better!" her eyes were dancing and her cheeks were bright. "Never!"

"To *me*," Leonidas accented the word, "you don't

look well! To me, you look as if you were going to faint!"

"Faint? Why, I never fa—"

"Faint!" Leonidas interrupted firmly. "I—er—don't think you look as if you were going to faint at once, but—what's that, sir?"

The bald man triumphantly held out a tea strainer that had been passed from hand to hand along the crowd.

"Tea strainer!" he said. "Sheffield, with a crest. Be as good as new after it's been cleaned up a bit."

"Long-handled dipper," Leonidas took it from Jinx and gravely presented it to him. "A patriotic citizen would probably donate it to the scrap heap. Now, what about my Lady Baltimore cake?"

While the bald man held a spirited discussion with two dozen people at once, Leonidas again stared at Jinx.

"Say, Mr. Witherall, do I really look sick? Because I don't feel sick!"

"While I do not think you will faint until our friend, who," Leonidas said, "I find is Haymaker's lawyer—"

"Oh," Jinx said. "Oh-oh!"

"Until he has completed my swop," Leonidas continued, "I'm afraid you'll collapse shortly thereafter. Let me assure you that I'll tell you if I think I see you sway. And mind," he whispered in her ear, "you don't giggle! Now," he turned to the bald man, "what about my cake, sir?"

"They feel that any cake with frosting that thick," the bald man said, "is worth an easy two dollars. You think that's fair?"

"I'm quite willing to abide by the consensus."

"I wish," the bald man said wistfully, "I hadn't already swopped. I'd have given you an almost brand new driver for it. Splendid club. Worth about ten dollars—too bad! Well, the offers are a bridge lamp, and about a dozen other lamps—"

"No lamps." He couldn't, Leonidas thought, cart a lamp around the rest of the night!

"Well, what about food? You're offered an assortment of preserves, pickles, fruits, vegetables, and a crock of sauerkraut!"

"Er—I think not. Although," Leonidas added, "I think I know that sauerkraut, and it's excellent, I'm sure."

"Pair of antlers? Oil painting of—what are those, cows? Yes. Oil painting of cows. Nice gilt frame. Scooter in good condition. Bathroom hamper. Care for a statue? Tables? Chairs? Nice umbrella stand? What's that, back there? Tell the little boy to speak up, I can't hear him. Speak up, son—you've got a lion? How's for a lion, Witherall? Boy says he has a lion. Oh. Lion's *head*. Kind you put on for a play, or a masquerade. What's it made of?"

A papier-mâché lion's head sailed through the air, and the bald man caught it expertly.

"Light as a feather," the bald man stuck it over his own head, then took it off and held it out for Leonidas's inspection. "Very realistic. Fits all head sizes. Nothing like a good lion's head around the house to scare your friends and mother-in-law with, ha ha!"

"Done." Leonidas took it, and everybody had a good laugh.

At least, he thought, the thing didn't weigh as much as a crock of sauerkraut or a nice umbrella stand!

"Here's the cake—pass it back to the little boy, folks!" the bald man said. "Careful with it—now, Jimmy, help get these good people out. Make way for Frank Buck with his lion's head—"

"Jinx!" Leonidas took her hand. "Jinx, are you all right? Jinx, are you going to faint?"

"I feel—I feel funny!" Jinx closed her eyes. "I feel —oh!"

It was an artistic faint, and Leonidas viewed it with pride, almost as if he'd done it himself.

"Oh, the poor kid!" the bald man leaned over her solicitously, and then at once straightened up and became executive. "Come, come, now, don't crowd! Stop crowding! Let her have air! All of you step back at least fifteen feet, except those who've had first aid! Everybody back except the first-aiders!"

It seemed to Leonidas as if everyone in the hall surged forward as one man.

"*All* of you first-aiders? Oh." But the bald man was only momentarily disconcerted. "Well, then, you all ought to know better than to crowd! Move back, now, and give her air! Jimmy, she's light. You pick her up and carry her out into the back room."

The casual way in which the policeman picked Jinx up evoked a certain amount of spirited and critical comment from the first-aiders in the immediate vicinity. Their words, reaching the bald man's ears, caused the latter to assume a light-purple hue.

"Well, if *you* people won't move back," he said defensively, "then we've *got* to move her, haven't we? All right, all right! So her head should be lower than her feet! Two of you—you *experts* come along and look after her!"

Two sturdy women in gray-green Volunteer Corps uniform beat the rest to the door, and superintended the policeman while he placed Jinx on a battered couch in a small, musty smelling back room.

"Now," the taller woman said in a low, serious voice, "you men leave her to us. We are quite able to take complete charge!"

"I don't see what there is to take *charge* of!" the bald man resented being edged toward the door. "Nothing but a simple faint. Just the excitement and the crowd, and so forth! She'll be all right in two seconds!"

"I'm sure," Leonidas added hurriedly, "she'll be coming to almost at once!" It was not a part of his plan to have Jinx immobilized for any longer period than he needed to pump the bald man. "Just—er—give her some water, or something, and let her rest for five or ten minutes, and then we'll call a cab and be on our way."

The taller woman looked at him with an expression of pitying scorn.

"*Please!*" she said. "Leave her to *us!*"

Leonidas, the policeman and the bald man found themselves out in the hall, and the door was shut firmly in their faces.

"Jimmy," the bald man said, "go out and tell everyone to keep on swopping, and everything's fine. Honestly, Witherall, don't these women get your *goat* sometimes? Way they acted, you'd think a little thing like a girl's fainting was a major catastrophe! She's a good-looking kid, all right—what'd you say her name was?"

"I'm sure you've seen her before," Leonidas deftly avoided the question. "She's an elevator girl at Haymaker's. Rather a coincidence you should mention his will. Er—I made one myself, recently."

The bald man, looking anxiously at the closed door, said shortly that everyone ought to have a will.

"What the hell," he added, "are those fool women doing in there?"

"I can't imagine, but I feel positive," Leonidas said truthfully, "that Jinx will—er—recover in spite of their ministrations. Of course, the disposition of *my* property was simple indeed, compared with the complications of Haymaker's estate. It must be very difficult for a man of such property to—er—devise and bequeath, particularly when he has no immediate family."

"Certainly was a job. Made me thank God," the bald man said, "that I'm poor. Hey!" he raised his voice. "Hey, you in there! You all right?"

Leonidas sighed. It would be so much easier not to circumnavigate, to come out into the open and frankly tell this man about Haymaker, and to ask him point blank if any beneficiary might also conceivably be a suspect. But after delivering a poignant bond appeal, and after swopping a dipper and a cake for a tea strainer and a lion's head, no man born of woman could come out with the casual statement that he was trying, all the time, to track down the murderer of R. H. Haymaker! If he were the bald man and if that tidbit were imparted to him, Leonidas thought, he would unquestionably summon Jimmy, the pride of Pomfret's police force, and tell him to carry poor Witherall to the psychopathic ward with all possible haste.

"Hey, you in there!" the bald man knocked on the door. "Hey!"

One of the women opened the door a scant inch and told him severely to be still.

"She has come to, but she's not acting at all the way she should!"

"You—er—mean that she is normal," Leonidas inquired, "or that she is not?"

"She's *too* normal! She wants to get right up! *We* feel she should have absolute rest and quiet—so you be still! After all, you don't want the girl to faint again, do you?"

"Think I better call a doctor?" the bald man asked. "Probably there's one out in the hall—oh, I keep forgetting we're down to old Eastman and Pincus. Well, you think I should phone one of 'em?"

"We're perfectly able to handle this! Just you be *still!*"

"Amazing man, Haymaker." Leonidas decided to try a new tack. "I'd always thought he was a bachelor, and only very recently learned about his marriage. But of course you probably know all about Mrs. Lately?"

The bald man bit.

"You know," he said confidentially, "I've been wanting to ask someone from Dalton more about that —of course, I couldn't ask just anyone, but I can ask you. Now frankly, did you guess he still loved her?"

"Well," Leonidas began cautiously, but the bald man didn't wait for his answer. Clearly, Pink Lately was one of his favorite topics.

"Why, Witherall, in all the years I've worked for Haymaker, I never heard him mention her name until she came back to Dalton! *I* always thought *he* thought she'd pulled a pretty dirty trick on him. *I* never guessed that he still loved her!"

"Er—"

"Why, Witherall, think of his remembering her for thirty years! It's incredible. Of course, she's still a good-looking woman. I grant that. She doesn't begin to look her age. I've been wondering and wondering —was it his finding her looking so much the way she did," the bald man said, "except for her hair, or did he get sort of patriotically inspired by the family that might've been his? You know, she's got five sons, all in the service."

"M'yes. So I heard. Er—"

"Bill Lately wasn't a bad fellow," the bald man went on. "Lot of fun, and a pretty good engineer. But he left her practically nothing. Her mother always helped out with the boys. I tell you, Witherall, you could have knocked me over with a feather when Haymaker called me, the week after Pink Lately came back, and said he was going to draw up a new will because of her! Why, I nearly dropped the phone—did you say something?"

"Er—this tickle," Leonidas said in a choked voice. "I have this little tickle in my throat. It bothers me, sometimes."

"I had a tickle last week." The bald man obviously had no idea of the effect that his tidings had on Leonidas. "Cleared it up with some sort of red stuff my wife got at the drugstore. Well, that money'll be a fine thing for Pink Lately and the Lately boys. They certainly can use it! But I still think Haymaker should figure out that when she gets that money, an awful lot of old dead gossip'll get dug up. There'll be more talk than there ever was. People'll say Pink Lately only came back to charm him and get his money. But Haymaker says they'll say that no matter who he gives—say, that red-head ought to be all right by now!"

"Perhaps they're right in making her rest." Leonidas moved just enough toward the door so that the bald man couldn't quite reach past him to knock. "I wonder what Mrs. Lately's reactions might be. Has she—er—any inkling of the situation?"

The bald man shrugged. "I told Haymaker I thought before he did something like that, he ought to—well, hell, not exactly talk it over with her, but at least sort of sound her out on the subject! I pointed out that no matter if she needed money, she mightn't like the idea of having his thrust on her. But Haymaker said he knew what he wanted to do, and if I didn't like it, I could lump it. Or words to that effect. Said he didn't care who knew about it, that he wasn't making any secret of it, and had no intention of letting it all burst on her like a bombshell in order to embarrass her later."

"I wondered about that angle," Leonidas said. "It could well be a rather subtle bit of revenge, couldn't it?"

"He didn't mean it that way. And I know he's told people, because a couple of 'em have hinted at it to
110

me. Whether he told Pink Lately, or whether she's heard about it, I wouldn't know."

"I must confess," Leonidas said, "that I am surprised. Er—not the store, too!"

"Oh, no, the nephew gets the store. I don't know what the hell he'll do with it," the bald man said. "He doesn't want it, and wouldn't work in it. They had a great old scene the day he left. Dave said you had no right to consign a man to the drygoods and department-store business just because his name was Haymaker instead of Smith or Jones, and Haymaker told him that if you were a Haymaker, it was the only business you were ever any good at, and that Dave would find it out sooner or later. I guess Dave has, all right. He had a car agency, and then the war came and washed him out of that. Then he started some sort of plastics business in a shed over Carnavon way—by the way, Witherall, I wish you'd tell me where Haymaker is, will you, so I can tell Dave if he comes back here looking for him again."

"Er—he's in Dalton," Leonidas said. "Has Dave been hunting him?"

"All over the place. Haymaker phoned him this afternoon—wanted to see him on something important, Dave said, though Haymaker hadn't said what. So Dave drove right over, because Haymaker doesn't call on him for anything more than once a year. But he couldn't find him at the store, or the club—seems to me he said he'd gone to your house, too. Somebody at the club thought Haymaker'd gone to see you."

"Indeed!" Leonidas said.

"He wandered around, and then he drove over to my place, and my wife sent him here. I told him I was sure it couldn't be anything very important. Probably just some errand. Privately, I don't even think it could have been much of an errand, for Turk does Haymaker's odd jobs."

"Er—where did Dave go from here?" Leonidas tried to make the question sound casual.

"Back to Dalton, I think, to have another hunt around. I guess he'll find Haymaker, all right. Witherall, enough is enough. I'm going in and see how that red-head is. Those two amateur Florence Nightingales may be putting a traction splint on her!"

He shoved the door open, and Leonidas followed him into the musty little room.

Jinx was still lying on the couch. At its head sat one woman, and at its foot sat another. Both of them, Leonidas thought, looked like gray-green ramrods.

"What goes on?" the bald man demanded. "Playing Quaker Meeting? Is she all right?"

"She's resting."

Jinx sat bolt upright. "I'm all right! I'm perfectly all right, but they won't let me get up, Mr. Witherall! Can't I—"

112

The woman at the head of the couch reached out and pushed her down.

"This girl's got to rest! And, furthermore," she said, "she's *going* to rest!"

It was evident to Leonidas that Jinx was going to rest over their dead bodies, if need be.

"Well," the bald man said, "I suppose she might as well rest—what's the matter, Jimmy?"

"It's two women." The policeman spoke from the doorway. "They're fighting over this swop of a piano stool and a charcoal picnic grill. *I* can't do anything with 'em, and you don't want me to get tough, do you? They *said* they'd do what you said, so maybe you better come."

The bald man, muttering something under his breath, hurried out, and Leonidas turned to the tall woman and put on his pince-nez.

"Do you know," she said suddenly, "you look just like Shakespeare? All the time you were talking, I kept trying to think who you looked like. Somehow I thought of you in a library!"

"Ah, yes. You were recalling a—er—bust of the Bard!" It was amazing, he thought, that he could still insert some spontaneity into that sentence after saying it several thousand times.

"How'd you know?" she demanded. "Did anyone ever tell you you looked like Shakespeare before?"

"Some—er—literate few," Leonidas said politely,

113

"have noticed a resemblance. May I ask a favor of you?"

"If you want me to let this girl up, the answer is no!"

"Ah, but I agree with you that the child should rest. M'yes, indeed!" He ignored Jinx's splutter of indignation. "No question about it, rest is imperative. But since her resting will delay us, I wonder if you'd be good enough to go to a phone and call for me the number I am writing down? And tell the person who answers that we will be late—and the reason why. I deeply regret the necessity for asking you, but I'm sure you'll be able to explain the situation far more satisfactorily than I. It may—er—take time."

He knew it would take time. He had written down his own number.

After the woman had marched out, he turned to Jinx.

"Now, I've been wondering if your pocketbook— dear me," he added hurriedly before Jinx could say that she had no pocketbook with her, "it isn't here! You had it on the platform, didn't you? Dear me, I'm afraid that if I go out and start asking for it, I may cause people to think you've been taken seriously ill. I don't want to cause any panic, but we must find your pocketbook! Now how can we solve this little problem!"

"I could go," the short woman suggested.

"Could you? Perhaps at the same time you could

reassure people as to the child's condition. It's a brown bag, and—er—describe your pocketbook, Jinx."

"It's an alligator pouch," Jinx said, "with my name in gold letters—" she went into an intricate description of the frame, the fittings, and the bag's contents.

"I'll get it. I think I know what it looks like."

The short woman trotted away.

"Now," Leonidas said briskly, "come along! Is there a back door to this structure? There must be. There always is a back door. Pick up your tea strainer and hurry!"

They slipped along the hall. Two minutes later they were hurrying along an uneven brick sidewalk at the rear of the building.

"Well, gee," Jinx said, "I never lived through anything like those two, not even in the Christmas rush! Wow! You remember when Haseltine was fighting sharks somewhere in the South Pacific after bailing out, and then that rubber boat bobbed up from nowhere? Well, when you came back just now, your face looked like a rubber boat to me!"

"Helen," Leonidas said, "thy beauty is to me like a rubber boat. M'yes, indeed!"

"Is that Shakespeare?" Jinx asked suspiciously.

"No. I'm truly sorry that you were forced to suffer, Jinx, but your sacrifice was worth while. I've learned from our bald friend—"

"What's his name?" Jinx interrupted.

Leonidas shook his head. "I still don't know. Our

115

conversation provided no opportune steppingstone where one might have paused and—er—casually asked him. To have done so might have undermined some of the boundless confidence he apparently had in me. But he is Haymaker's lawyer, and he told me that Mrs. Lately—"

"You mean," Jinx broke in, "the one in the elevator that made the cake and had the sword, and we missed in the beachwagon when we left the junk?"

"Exactly. That Mrs. Lately. She inherits Haymaker's money, it seems."

"Gee! And it was her sword—say, you don't suppose she did it all the time!"

"No, I don't. But the fact that she stands to gain by his death is going to add certain complicating factors. I also learned that Haymaker has a nephew who will get the store."

"Oh, everybody guessed that," Jinx said. "We all know Dave. He worked in the store nearly a year, you know."

"What," Leonidas asked, "is Dave like?"

"Oh, he's quite tall, and thin, and he wears glasses. He isn't a bit good looking. And he wears funny clothes. They never match. And a funny little round hat. A pork pie. He lives in Carnavon."

"And what was he like?"

"I just told you—oh, I see what you mean. Well, he didn't like working in the store. He was always wanting things changed over, and nobody would let

116

him. Funny thing, though, after he left, all the things he suggested were done. All the fancy lighting, and the modern showcases, and the mirrors and all."

"So! And after leaving the store, he hasn't been very successful?"

"Why," Jinx said, "he's done fine! A lot of the boys from Lower Falls work at his factory. They have guards outside, too. I don't know just what it is they make, but it's got to do with the war. Say, Mr. Witherall, where are we walking to, anyway?"

"We are walking," Leonidas said, "for what might be termed your health. As soon as we've proceeded a safe distance from the Lady Volunteers, we are going to take a cab back to Dalton. Dear me, it is going to be phenomenally hard to convince anyone I was at the Lyceum Hall swop from the time the doors opened!"

"Why worry?" Jinx said cheerfully. "You can always convince 'em you were at *this* swop. Nobody in Pomfret's going to forget your fireside chat in a good long while. What's it matter which swop you went to, anyway?"

Leonidas stopped and looked at her.

"I think," he said, "that you have something there. M'yes. M'yes, indeed. D'you know enough about Pomfret to know where the station is? I assume that's the most logical place for us to find a cab."

"There's almost as many Pomfrets as Daltons," Jinx said, "and they've all got stations. I could tell

117

in a minute where Main Street was if the knitting mill's big electric sign wasn't blacked out. Probably we'll find something if we just keep on walking."

"Jinx," Leonidas said, "I keep brooding about Haymaker's note. When he gave it to you, when he left, did he appear at all worried or upset?"

"No. He just looked like he was thinking hard, but that's the way he always looks. He wasn't worked up or anything. Not until he saw the stocking sale, and that got him sore, I think."

"Why?"

"Oh, I guess because somebody forgot to tell him about it. One day last week there was a perfume sale he didn't know about, and it made him good and sore. It was one of Dave's ideas."

"Er—the perfume sale?"

"No, having sales every day or so that weren't advertised. Dave said it'd get people into the habit of dropping in regularly and looking around. Every now and then someone does it—I don't know why it makes Mr. Haymaker mad. I guess he likes to think the store's still little, and he knows what everyone's doing and where everything is, and all. My grandmother said that old R. H. used to wait on customers himself, and he knew where every button was. Mr. Witherall, what you going to do with that lion's head?"

"I don't know," Leonidas said honestly. "And it's far heavier than I thought, at first. But at least it does not have to be tenderly extended at an arm's

118

length, like Lady Baltimore, and I suppose I can always put it on and wear it when I'm tired of carrying it."

"It's funny Turk wasn't around to get that note," Jinx said. "I never saw him all day. Mr. Haymaker must've expected him, too. He wouldn't of given me the note if he didn't think Turk'd be there." She paused at a street intersection. "Which way?"

"Take your choice," Leonidas said. "If we could only achieve a hill, we might figure out our bearings. On the level here, the direction of more populated districts is any man's guess. Pomfret's dimout is very definitely a black beauty."

"Let's go this way, then."

Jinx turned, and Leonidas followed her up the brick sidewalk of a wide street flanked by big, old-fashioned frame houses. The gas street lights, turned down to a pin point, didn't even cast sufficient glow to distinguish the corner signpost, let alone the name on it.

As they walked along, Leonidas tried to take stock.

If what the bald man had said was true, and there was no reason to think that he'd lied, then the person who literally stood to gain the most by Haymaker's death was Pink Lately. Pink was mixed up in that inexplicable hamper incident. Her sword was the murder weapon. She had been roaming around during the blackout. On the other hand, Leonidas reminded himself that he was equally involved from a circumstantial basis. And if the police found Haymaker's body, and then set out to investigate his own actions since four-thirty, and up to and including the present—Leonidas shivered involuntarily.

"Cold?" Jinx asked.

"No," Leonidas returned. "Er—no. I'm merely thinking congealing thoughts."

The way the bald man told it, it had at first sounded as if Haymaker's slightly disgruntled nephew, having left the store and failed in his subsequent business undertakings, might have a sterling motive to recoup his fortunes by killing his uncle. It was, after all, one way to get a job.

But Jinx said that the fellow's enterprise was flourishing. And if he rushed to his uncle when his uncle summoned him, there certainly couldn't be too many hard feelings existing between them!

"Still," Leonidas murmured aloud, "if he came to my house this evening—Jinx, I think that perhaps we well may—er—digress long enough to make some effort to track down Dave Haymaker. Did you say that he lives in Carnavon?"

"Yes. I don't know where, though. Which way do we go now? It looks to me as if it was a little bit lighter over there."

Leonidas followed her without paying very much attention to the direction she took. His mind was again busy mulling over the contents of Haymaker's note.

If accounts really were at the root of things, of

course, neither Pink nor young Haymaker could by
any stretch of the imagination—

"Say!" A man stepped suddenly out from behind a
tree, and Jinx squealed. "Oh, sorry. Didn't mean to
frighten you, young lady. Either of you happened to
see an oil truck around here anywhere?"

"Er—no," Leonidas said. "No, we haven't. Er—have
you lost one?"

"Dammit, no, I'm trying to *find* one! You know
what *I* think?"

"About the current oil situation? Doubtless," Leonidas said sympathetically, "you also find it rather trying."

"Trying! *Try*ing! Look here, I was as resigned about
it as the next man. I said well, if we haven't oil we
haven't oil, and make the best of it. That's what I
said. But what do they have to go lousing it up with
women for? I *ask* you! Women are perfectly all right
on some jobs. I couldn't ask any better workers than
my girls at the mill. Damn fine girls, all of 'em. But
oil *women!* God deliver me from oil women!"

Leonidas, who had started to edge past the man,
abruptly stopped.

"Er—oil *women?*"

"That's what I said to my daughter. Oil *women!*
Minute she told me we'd had an oil *woman,* I knew
something would go wrong. Well, I won't keep you
listening to *my* troubles, but if you see that oil truck
—*think* of it, minding the baby!"

121

"Er—the oil truck?"

"No, no, the oil *woman!*" the man said. "That idiot fool *woman!* If I get hold of her—but I'm keeping you. My wife says it's a wonder someone hasn't taken a poke at me before this for talking their ears off!"

"Let me assure you," Leonidas said, "that I am genuinely interested in knowing what happened!"

"Well, this fool oil woman came here this afternoon—that's my house, on the corner." He waved toward a massive frame house that bulged with bay windows. "My daughter was waiting for my wife to come home from shopping and take care of the baby, so she could go to the hospital. She does volunteer work there twice a week. Well, my wife didn't come and didn't come, and my daughter was steaming around—and what do you think? This oil woman says *she'll* tend the baby till my wife comes back!"

"How very accommodating of her!" Leonidas said.

The man made explosive little sounds in the back of his throat.

"Can you beat it?" he demanded, "I said was she stark crazy, leaving the baby with a stranger? And my daughter had the nerve to say she was a nice girl! Can you *beat* it? Leaving my grandson with the first oil woman that comes along! Well, my wife came home, and the oil woman left—and what do you think? No oil!"

"You mean that she neglected," Leonidas asked interestedly, "to fill the tank?"

"Ran dry as a bone an hour ago! Now I ask you, can you beat it!"

"Well," Leonidas said, "one must be fair. After all, she looked after the baby."

"My wife said the baby loved her. My wife thought she was a nice girl, too. But no *oil!*" the man said vehemently. "No *oil!* I grant you that a man might not stop to tend the baby, but dammit, if he came to leave oil, he'd *leave* oil! He wouldn't go flouncing off forgetting what he came for!"

"Whose oil was it?" Leonidas inquired. "Er—any company I know, I wonder?"

"Quarl's. Quarl's Quality Oil. Huh! Quarl's Quality idiots! I told 'em a little bit over the phone, but I've got an awful lot more saved up to tell 'em about Quarl's Quality! Well, if you catch sight of that oil truck, just you yell at it and send it on to me, will you?"

"We will indeed," Leonidas promised. "By any chance," he added, remembering Pink's positive declaration about the girl in his cellar, "by any rare chance, was your oil woman blonde?"

"So they tell me. A beautiful young blonde. Lovely expensive perfume, too." The man snorted. "Why, you'd think they'd had a movie star visiting 'em, the way they raved about that fool oil woman!"

"Er—she didn't wear a mink coat, did she?"

The man whooped with laughter. "Oh, that's one I forgot to ask 'em!" he said delightedly. "I said I supposed she had lovely white hands and a nice mani-

123

cure, and they said, yes, she did. Oh, I'll have to ask 'em about the coat! Well, so long!"

"Perhaps you'd be good enough to tell us how to get back on to the main street?" Leonidas asked. "We've rather lost our bearings in the dimout."

"First right, then straight ahead. Other times, I'd offer to drive you over. But it isn't far. And listen, you want to know my advice to you?"

"What?" Leonidas asked obediently.

"You convert right back to coal! They'll have a hard time getting lady coal heavers!"

"Mr. Witherall," Jinx said as they set off again, "you told me something about that girl in your cellar and the mink coat—gee, do you think she really could've been an oil woman?"

"D'you think," Leonidas returned, "that an oil woman, even a beautiful blonde oil woman, would be inclined to go about her chores wearing a mink coat?"

"Well," Jinx said thoughtfully, "you can't always tell, these days. There's a lady meat cutter in the chain store we trade at in Lower Falls, she wears a diamond as big as an egg, and Mae's sister that works on the jewelry counter at Haymaker's, she says it's real. And one day Mae and I went for some pork chops, this woman was wearing a corsage of two orchids." She giggled suddenly. "I keep thinking about that bum, Beeding. You suppose he's called that damn morale class to check up on me?"

"It is my impression," Leonidas said, "that Major Beeding is now in bed licking his wounds, having first rubbed them down a bit with arnica—why is he not in active service, I wonder? I've heard him boom about on the beauties of Army life, but it never occurred to me to ask why he was working at Haymaker's!"

"Oh, he was in the regular Army," Jinx said, "and then he left it to work at the store. Then when the National Guard got called up, he went off with that, and then it turned out he had something the matter with him. A bad foot, or something. So he had to leave, and then he came back to the store again."

"After watching his agile pursuit of you this evening," Leonidas commented, "one would never suspect that he suffered from any physical disability. Didn't our oilless friend say first right? This must be it."

"Gee, all these streets look alike!" Jinx said as they rounded the corner.

"They do possess a certain universal drabness," Leonidas agreed. "Even its Chamber of Commerce could not recommend Pomfret's streets as any scenic tour. But at least our little detour has apprised us of the fact that Quarl's Quality Oil employs women. Whether we may stretch the long arm of coincidence to a point of making the unequivocal statement that the blonde girl who said she came to my cellar to retrieve a mink coat was also the Quarl's Quality blonde oil woman who minded a baby in Pomfret—hm. That has a certain Haseltinian quality!"

Halfway along the next block, Jinx quickened her steps.

"I'm sure there's lights ahead. What are you going to do, Mr. Witherall? Take a cab back to the right swop in Dalton, or what?"

"I'm going to telephone Dave Haymaker and see if he can be located. If so," Leonidas said, "we shall locate him, and then proceed to the swop."

"Are you going to telephone from a drugstore?" Jinx asked eagerly.

"M'yes, I suppose so. A drugstore, or any available phone."

"Well, if it was from a drugstore, then do you think maybe we could take enough time out to get a bite to eat?"

"My dear child, haven't you had dinner? No? You must be ravenous!" Leonidas said. "I should have inquired—dear me, that's amazing! Now that I stop and consider the situation, it occurs to me that I neglected to dine, myself!" He gripped the lion's hempish mane and lengthened his stride. "By all means, let us get a bite to eat!"

They found a drugstore on the next corner.

Leonidas paused while Jinx climbed up on a stool at the counter, and indicated the telephone booths at the rear of the store.

"I'll make a preliminary survey of the Haymaker situation while you order," he said. "If he is not available, I'll have a cab pick us up here."

Jinx caught up with him before he reached the booths.

"Say, gee, Mr. Witherall, all they have left is chop suey. Meatless."

"Then by all means let us have chop suey, meatless. Er—any coffee?"

Jinx shook her head. "There's only milk. I'm going to have a double chocolate malted."

Leonidas winced, then looked at the lion, and smiled briefly.

"Ah, well, let us go whole hog," he said. "Chop suey, meatless, and a double chocolate malted for me, too!"

One of the two telephone booths was empty. Leonidas entered it, and then, after two vain attempts to take the lion's head in with him, he gave up and put it on a small table near by.

The black hat lying on the table caught his eye. Leonidas had a fondness for good hats, and this was one of the most beautiful Homburgs he had ever seen. Definitely, he thought, not the sort of headgear one might expect to find on a none-too-clean glass-topped table in a Pomfret drugstore. That hat was born for Ritz check rooms, for the mahogany shelves of directors' rooms!

Putting on his pince-nez, Leonidas leaned over to peek at the maker's name.

But it was the owner's name that rose up and hit him in the face.

"R. H. Haymaker," the small gold letters said.

CHAPTER 6

Leonidas blinked, then deliberately turned and stared for thirty seconds at a small showcase of cameras and flash bulbs.

Then he looked back at the hat.

But the small gold letters were no mirage.

They still said "R. H. Haymaker."

Slowly, Leonidas swung on his heels and surveyed the occupied telephone booth. Because the folding door was open a few inches, the inside light had not flicked on, and neither the booth's occupant nor its interior was visible. Only a boot showed by the crack of the door. A workman's boot, clumsy, hard-toed, and mud-caked. Around the ankle was a cuff of frayed, grubby dungarees.

Could Haymaker's elegant Homburg be in any way connected with the owner of that very utilitarian boot? Had *he* left the hat on the table?

If he hadn't, *who* had?

And where could the person have got it, in the first place?

And what, Leonidas thought, was the man doing in

the booth, anyway? He certainly wasn't talking. He wasn't saying a word. He wasn't even making the usual "uh-huhs" and "nun-uhs" of someone being talked to.

Leonidas twirled his pince-nez for a moment, and then sat down on a stoollike chair directly in line with the booth's door. It was a good strategic position, and he intended to hold it and await any developments that might ensue.

It occurred to him suddenly that the man was just standing there dialing. Dialing and dialing.

At last the door was slammed open, and the booth's occupant stepped out and reached for the Homburg hat.

He was a tall thin young man with glasses, and neither his long thin face nor his long well-kept fingers resembled those of any workman Leonidas had ever seen.

Picking up the hat, he turned, saw Leonidas, and a wide grin spread over his face.

"Prithee, Master Will, why bearest thou yon lion's head?" he inquired politely. "Offhand, I know three quotes about horses, a couple about mice, and even one on elephants that your looksake wrote, but that lion's head has me stumped—by the way, you *are* Witherall of Dalton, aren't you?"

"M'yes," Leonidas said, "I am. And may I ask who you are?"

"I'm Dave Haymaker—my God, I've called your

130

house, and called, and called, and called! I could dial your number in my sleep. Probably will. Look, sir, can you tell me where my uncle is?"

Leonidas looked at him thoughtfully.

"It is not my intention to answer you in song, so to speak," he said, "but—er—where did you get that hat?"

Dave Haymaker looked thoughtfully back at him.

"Something's happened, hasn't it, sir?"

"M'yes," Leonidas said. "Something most assuredly has."

"I felt it." Dave Haymaker sat down in a stool-like chair opposite Leonidas. "I felt it in his voice when he phoned me this afternoon. Ordinarily I'm one of the least psychic people in the world, but something in his voice made me rush off from the shop without bothering to change my clothes. And when I couldn't locate him, I got good and panicky. You can always put your finger on uncle, you know. You can always find him. Then when I stumbled on that hat, I knew that whatever the worst was, it had happened. Uncle never left hats around loose in his life. Not one of his precious black Homburgs!"

"I see," Leonidas said. "I see. Er—d'you mind glancing at the soda fountain and ascertaining if a young red-headed girl is sitting at the counter, and presumably all right?"

Dave leaned over and craned his neck.

"Oh, I know her! That's Jinx. The songbird of

Lower Falls. Yes, she's there, and she seems to be munching happily away—look, sir, what's happened?"

"First," Leonidas said, "d'you mind very much answering a few questions?"

"Not at all. Only I wish you'd tell me if uncle is all right, or hurt, or sick, or anything. Ever since he phoned, I've been quietly going mad!"

"There is nothing," Leonidas said, "that you can do for your uncle now, believe me. But I think, on the other hand, that there is much *we* may be able to do for him. Now, can you tell me where you were from—oh, say four this afternoon until that apparently false blackout and alert which took place in Dalton this evening?"

"I spent most of the afternoon with a government inspector," Dave said. "Fact is, I was with him when uncle telephoned, a bit before four. Then I rushed—"

"What did he call you about?" Leonidas interrupted.

"He said that there was a matter pertaining to business in which he required my presence—you know how very precisely he always put things. I told him I'd be over at once, and he thanked me and said it was very good of me, and that he'd be at the club, and would explain the situation there."

"But he didn't tell you what specific business was involved?" Leonidas asked. "Or why he wished to see you in person?"

"No. He's not inclined to be chatty over the phone,

132

ever," Dave said. "I think he still faintly mistrusts
Bell's Folly. Anyway, that was all he said. But there
was something in his voice—a sort of urgent note—
that hit me like a ton of bricks. I can't explain it any
better than that, but I somehow just felt that the old
boy really did need me. I rushed out and grabbed my
beachwagon and went tooting over to Dalton, to the
club. I got there perhaps a bit after four-thirty. But
uncle had already been there, and left!"

"Alone?"

Dave nodded. "And he hadn't left any message for
me. I went up to the cardroom to see if he'd told anyone where he was going, and old man Newton said
that uncle had murmured something about seeing
you. So I got your address and drove up to Birch Hill
Road, but nobody was there."

"I was in a hamper," Leonidas said a little apologetically.

"In a—" Dave paused and stared at him. "You
know, it sounded to me as if you said you were in a
hamper, sir!"

"I did. I'm truly sorry," Leonidas said sincerely. "I
have no desire to confuse the issue by inserting my
story until you're through. Er—what did you do then,
after visiting my house?"

"I went back to the club," Dave said. "I decided that
uncle probably hadn't expected me to get there so
quickly, and that he'd probably popped across the
street to the store on some errand or other, and that

he'd probably have popped back to meet me. After all, old man Newton wasn't *sure* that uncle had gone to see you. He just had that impression—by the way, sir, he gave me a very vivid description of you."

"I'm sure he did," Leonidas said. "Theodore Newton has always faintly resented me. He firmly believes that Bacon wrote Shakespeare, and somehow it makes him feel that I am a rank impostor."

Dave chuckled. "As a matter of fact, he did manage to insinuate that there was something slightly spurious about you. He said that you resembled Shakespeare to a marked degree in an expurgated sort of way."

"And of course you asked him what he meant, and he murmured something about Shakespeare in Modern Dress," Leonidas said. "It was one of the happiest days of his life when he came on me picnicking with the Sixth Form at Dalton Falls. I had a burned hot dog in one hand and a charred marshmallow in the other, and Newton crowed with pleasure and said, 'Ah! Shakespeare, the Inner Man.' But let us not digress. You returned to the club, and your uncle still was not there."

"Then," Dave said, "I drove up to his house. Annie said he'd phoned her that he'd be out for dinner, and would probably be quite late returning. She thought he meant to dine at the club. So I tooted back there. No soap. Then I went to your house again—was

134

that you who answered the bell and spoke into that tube thing?"

"M'yes. That was I."

"Well, you just sounded dazed when I mentioned his name, and kept saying 'Haymaker? Haymaker? R. H. Haymaker?' as if my asking for him all but floored you, so I decided old Newton was crazy thinking uncle spoke of going to see you, and bounced off again."

"Er—just where were you," Leonidas asked, "at the time of the Alert?"

"I'd just got back to the club, and was parking the beachwagon. That new bellboy—well, you couldn't exactly refer to him as a *boy*, could you? He's the grandfather of the bellboy that went into the Navy. Anyway, he and Judge Thackaberry rushed out with truncheons and tin hats and bustled me inside. They stood guard over me in the lower lounge till the All Clear sounded," Dave said with a reminiscent grin. "As if I were something very precious, like a pearl of great price, or a gram of radium, or something. They wouldn't even let me go get a sandwich and a drink."

"Consider yourself fortunate," Leonidas told him, "that they didn't send you to the shelter in the cellar. Professor Bradbury presides over that, and practically forces you to take two vitamin B pills as you enter."

"For the love of God, why?"

"He says it's for your nervous system. Having spent

much of his life segregating one vitamin or another," Leonidas said, "he puts a vast amount of faith in them. What did you do after the All Clear?"

"I drove back to Carnavon," Dave said wearily. "I wondered if uncle might possibly have driven over to catch me before I left the shop. But he hadn't. So I went back to the club, had a sandwich, and then went to his house once more. Then I came over here to Pomfret to see Gidding. His lawyer. You know Gidding?"

"Intimately," Leonidas said, "though not by name. I have just attended his swop."

"Well, Gidding pooh-poohed the idea that anything might be seriously wrong. He said that uncle was coming over here to make a bond speech, and that he'd probably called me because he wanted *me* to make a bond speech at some other swop. Seems there's a lot of 'em going on tonight. It's the County Victory Drive, or something like that. Gidding said that was probably why uncle said he'd be out for dinner, and late returning home, and all. Then he went on at a great rate about mountains and mole-hills, and said if anything untoward had occurred, uncle would undoubtedly have phoned him. Well, Gidding has a right to his own opinions," Dave said, "and on the face of it, my getting so steamed up probably did look silly as hell. But I was still worried. I decided to take another crack at finding you, so I drove back to Birch Hill Road."

136

He stopped, and a peculiar look flitted across his face.

"Did—er—anything out of the ordinary take place?" Leonidas inquired.

"Well, sir, that's unquestionably one of the best sections of Dalton, and without doubt the best people live there, and they're all lifelong customers of Haymaker's," Dave said.

"A beachwagon and a Buick in every garage," Leonidas murmured. "M'yes, indeed!"

"Exactly. But by God, Bill Shakespeare, that's a crazy neighborhood! You know what it made me think of? Haseltine. It was exactly like a chapter out of the adventures of Lieutenant Haseltine—but then I don't suppose the head of Meredith's Academy would know about that merry blood-and-thunder epic."

"I could practically quote Haseltine to you," Leonidas said, "by the yard. The excellent Lieutenant is very dear to me. M'yes, indeed! Er—what happened?"

"Well, first a posse of cops held me up at the corner of Oakhill Place and Birch Hill Road. Made me get out, and—oh, they went through the usual routine. Where'd I think I was going, huh? Did I have a license, huh? Well, show it to 'em, show it to 'em, they didn't have all night to wait for me to show 'em my license!"

"What," Leonidas inquired, "appeared to be their basic motive?"

Dave shrugged. "That's what I asked 'em. I was

137

proceeding at not more than twenty-five miles an hour on the proper side of the street, and my lights were properly dimmed. My windshield had an A sticker, a C sticker, a state inspection tag, a federal tax stamp, and a permit to enter an area where military equipment was being manufactured. And—"

"That's a new one to me," Leonidas said.

"I have to have it to get into my own shop yard," Dave said. "I had a State Guard sticker, and a sticker saying I was pledged to drive not over thirty-five, and a sticker saying that I shared my car with defense workers, giving their names and addresses, and a sticker about my tires. Furthermore, I'd come to a complete stop at the intersection. I wasn't breaking any rules I ever heard of. Well, while they looked at my license and my registration and my stickers, they kept muttering a lot among themselves, and pointing to my boots and dungarees and jacket. They seemed fascinated by my boots. They kept circling around me saying 'Mud—*see?* Mud—*see?* Mud!' Just as if a bit of mud befuddled them."

"Bemuddled," Leonidas suggested, "would be more apt. What was their purpose in treating you like a man from Mars?"

"I asked 'em, with great politeness," Dave said. "I asked 'em several thousand times. Finally they broke down and said they thought I was a prowler. I pointed out that the average prowler didn't prowl in a beach-wagon, complete with all the proper stickers and all.

Left 'em completely unmoved. They looked at me in a sinister fashion and asked where I was going. I told 'em to see you, and they said, well, why didn't I go see you, then? And trooped after me with their hands suggestively hovering over their holsters while I went and rang your front-door bell for the third time. At least, I think it was the third time. I'd lost count."

"Er—then?"

"Then—well," Dave said, "frankly, I was irked by those cops. I was irked right down to the bone. And I began to wonder if their hunting a prowler might conceivably have some connection with my inability to locate uncle. I wondered if anyone might have threatened the old boy, and that's why he wanted me. Uncle has a really reckless habit of carrying around a lot of money, you know. It seemed to me entirely possible that he might have gone from the club to see you, and have been waylaid on the way by this prowler. But—"

"Yes?" Leonidas said encouragingly, as Dave paused.

"But I was damned if I'd stick my neck out by telling my suspicions to those dumb cops, after they'd been so suspicious of me, and after my telling 'em I'd only come to see you. I had a hunch they'd just ball things up by grabbing me again. And this feeling I'd had all along that something was awfully wrong kept growing on me. I didn't want to waste time with a lot of explanations—I didn't have anything concrete to explain, anyway. So I decided to look into the situa-

139

tion on my own hook. I drove around the block to the next street, and parked the beachwagon, intending to slip back to your house through the woods."

Dave paused again.

"It's just occurred to me," he continued, "that I didn't really know why I went back, or just exactly what I expected to find. I was so worried, I wasn't thinking very clearly. And I was a lot more worried when I caught sight of this figure slipping out of the woods just as I slipped into 'em!"

"It wasn't, by any rare chance, a blonde oil woman wearing a mink coat, was it?" Leonidas inquired interestedly.

"A blonde oil—a *what? What* did you say?" Dave demanded.

"I'm sorry," Leonidas said contritely. "Forget it, please. I didn't mean to distract you again. Whom did you see?"

"Well, it was a fellow in a turtle-neck sweater," Dave said, "and I'd almost be willing to swear on a stack of Bibles that it was Turk, uncle's man Friday —do you happen to know Turk?"

"Er—no, but I'm beginning to feel that I do," Leonidas said.

"Before I had a chance to call out," Dave went on, "he slid back into the woods like a snake and disappeared. Honestly, just assuming from that sweater that it was Turk had the oddest effect on me—I was sure then that uncle must be around in the neighborhood somewhere! I yelled at him, and set out in the direction I thought he'd taken. Perhaps a dozen yards later, I saw something moving—and then, wham! The fellow lunged at me!"

"And it *was* Turk?"

Dave smiled.

"It was one of those funny little things that happen so quickly, and yet take a year to tell. As this fellow lunged at me, he said something—it wasn't an actual word you could distinguish, like 'Hey' or 'You' or anything like that. It was sort of a grunting sound and a word, all run together. And believe it or not, I recognized the man at once. There was just enough of his usual boom in the tone, as if he was belching out an order."

"Not Beeding!" Leonidas said. "Not Major Beeding!"

"You know that jackass? He's one of the reasons I left Haymaker's store," Dave said. "I knew in my bones that sooner or later, I'd paste Comrade Beeding smack on the snoot in public, which would have been very bad for the store's good name."

"Why in the world did he lunge at *you?*"

"I don't know." Dave shrugged. "He just lunged. But when he made that sound, I knew him. And I'm happy to say that with a bit of fancy footwork, Mrs. Haymaker's boy Dave gave him a snappy left to the jaw before getting the hell out of there. I remember thinking as I loped away that just flattening Major

141

Blimp was enough to make any evening a success. It wasn't till a lot later that I started wondering what in blazes Beeding was doing out there in the woods, lunging at all comers!"

"Perhaps," Leonidas said thoughtfully, "I have been guilty of underestimating the Major! In my mind, he has for some time been in bed with an electric pad clutched to his sore shoulder. M'yes, indeed, he seems to be far more resilient than I suspected!"

"But what would he be doing out in those woods!" Dave demanded.

"I rather think—m'yes, I feel quite certain that he was still aiding the police in their effort to track down that prowler of his!"

"Of *his?*" Dave said. "Why *his?*"

"For all Major Beeding knows," Leonidas informed him, "he was somewhat roughly handled by a prowler this evening."

"I don't get it—did somebody muss him up?" Dave said. "Who?"

"Er—I did, assisted by a plant stake. I fear," Leonidas said, "that if Beeding ever does happen to catch a genuine prowler, things will go hard for the poor creature. After tonight, Beeding's aversion to prowlers will very likely amount to a mania. Er—what did you do then? And where did you find your uncle's hat?"

"I'm just coming to that part. I must have got twisted after smacking Beeding," Dave said, "because when I came out of the woods, I was right behind your house, on Birch Hill Road. I decided to walk around the block instead of getting twisted in the woods again, so I went down your driveway. I don't know what impelled me to jump over your hedge—"

"Everybody does," Leonidas interposed. "The grocer boy, his successor, the grocer girl—everyone goes just so far down the driveway, and then some gremlin whispers in their ear and tells them to jump over Mr. Witherall's hedge. I replace those corner privet plants every other year. There's a gap there now named 'Jesse's Gap,' after my vegetable woman."

"Well, right there on that triangle of lawn," Dave said, "I saw uncle's hat. It was just on the edge of the little puddle of glow that the street light gives out. I picked it up—of course I recognized it! There's not another hat in Dalton like that! And while I was standing there trying to figure out what in God's name could have gone on, with uncle's hat there, and Turk sneaking around in the woods, this man materialized. I don't know where he came from. He may have landed with a parachute. But I looked up, and he was running toward me, waving his arms and yelling like a madman. I started to run. I don't quite know why now, but it seemed the only logical and sensible thing to do just then."

"Er—who was he?" Leonidas personally had his own suspicions.

"He was a warden in a tin hat," Dave said, "and he kept screaming something about a report. I think

143

he wanted me to make one out—I give you my word, sir, things like that don't happen over in Carnavon!"

"Henry S. C. Compton," Leonidas said, "is the sort of man who would have held his finger in the dike even if something far handier had been available. He would have stood on the burning deck even if a fire extinguisher were within easy reach. Henry is a man of incredible perseverance. He desires to have a report made out. I can clearly see where he is going to have that report made out even if he has to chase some innocent bystander to do it. Er—did he catch up with you?"

"No," Dave said. "It suddenly occurred to me that there was no reason why I should run away. After all, I didn't smack Beeding until he made a pass at me. That's justifiable self-defense in any court. So I turned around and walked back toward him. He panted up, flapping this paper at me."

"What happened?"

Dave grinned. "I stuck my tongue out at him," he said simply, "and turned and left. He was still staring after me when I turned the corner. I went back to the beachwagon. I rather wanted to see if I couldn't find Turk, but then I heard those cops whistling, so I drove off back here to Pomfret, to see Gidding. But before I had any chance to tell him about finding that hat, he said that you'd been there to the swop and made a bond speech, and that uncle certainly was all right, because you'd just come from him, or words to that effect. So I came here and started phoning your house. If I couldn't get hold of you, I intended to go and see if you were at the Dalton swop. If you weren't there, I had every intention of braving that crazy neighborhood of yours again, and sitting on your front doorstep till you came home. Hello, mama, hello, papa, I made it!" he concluded with obvious relief. "I didn't think I could stagger through that narrative, and I'm not sure that it's all clear to you, but it's the best I can do. Now, sir, what *has* happened?"

Leonidas drew a long breath.

"If you succumb to what I fear will be your natural inclination to interrupt," he said, "we will remain in this somewhat untidy drugstore till doomsday, at the very least. In short, let me tell you the tale in its entirety. I shall start with a mislaid umbrella, and I shall boil it all down as much as possible."

Six minutes later, Leonidas stopped talking, and Dave Haymaker stared at him, and then shook his head.

"I don't suppose," he said, "that my lower jaw will ever permanently return to its original position up there in my mouth—oh, it's unbelievable! The old boy and I had our troubles from time to time, but I was very fond of him! I really was very fond of the old boy—oh, if only I could have reached him in time! Why didn't he call me sooner? Why didn't he give me some hint of what was going on? Why didn't he tell you in that note?"

"It is my impression," Leonidas said, "that while he might have guessed that something was wrong, he neither grasped the extent of its importance, nor understood what peril he was in—you can't think of any specific person whom you might term his enemy, can you?"

Dave made a little gesture of futility.

"I suppose any number of people may have wanted to kill him, over a period of years. He was a sharp Yankee horse-trader, and Haymaker's hasn't grown to its present size because the Haymaker family thought it beneath 'em to lift out a few eye teeth. The first Haymaker started in as a tin peddler, you know. Went from door to door, dickering. Uncle used exactly the same methods, only he sat behind a mahogany desk under a Mawson portrait of the tin peddler dressed like a deacon. There are very few people who ever got the better of a Haymaker in trade, and never twice."

"Can you think of anyone in the store, perhaps, who might have some grudge against him?" Leonidas asked.

"I think most of the employees were rather fond of him," Dave said. "He was always very fair with them—a lot fairer than he was with his business associates. He did nice, paternalistic things, like sending all the girls home in cabs when there was a bad storm. And he was grand to old employees. They usually made more out of him after they left than while they were here. What do you think about all this, Bill Shakespeare?"

Leonidas twirled his pince-nez. "The obvious course was to try to discover who stood to gain by his death. Gidding said that Pink Lately—"

"I know. You said she got the money. But it can not," Dave said with finality, "be her."

"You know her?"

"No. I never met her. But I went to school with a couple of the Lately boys. Archie and Tad. Would you believe it, but the whole affair of uncle's blighted romance was so hushed up in the family, I never knew about it till Archie and Tad told me, out in California? But it couldn't be Pink Lately. If the Haymaker money had meant anything to her at all, she never would have gone running away from it with Bill Lately!"

"That," Leonidas said, "also occurred to me. And you, as the other beneficiary, were at the club during the period of the blackout. The obvious course, in other words, has come to a dead end."

"Haven't you any ideas?" Dave asked. "Other ideas?"

"I toyed with the notion that some good honest burgher might have been consumed with jealousy at the jobs and directorates that have been coming my way—specifically, that Haymaker directorate—and taken out his wrath on your uncle by killing him, and on me by leaving the body in my house. But

147

that," Leonidas said, "is an assumption too full of flaws."

"Well," Dave said, "I didn't, you didn't, Pink Lately didn't, and I'm sure Turk didn't. Turk would cheerfully cut off his right arm for uncle—one Haymaker or another has been bailing out the Turk family for years. If anyone killed uncle, it's a wonder to me they didn't have to kill Turk first. I can't imagine where Turk was, and why he wasn't around."

"If the note your uncle wrote me was left for Turk," Leonidas said, "one might suppose that Turk was expected. Hm. I feel that a recapitulation is in order. I hoped, when I set out, to find Haymaker's lawyer—"

"Check," Dave said. "You got all he can tell you that matters at all."

"I wanted to find who called and asked for Haymaker at my house."

"That was me. Check."

"The oil man, or," Leonidas said tentatively, "oil woman."

"That throws me," Dave said. "I think it's possible you may have had an oil woman, yes. But even if an oil woman in Pomfret played with a baby, I don't think that it necessarily follows that the same oil woman in Dalton would leave a mink coat behind her. Not even if they were both blondes, well-scented, and characterized by a congenital inability to deliver their goods."

"I wanted to discover the identity of the prowler," Leonidas said, "and also to find out if he were in my cellar."

"I'm putting my money on it's being Turk," Dave said. "It's that turtle-neck sweater. That's practically Turk's trademark. And if I was hunting uncle around your house, Turk may well have been hunting him there, too. And for the same reason."

"A chance remark about the Dalton Demons caused me to wonder if it couldn't be Turk," Leonidas said, "but on the other hand, d'you think Turk would be inclined to break into cellars?"

"Every last member of the Turk family," Dave said, "has a record as long as your arm. If Turk thought uncle was in someone's house, and if he wanted to get in, his mode of entry wouldn't bother him a whit. I wouldn't put it past him to skip lightly into the second story by way of a wisteria vine, if one was handy. As far as I'm concerned, and until a more likely candidate comes along, Turk is the prowler."

"Then, of course, I had that hamper problem," Leonidas said. "Every now and then, that comes to my mind and frightens me. All those loaves of bread!"

"I think you pretty well figured out all the mechanics of that," Dave said. "The employee's lunchroom is on the sixth floor, and a part of it opens out on to a wide corridor. The room where the Lost and Found stuff is kept—it's really an oversized closet—has a door leading to the same corridor. And there al-

149

most always are parcel trucks or hampers in the corridor, since it leads directly to the freight elevators.
Without any doubt, you and Pink got stuffed into
hampers and stuck out there, and then someone just
came along and whipped off with the hampers. The
actual action's clear enough. But why it happened is
beyond me!"

"Would you know," Leonidas asked, "what employee might have done the whipping?"

Dave shook his head.

"Probably they have lady porters, now. But I don't
think that part matters. If no one spotted you, I doubt
if anyone guessed that you and Pink Lately were inside. Those hampers and trucks are heavy things. I
know. I shoved 'em around for three months when I
started in to work. Where do we go from here, Shakespeare?"

"First, to the Dalton swop. I should be seen there,"
Leonidas said, "and we should reassure Pink that we
have neither forgotten her nor been diverted from our
main interest. Then we will have to tackle things
from a slightly different angle."

"Like," Dave said, "from what?"

"From the angle of the Haymaker accounts. While
it seems incredible that my innocent question in the
directors' meeting might have led to the discovery of
actual irregularities," Leonidas said, "the fact remains
that the only suggestion I made, the only thing I
opened my mouth to speak of during the entire meet-

150

ing, was accounts. That must be what your uncle referred to in his note."

"Hey," Dave said. "I have a brain wave. Do you suppose the old boy could have been collecting you and me in order to confront someone? He means to talk things over with you—at the club, or at your house. Then he means to go and see someone else. Uncle was no fool. Uncle believed in witnesses. Uncle—does this make any sense to you, Shakespeare?"

Leonidas nodded. "I think you might go on," he said. "Uncle wanted a witness, and uncle—for some reason or another—wanted someone not connected with the store. You are not. And my connection is so recent as to be very thin indeed. M'yes, indeed. But after reaching the club, uncle regretfully changed his mind and set off by himself. Now, I wonder about that hat, Dave. If I were your uncle, that hat is the last possession I would toss on my lawn. Or anyone else's lawn. And I doubt if anyone, after killing him, would deliberately toss it there."

"How'd it get there, then? I've racked my brains over that one," Dave said.

"If you were going to my house with someone whom you did not entirely trust," Leonidas said, "but if you had left a note for your faithful henchman, who would presumably shortly arrive to deliver it—well, suppose if your fine black Homburg blew off, you let it blow. Suppose you even gave it, so to speak, a head start?"

151

"You mean that uncle might have done that deliberately, so that Turk would spot it? God knows if Turk saw uncle's hat lying anywhere without uncle, he'd tear a house down with his bare hands to see what the matter was!"

"Exactly."

"But why did uncle go *in?* And how did he and this person get into your house, anyway?"

"That," Leonidas said, "is something we cannot even guess at—who has charge of Haymaker's accounts?"

"Dear good old honest John Meiklejohn," Dave said. "To think he might have had anything to do with any possible shortage would be like—well, accusing the Bank of England of selling wildcat oil stock. It's possible that someone might be lousing up the figures they gave John, but John wouldn't be involved."

"What d'you think happened," Leonidas asked, "when your uncle, consulting the notes he'd made during the directors' meeting, found a notation about Witherall and accounts?"

"He told someone to get John," Dave said, "and John sent him in the figures he wanted."

"Ah, then John would know about shortages!"

"Not necessarily. John is concerned with figures. His not to reason why."

"We will go to the swop," Leonidas picked up the lion's head, "and then we will call on honest John—

152

dear me, Dave, I forgot poor Jinx! How unutterably careless of me! Is she all right?"

Dave craned his neck.

"She isn't there any more," he said. "She's gone!"

Gripping the lion's head, Leonidas started for the front of the store. Dave, with the black Homburg, followed more leisurely.

"Where," Leonidas asked the counter girl, "is the young woman who came in with me? What became of her?"

"She left," the counter girl said. "That'll be a dollar twenty, plus tax, please. She didn't pay. That's two chop suey, meatless, and two double chocolate malted milks."

"When did she go?" Leonidas demanded.

"Oh, a long time ago. Fifteen minutes. While you and him was talking."

"You mean," Leonidas said, "that she—er—devoured two chop sueys and two double chocolate malts, and—er—just left?"

The counter girl giggled. "It's all right, gramp," she said. "Your girl friend didn't go off with no fellow. It was just two women."

"Two *women?*"

"From the Volunteer Corps. You know, with that gray-green uniform."

"Those women!" Leonidas said. "They—oh, my, no! They couldn't have tracked us down from Gidding's swop! We're miles from that!"

"Miles?" Dave said. "Why, it's practically just back of us!"

"It can't be," Leonidas said. "We walked miles away from it. Blocks and blocks. We—"

He thought back. There had been a right turn, then another turn, then a right turn, then another right.

He looked at Dave.

"Honestly, Shakespeare, the hall's just back of us. That's why I was phoning from here. It was the nearest phone."

"We walked in a circle," Leonidas said, "and those women—tell me," he said to the counter girl, "did she leave willingly? Er—of her own free will and accord?"

"Well, she went out with 'em," the girl said. "She didn't *say* anything. You needn't worry, mister. One of the women was in here a little while ago. She was trying to get a phone number in Dalton. I talked with her then. She's all right."

Leonidas turned to Dave. "We can't leave that child here! Dear me, they know me—er—d'you know any Lady Volunteers?"

"God forbid!"

"Capital! Now," Leonidas said to the counter girl, "will you sell me one of those long white aprons? And a white coat? And a white cap?"

"*Sell* them to you? What *for*?"

Leonidas put a ten dollar bill down on the marble slab.

"I do not," he said, "desire any change."

Five minutes later, when he and Dave left the store, Leonidas was carrying a white apron, a white coat, and a cap, in addition to the lion's head.

"What's the idea?" Dave demanded. "Who's going to wear those?"

"Er—you are," Leonidas said. "You are Doctor Hasenfus, the faint specialist, and I have imported you from Dalton. Seized you, in fact, from your laboratory, where you labor for mankind. Be sure, by the way, to keep those boots as much away from the light as you possibly can. Where's that back door? Ah, yes. Will you open it? My hands are rather full."

"See here, *I* can't be a doctor—I don't know what to say!"

Leonidas pushed him into the hallway.

"Hurry, please, and don this outfit. You will go in and look at Jinx—I am sure those two women will have her back on that lumpy couch—and then you will say in a shocked voice that the girl has unquestioningly had an overdose of a sulfa drug."

"Of a what?"

"Sulfadiagermis—no," Leonidas hurriedly tied the white apron around Dave's waist and held out the white coat. "I don't like the sound of that. Sulfa—sulfa—ah, I have it. Sulfabenzoparbethen. Say it. Sulfabenzoparbethen. Got it?"

"What *is* it?"

"I made it up," Leonidas said, "and you must admit

that it has a splendid, medical ring. Sulfabenzoparbethen. She's had an overdose of—can you finish it?"

"Sulfabenzoparbethen," Dave said obediently. "Then what do I do?"

"Tell those two women that unless she is violently exercised, at once, the poor child will slip into a deep sleep from which there is no recovery. Then grab her, and walk her up and down."

"Suppose she doesn't catch on?"

"Jinx," Leonidas said, "is a very quick catcheronner. Then tell the two women to rush out for Gidding and a policeman. Get them out of the way. Then rush back here and we'll—er—scram."

"Sulfabenzoparbethen," Dave said. "We can't get away with it, Shakespeare! Sulfabenzoparbethen!"

"You've got to get away with it. The child was miserable enough the last time she was pinned down on that couch, and she's done yeoman service, getting your uncle's note to us. This is no time to leave her in the lurch. Besides, I doubt if she has the fare back to Dalton. Sulfabenzoparbethen. Run along."

Holding the lion's head and the black Homburg, Leonidas waited in the hall.

He had, he told himself, been inexcusably negligent. It was all his fault for leaving the child to her chop suey, meatless, while he talked and talked with Dave Haymaker. True, there were things which it was necessary for him to have found out about. There were things which had to be discussed.

156

"On the other hand," Leonidas murmured, "I wonder if perhaps that is not, in a sense, an omen. We talk and talk, and things happen. Perhaps it will be wiser to talk less, from now on, and do more. M'yes —what's the matter? What's wrong?"

Dave Haymaker was racing down the hall as if several packs of starved wolves were taking hungry nips out of his heels.

"Quick!" he panted. "*Out!*"

Leonidas tugged at the heavy door, swung it open, and the two of them dashed outside on to the brick sidewalk.

"This way!" As they pounded along, Dave reached out and relieved Leonidas of the lion's head. "Hustle, Shakespeare, hustle!"

Leonidas could hear angry shouts rising behind them as they turned the corner.

"Here!"

Dave opened the door of a beachwagon, tossed the lion's head toward the rear, slid across the seat, and kicked at the starter, all in one rapid motion.

The engine purred, the car jumped forward, and then Dave slammed on the brakes so hard that Leonidas was nearly thrown onto the floor.

"My God!" Dave said. "This—"

"Do get along, please!" Leonidas interrupted. "Rapidly! Those shouts are getting nearer!"

"But this—"

"Jimmy, the pride of Pomfret's police," Leonidas

157

said, "is rounding that corner after us! Hurry! Drive on, quickly!"

"But—"

"Oh, hurry!" Leonidas said. "Hurry!"

Dave shot the beachwagon up the street just the fraction of a second before Jimmy jumped for the running board.

"Dear me!" Leonidas peered out the back window. "I fear he—no, he's not hurt. He's picking himself up. But I do rather feel that the quicker we leave Pomfret, the—er—better!"

"Would it move you," Dave said in a strange voice, "to know that—"

"I think—ah, it's all right," Leonidas said with relief. "I thought for a moment that we were being pursued. But that car turned away. Whatever happened, back there at the hall?"

"Well," Dave said, "I went into that little room, and there was only one dim light, but I could see Jinx lying there on the couch with a cold towel or something draped across her head, and two women in uniform were sitting beside her. I spoke my piece about the sulfa-whatever-it-was, and they were visibly impressed—I got the impression they were expecting a doctor, anyway. I reached out and jerked Jinx to her feet—"

"And—er—what happened?" Leonidas inquired as Dave paused.

"It wasn't Jinx," Dave said simply.

"Not Jinx! Where *is* she? Who was it?"

"When I lifted her up," Dave said, "that towel fell off, and I realized it wasn't Jinx at all. It was a woman with black hair. I let go of her and started to beat it out the door—after all, we didn't want to walk *her* out! Then she yelled, and the Lady Volunteers yelled, and that cop came rushing in. I told you it wouldn't work out, Bill Shakespeare! We've gone and got ourselves in a jam, having to rush off this way!"

"I should not refer to it as a jam," Leonidas said. "True, we'll have to turn back and find Jinx—dear me, I wonder where she can be?"

"Wherever she is, we are not turning back!"

"Oh, but we must!" Leonidas said. "Hm. I suppose she dodged those two women—she's a very artful dodger. She dodged Beeding all over my lawn. But we can't let the poor child roam the streets of Pomfret!"

"It's a lot better to let her roam the streets of Pomfret," Dave said, "than to have you and me roaming the dank corridor of some jail! That black-haired woman was Gidding's wife. She didn't recognize me in this white coat get-up, but I knew her."

"The offering of medical advice," Leonidas said, "is no crime. It's purely a humanitarian gesture. Think of all the people who make helpful suggestions about colds, for example! You committed no crime!"

"I'm not thinking so much about Gidding's wife," Dave said, "as I am about this beachwagon. That's

159

why I braked so hard. I realized I'd grabbed the wrong beachwagon the minute this started. Mine lost its purr years ago."

"Not yours?" Leonidas said. "Er—to whom does it belong?"

Dave took a hand from the wheel and pointed to a stencil on the dashboard.

"It's the property of the United States Navy."

"Oh," Leonidas said. "Oh! Dear me! How unfortunate! But I am mercifully acquainted with Admiral Coe-Chester."

"One of my best friends is a chief machinist's mate," Dave said, "and I know all the words to 'Anchors Aweigh.' But I doubt if that'll help us any if we're caught with this thing. I knew I ought to have stopped at once, but then I thought of all the explanations and to-do, with that cop racing after us, and you were yelling in my ear to hurry, hurry—that's the trouble when you jump into some crazy fool stunt like that sulfagoofathiamin business. All of a sudden you're jumping into something else that's got worse consequences!"

"M'yes, indeed," Leonidas murmured. "Crime does not pay—er—why are you stopping?"

"We're going to get out of this before someone catches up with us!" Dave said.

"Don't you think," Leonidas said, "that we might as well be—er—hanged for sheep? Lyceum Hall is a scant mile beyond here. You might park on some unobtrusive side street where no one will see us emerge. After all, no one *did* set out in pursuit of us!"

Ten minutes later, Leonidas paused on the steps of the hall and held out his hand for the lion's head which Dave was carrying.

"I'll take it," he said. "You see, it all worked out, despite your trepidations. At this point, I think you may cease darting those nervous little glances over your shoulder, as if you expected any moment to be seized by the Secretary of the Navy, and clapped into irons. Er—before we go in, I must warn you to keep a sharp lookout for Henry Compton. I must at all costs avoid meeting Henry Compton face to face."

"I'm not crazy to meet him again, either," Dave said. "I'm sure I don't know what you'd say to someone you stuck your tongue out at—Bill Shakespeare, d'you really think we got away clean with that beachwagon?"

Leonidas indicated the empty street.

"Voilà!" he said. "And although I'm convinced that Major Beeding is now home nursing his jaw as well as his shoulder, it might be wise for us to watch out for him, also."

"When you come right down to brass tacks," Dave said, "we'd better avoid cops and sailors, too—anything in a blue uniform. Perhaps it'd be simpler to figure out who we could be seen by."

"Not who," Leonidas said absently. "Whom. We want to find Pink, if she's here, be seen by a few people, and then we shall call on honest John Meikle-john. Dear me, I do hope that Jinx has carfare! I'm going to worry about that child!"

Pink Lately jumped on him as he entered the crowded hall.

"Shakespeare, I've gone *mad!* I've been sick with worry! I was never so upset about the five Lately boys in all their lives! Listen—I found out, just as I said I would, and I was right!"

"Er—about what?"

"The blonde girl. I've found out who she is. And think of it, I was right! She *is!*"

"Is what?" Leonidas asked.

"Haymaker's ward!"

CHAPTER 7

"WARD?" Leonidas said. "Ward? *Ward?*"

"You sound like a parrot—don't you remember," Pink said, "I said that in a book the blonde would turn out to be Haymaker's ward, and he'd have spent all her money in riotous living? Well, she's his ward, all right, although I don't know about the riotous-living part. You'll have to look into that. Oh, is this young man with you?" she stopped as she suddenly became aware of Dave, standing by Leonidas's elbow.

Leonidas introduced him, and Pink's eyes lighted with recognition.

"I knew your mother—she was a bridesmaid of mine. And of course, you knew Archie and Tad. They've sent me messages for you that I never got around to delivering," Pink said.

"I'd be with 'em," Dave sounded a little apologetic, "if it weren't for this plastic gadget I'm making. I always feel I ought to wear a sign on my back."

Pink lightly touched the row of "E" pins on his jacket lapel.

"You don't need a sign on your back," she said.

"Bill Shakespeare, *what* are you doing with that lion's head, of all things?"

"That's Lady Baltimore," Leonidas told her. "About this girl—"

"You swopped my beautiful cake for that thing? Well," Pink said philosophically, "in a way, I'm relieved. I got carried away and swopped your Uncle George's Dahlia Cup for the loveliest little old-fashioned music box. It only plays a few notes, but I think I can unstick it—where have you been? What've you been doing? I thought your greatest desire in life was to establish yourself as being at this swop!"

"I established myself at another." Leonidas pointed to an empty corner. "Let us get out of this milling throng—how do you do, Mrs. Agry! And I'll tell you all about things. First, however, I should like to know more about this ward of Haymaker's!"

"I never knew uncle had a ward!" Dave said blankly. "That's news to me!"

"He only acquired her a few weeks ago. Her father went off out of the country to do something about oil for the government, and before he left, he made Ross Haymaker her guardian."

"Oil?" Leonidas said. "Er—what's her name?"

"Quarl. Her—"

"Suzanne Quarl?" Dave asked. "Not Suzanne Quarl! It kept sounding like Suzanne Quarl, but I knew it never could be! Not Suzanne!"

"Why, yes, that's her name? Do you know her?"

164

"I used to know her," Dave said, "rather well. Her father owns Quarl's Oil. She's blonde and beautiful, and probably has a gross of mink coats, but never in this world did that lily of the field—"

"And, Bill," Pink interrupted, "you know I told you I thought I'd seen an oil woman? Well, Elspeth Agry just said she'd actually had one—she'd spent a frightful day just because of her. You see, she wasn't home when the oil woman came, but the maid let her in, and she let out Toots and Caspar, and Elspeth and the maid and all her neighborhood have spent the whole day getting them back!"

"Dogs?" Leonidas inquired.

"No, Elspeth's pet skunks. The oil woman simply let them out, and she didn't leave any oil there, either! What do you think of *that?*"

"There's only one thing you can think," Dave spoke before Leonidas had a chance to answer, "and it stuns me. It knocks me off my feet. It's all the same oil woman, from the Pomfret baby to the Agry skunks to your cellar, and it's all Suzanne Quarl herself, and I practically can't make myself believe any of it!"

"You mean," Pink said, "she just wasn't after her mink coat up in Bill's cellar, she was the oil woman, *too?* Oh, but no one said *she* was an oil woman. The Quarl girl, I mean. No one told me that. They just said that there really were oil *women!*"

"Pink," Leonidas said, "I wonder if you'd be good enough to go over to that group bickering over the skis and snowshoes, and ask Elspeth Agry if her oil woman was by some chance a beautiful blonde creature!"

Pink trotted off.

"I suppose," Dave said, "you're thinking that I should have told you when I thought of Suzanne, but —how can I explain it to you, I wonder? Suzanne never did anything more strenuous in her life than pinning an orchid on her coat. I mean, you had a feeling that maybe she could, because she could play a slam-bang game of golf when the spirit moved her. But I wouldn't have said that she knew what an oil truck was—and as for minding a baby! I can't think of her delivering oil. The last time I saw her," he added, "was at a party in New York where she was getting engaged to a prince who clicked his heels and bowed from the waist and kept looking at her square-cut emerald bracelet as if he couldn't wait to bite out a chunk and hock it."

Leonidas, twirling his pince-nez, looked at him quizzically.

Dave grew pink.

"Yes, I was an also-ran," he said. "I admit it. And I don't mind admitting that I rather look forward to seeing her now that she seems to have—uh—well, now that she—uh—"

"Seems to have suffered a sea change?" Leonidas suggested.

"Something on that order. Shakespeare, there's an

awful lot I don't get, even if it turns out that Suzanne really is the oil woman. I can easily understand
her not remembering to leave oil—I think it's God's
wonder she even got to the places where oil was supposed to be delivered. I can understand her letting out
skunks—after all, who wouldn't let out a skunk? But
what was she doing in your cellar, coming *for* her
mink coat? Why'd she gone off and left it there in the
first place?"

"None of that," Leonidas said, "amazes me as much
as the fact that your uncle, providing he actually was
her guardian, should have permitted her to act as an
oil woman, with or without mink coat."

"I never thought of that angle!" Dave said. "Uncle was all for having women work in jobs he considered fitting. He had the first woman elevator op-
erator in Dalton, for example."

"So Jinx said. Dear me," Leonidas said, "I brood
about that poor child wandering about the streets of
Pomfret! And it isn't as if she liked the streets of
Pomfret much, either. They bored her."

"On the other hand," Dave continued, "uncle was
violently opposed to lady cab drivers. I'm sure he'd
raise the roof at a lady oil-truck driver—Shakespeare,
I've got it! Suppose she goes to your house and uncle
turns up. Say that she's being an oil woman, and he's
forbidden it, see? Just his coming there would be
enough to send her scooting away. No," he added,
"that won't do. There'd be no reason for her to sit

167

down and take off her coat before she scooted, would there?"

"I wonder," Leonidas said. "As I recall, I was so delighted to see Quarl's Quality Oil show up, I called down and urged the driver to have a bottle of beer. Suppose Miss Quarl, bowed down by baby tending and that skunk episode, took me at my word and sat down to refresh herself with a bottle of beer—dear me, that won't work out, either. There would be no earthly way by which anyone in the cellar could possibly see a person approaching my front door. She couldn't have seen Haymaker."

"Perhaps he approached from the rear," Dave suggested. "Anyway, it would seem that she was there, and that she must have fled—"

He broke off as Pink trotted back.

"Elspeth Agry says the oil woman was blonde, and she's sure she must have been Suzanne Quarl. It never entered her head at the time, but the maid's description fits Suzanne perfectly. Bill, I haven't told you why I left you in the lurch, back there on Birch Hill Road. Brother appeared out of nowhere and asked where I was going. I said to the swop, and he promptly invited himself along. I simply couldn't do a thing about it."

"M'yes, I rather assumed as much," Leonidas said. "Is he still violently hunting me?"

"Goodness, yes! He came here to look for you," Pink said, "and then he went bouncing off when he heard about Haverstraw's prowler, and he's been back again several times. But I think you're safe from him now. When I saw him last, he was planning to take a shooting stick and camp on your front doorstep. He's furious with you. I don't think he exactly intends to rend you limb from limb, not until you've made out that report, at least. But—"

"In the interim," Leonidas said, "I dare say he is dreaming of an Iron Maiden about my size. Now, I must briefly circulate and be seen by a few of the best people, and then we—"

"Hey!" Dave said. "There's a sailor—wow, scrambled eggs and a sleeveful of gold braid! Shakespeare, that's an admiral who's just come in the main door, and he's probaby the most suspicious-looking man I ever saw! I *bet* you someone saw us take that beachwagon. I *bet* you they chased us!"

Leonidas whipped on his pince-nez, looked across the hall, and frowned.

"Pink, stand in front of me!" he said quickly. "It's Admiral Coe-Chester! Duck down, Dave. Bend over and stare at the floor!"

A moment later, Pink craned her neck.

"He's going—yes, he's gone. He's been here several times this evening," she said. "Hunting his cousin, I heard him tell someone. It's that Mrs. Gidding, over in Pomfret."

"Basil Gidding's wife is the admiral's cousin?" Dave asked in a choked voice. "Did you hear that one, Bill

169

Shakespeare? That woman I jerked to her feet and told about the sulfa stuff—Gidding's wife is the admiral's cousin! I told you so, I *told* you so! That lad is hunting us, that's what!"

"I'm quite sure," Leonidas said, "that he is doing nothing of the sort."

"Then why'd you duck?"

"Because I have a problem of his to solve," Leonidas said. "I faithfully promised I'd attend to it tonight, and thus far I've had no chance even to think of it. I rather feel that if he saw me sitting here among these bickering merrymakers, hugging a papier-mâché lion, he might just possibly get the impression that I was letting him down badly." He rose from the settee. "I am now going to circulate rapidly about the fringe of a few select groups and tell everybody how much better this Dalton swop is than the one I've been attending all evening over in the wilds of Pomfret."

"But I want to know what you've been doing!" Pink protested.

"Dave will tell you. He—er—knows all."

"Wait!" Pink said as he moved away with the lion's head tucked under his arm. "There's a fat woman I don't know over on the far side by the bond booth, and if you get a chance, you *might* try to strike up an acquaintance with her. At least *chat* with her."

"Gladly," Leonidas said. "But—er—why?"

"She has a pound of coffee," Pink said wistfully.

170

"In a tin, too. She's turned down every offer made her so far, including a really quite good six by sixteen tire tube with only a little patch. It might just be possible that a papier-mâché lion's head is the very thing she's been sitting there waiting for. Try, anyway. Does Dave know *every*thing that's happened?"

"Everything," Leonidas said, "and he tells a story well, if a trifle on the ungrammatical side."

He strolled off, and Pink turned to Dave.

"Go on. Be as ungrammatical as you please, but tell me! You can't imagine what I've been through, sitting here and worrying for two solid hours. And I simply couldn't lift a finger to try and help him, because when I started back to Birch Hill Road after him, I ran out of gas. Unless someone has a lawnmower they haven't milked, my beachwagon's going to stay there on Chestnut near Maple until the twenty-second of next month. Go on. Hurry!"

"My story is a then-I-went-er," Dave said, "and Shakespeare's sounds like a chapter out of Haseltine —do you really think he can solve this?"

"I don't know," Pink said slowly. "He has a certain bland assurance. Nothing jars him. And—well, lots of men aren't nearly as bright as they think they are, but I think Bill Shakespeare is brighter than he thinks."

"Funny," Dave said. "He laughs about his directorates and all that sort of thing, but Gidding thinks he's wonderful. He seemed to think it was awfully lucky for Haymaker's that he consented to be on the board.

171

I got the feeling that everybody had longed to get him into things, but they felt he'd turn 'em down, and so when the war came and gave 'em an excuse, they went for him with a scream of pleasure."

"He has a way of making everyone think he loves listening to 'em," Pink said. "He's already commiserated with Haverstraw about the prowler they had, and he's discussed oil women and pet skunks with Elspeth—oh, I've got to watch this! He's going up to the fat woman with the coffee—I wonder! Oh, dear, she's waving him away. Oh, dear! Go on and tell me things!"

Dave drew a long breath.

Ten minutes later he had got as far as the Navy beachwagon when Pink clutched his arm.

"Do you see that man coming in the main door—the man with the tin hat?"

"Wow!" Dave jumped to his feet. "Where's Bill? I said I'd watch out for Compton—"

"You go stall him!" Pink ordered. "Jump on his toes, knock him down—do *any*thing! Anything at *all*! Only keep him there by the door until I can find Bill and get him out of the way! Hustle!"

Dave knifed through two groups with a disregard for the proprieties that filled his wake with acidulous comments on the manners of the young, and Pink, having finally spotted Leonidas at the side of the hall, went for him like a greyhound after a tin rabbit.

Twenty seconds later, Leonidas felt the lion's head being wrenched out of his hand, and when he turned to look, Pink was jamming it down over his ears.

"Brother!" she said.

Leonidas's sigh was clearly audible through the brown-painted slit of screen that served for the lion's lips.

"Can you *breathe?*" Pink demanded.

"M'yes, indeed. Beautifully."

"Can you hear?"

"Dimly."

"Can you *see* all right?"

"While I should not want," Leonidas's voice had a muffled quality, as though he were talking into an empty rain barrel, "to—er—peruse the Lord's Prayer engraved on the head of a dime, I can nevertheless see, in a limited sort of way. How do I sound?"

"Like something the matter with the radio, but not a bad tube—oh, dear, Bill Shakespeare, I'm sure Dave's done his best, but brother's simply making a beeline for you! Oh, this is fatal!"

Leonidas sighed again.

"Dave couldn't think of any quotes," he said, "which pertained to a lion's head, but I feel quite competent to invent a few sterling sentiments on the spur of the moment. Er—for example—'How like an asse doth human man become, when toppèd—' you have to give that two syllables," he added parenthetically, " 'when toppèd by the head of that majestic beast who—' "

"Hush, he's *coming!*" Pink said.

" 'Who lurks in desert lairs and pounces un- awares—' really," Leonidas said, "I think this is rather good! 'Upon his prey. That same majestic head doth illy fit—' "

"Hush!"

"Now that," there was a note of pleased excitement in Compton's tone, "*that's* something I'd like to have! Hi, there! What do you want for that lion's head?"

"That's not a swop, Henry!" Pink said quickly.

"Of course it's a swop!" Compton returned. "By George, I've got to have that! What do you want for it, anyway?"

"I tell you," Pink sounded desperate, "it is *not* a swop. I—I just asked him."

"If it isn't a swop," Compton said, "what'd he bring it here for? Don't be absurd, Constance!"

Leonidas, completely unable to see the figures by his side, and not in the least wishing to turn around, wondered who Constance was, and then recalled that Constance was Pink's given name.

"Just because you want that lion's head yourself," Compton continued irritably, "is no reason for you to lie about it to me!"

"Henry Compton!" Pink was obviously losing her temper. "I'm not *lying!* I said it wasn't a swop, and it *isn't* a swop—"

174

"That's quite true," Dave came to her rescue. "Tried to get it myself, and the fellow wouldn't consider swopping."

"Well, I must say if someone doesn't *want* to swop something," Compton said stuffily, "he has no business bringing it *to* a swop! It very definitely said in the handbill that people should bring things here to *swop!* It didn't say to bring things people didn't *want* to swop! He's simply defeating the purpose of the whole affair, and I certainly must say that I, for one, do not think it's very patriotic of him! A swop is a swop. That's all there is to it. If this—"

"Oh, Henry, *hush!*" Pink said. "You're attracting attention!"

"I, for one, certainly think that a thing like this *ought* to be brought to people's attention!" Compton returned. "Why do you go to a bond rally? To buy bonds! Why do you go to a swop? You go to swop! The point I make is that if you don't swop—"

"I'm afraid, sir," Dave interrupted, "that you're off on the wrong track, if you don't mind my telling you so."

"Look here," Compton said, "just who are *you*, young man?"

"I'm awfuly sorry, didn't I tell you? I must have thought," Dave said, "that you knew. My name is Haymaker."

"Oh," Compton said. "Oh. The Carnavon one?"

"Yes," Dave said pleasantly. "Of course, perhaps

175

we shouldn't have done it, but everyone else except yourself has been rather amused and thought it rather clever advertising."

"Advertising? You mean that lion's head? Advertising what, I'd like to know?" Compton demanded. "What would you advertise with a lion's head?"

"Lions," Dave said simply.

"Lions? What lions?"

"The Lions' Frolic and Fair," Dave said.

Leonidas beamed with pride. He couldn't have done better himself.

"To be held in Carnavon," Dave went on, "next week. Three days. The twenty-first, twenty-second, and twenty-third. Tickets are a dollar ten, children half price. Special family book is three dollars flat. There will be door prizes daily, and a grand prize drawing on the last night in which every ticket holder will participate. We've just sold a raft of tickets over in Pomfret—perhaps you'd like one of the special family books? Bring your children over to ride on Jumbo. They'll love it. Put you down for a family book, shall I?"

"No, thank you." Compton, Leonidas thought, sounded defeated. "I didn't know there were Lions over in Carnavon," he added.

"Well, of course we're young," Dave said modestly. "Barely out of the cub stage, you might say. But we do our best. Sorry you don't want a ticket. Come along, Lion!" Leonidas felt Dave's hand on his arm.

"We shan't ask you to roar again here. We roared enough over at the Pomfret swop, I think."

Compton sniffed.

"I, for one," he said in the voice of one who was bound and determined to have the last word, "I, for one, feel it's rather bad taste of you to use *our* swops to advertise things. Especially *Carnavon* things!"

"We, of course, take the bigger view," Dave retorted. "We look on it as a *county* thing, you know. We don't feel that little interurban jealousies should be allowed to interfere with—"

Simultaneously with Dave's sudden pressure on his arm, Leonidas heard Pink's horrified gasp.

Turning, he saw bearing down on him the bald-headed Gidding, beaming widely, and still wearing his Master of Ceremonies button in his lapel.

"Ah, got it on, have you!" he said genially. "Becomes you, too, Mr.—"

"How do you do, sir!" Dave hurried forward with outstretched hand. "We've proceeded this far—may I have a word with you, sir?"

"Presently, my boy, presently! I want to congratulate my good friend—"

"We heard," Dave sounded desperate, and Leonidas found that he was holding his breath, himself. It was only a question of time before Gidding would mention his name. "We heard that your wife had fainted—I do hope that's not true, sir!"

"Oh, she's right as rain, right as rain," Gidding said.

"Just something she ate for dinner, I think. Some day she'll learn to stay away from lobster. Has our good friend made his excellent bond speech over here as yet?"

"Well, we weren't going to ask him to roar," Dave said. "We thought he was rather tired after roaring for your group."

"Roar—ha, ha," Gidding laughed heartily. "That's good. That's very good! But he must give these good people that speech. I tell you, our friend Wi—"

"Oh, dear!" Pink said suddenly. "Oh, my—quick, Henry, give me your arm! Oh—I feel so faint! I— oh, dear!"

Pink's crumble was even more artistic than Jinx's had been. And somehow, as she went to the floor, she had managed to bear Henry Compton along with her.

"Stand back, everyone!" Gidding's authoritative voice rang out. "Back, now! Give her air, give her air—Haymaker, push these people back!"

Mercifully, the crowd paid as little attention to his orders as the Pomfret crowd had paid. In the surge forward, Leonidas stepped back.

And continued to step back.

When he felt the wall behind his shoulders, he turned and painfully craned his neck until he saw the red light of an exit.

Then he sidled to it, unlatched the door, and stepped outside.

178

With a sigh of relief, he lifted off the lion's head, and wiped the beads of perspiration from his very warm brow.

He had, during the prescribed course of warden preparation which supposedly fitted him to man Oakhill's Post A-1, groped his way through a gas chamber with a gas mask on. But his heartfelt joy at getting that off was negligible compared to the feeling of deliverance he was experiencing now. Never, he thought, had it seemed so wonderful to breathe the fresh air of Dalton!

And it was through no genius on his part that he had escaped. Only Pink's quick realization that she was expendable had saved him. Somehow, she and Dave Haymaker would manage, Leonidas thought, to keep the hearty Gidding from apprising Henry Compton of his identity. Having succeeded at the critical moment, they should have no particular difficulty now that the real crisis was past.

He had intended to take Dave along with him to visit Meiklejohn, but it would be sheer folly to go back for Dave now.

He glanced at his watch.

It was quarter to eleven. He couldn't possibly wait around for Dave. He'd find Meiklejohn's address in a phone book, and go and call him at once.

Picking up the lion's head, he considered it thoughtfully.

It had, he decided, served its purpose. And much as

179

he regretted discarding anything which had played so vital a part in the events of the evening, the time had indisputably arrived when he could no longer bother to burden himself with such a cumbersome object.

He placed it on the sidewalk, gave it a farewell pat on the head, and then stiffened as a figure suddenly loomed in the doorway through which he had just emerged.

He recognized the woman instantly, and relaxed.

She was the adamant fat lady who had sat like a Buddha on the side lines, clutching her tin of coffee and waving away all offers with what amounted to regally imperial scorn.

"Oh, there you are!" she said. "I thought at first you'd just gone out for a breath of air, and then I began to worry that you might have left for good!"

"I was finding the atmosphere of the hall rather— er—discomforting," Leonidas told her with perfect truth.

"You know, I've spent the whole evening trying to find a nice birthday present for my grandson," the woman said, "and I was beginning to get awfully discouraged! What he really wanted was one of those shiny metal Haseltine guns they used to give away with six packages of Tootsy-Wheetsies. You know the kind I mean—they used to go grat-rat-rat! Grat-rat-rat!"

"M'yes, indeed, I knew them!" Leonidas had personally distributed a gross of them among Mere-

dith's lower forms and the boys of his own neighborhood—and lived to regret the day.

"My grandson gave his old gun for scrap, you see,
because it was broken, and then of course there
weren't any new ones. I thought there was a chance
that *some*one might bring one here—but nobody did.
And I was afraid if I said what I wanted, someone
might rush right home and take *their* child's Haseltine gun. And I didn't think that would be fair a bit,
do you?"

"Oh, definitely not!" Leonidas said. "No, indeed.
My, my, no—not unless the parents' eardrums were
on the verge of collapse!"

"They *were* noisy," the woman conceded, "but the
children loved those guns so! And what some people
would do to get a pound of coffee! Why, if I'd said I
wanted a Haseltine gun and a child, too, I think some
of those people would have thrown in their child
without batting an eye!"

"Tch, tch!" Leonidas clucked his tongue in sym-
pathetic horror. "But there are many other swops tonight, you know. Perhaps you still might have some
luck over in Pomfret. They're holding a very energetic
swop over there." He started to step away. "And now,
if you'll excuse me, I must—"

"Oh, but I've given up hoping for a gun," the
woman said. "I guess if anyone has a Haseltine gun,
they're just hanging on to it and making it last.
Tommy'll just have to do without. Of course, I *didn't*

181

at all like it at first, when you showed it to me."

Leonidas abruptly stopped edging away and took a step forward toward her.

"Er—the lion's head?" he inquired. "You mean, the lion's head?"

"I thought it was perfectly terrible," the woman said frankly. "I couldn't imagine why you'd bother bringing a terrible thing like that to a swop. But then I saw you put it on, and I nearly died laughing. I don't think I ever saw anything much funnier in all my born days! Why, it was funnier than the time my husband slipped and fell with his head in the bucket of paste the paper hanger'd left at the foot of the stairs!"

"That," Leonidas manfully strove to get the proper note of appreciation in his voice, "must indeed have been—er—hilarious. M'yes, indeed!"

"Well, of course *he* didn't think so," the woman said, "but I laughed till I cried. I was *sick!* I haven't laughed so hard since until I saw you with that lion's head on just now. Honestly, you just practically killed me, you looked so funny!"

"We—er—strive to amuse," Leonidas said. "And of course I suppose it—er—occurred to you what fun Tommy might possibly have with the lion's head? Halloween, and all that? And without doubt, I'm sure his mother will find the lion far quieter around the house than one of those infernal Haseltine guns. Dear me, yes! I'm sure that Tommy will derive a vast

182

amount of wholesome pleasure from the possession of this head!"

He picked it up from the sidewalk and held it out, and the woman presented him in return with the pound tin of coffee.

"Thank you, dear lady, thank you!" Leonidas's gratitude was heartfelt. "Of course, you should warn Tommy about the dangers of asphyxiation. Every now and then, the little fellow must remember to—er—pop out for air. M'yes, indeed. But Tommy will love his lion's head dearly, I'm sure!"

"I don't know what makes you think I want this," the woman said, "for Tommy!"

"Er—you *don't?*"

Leonidas clutched the tin of coffee and edged away. At this point, he firmly resolved, nothing short of a regiment of commandos could pry that tin of coffee from him!

"Why, I'm going to take this head home and hide it," the woman said, "and the *next* time my husband weaves in from lodge meeting at four o'clock in the morning, *I'm* going to put it on and scare the daylights out of him! Thanks a lot, mister. Good night!"

She disappeared through the doorway.

Leonidas leaned back against the cold brick wall and laughed till his sides ached.

Finally he wiped his eyes, and set off in the direction of Main Street.

Then he paused.

There had been, he remembered, a little variety store on the street where Dave had so timorously parked the Navy beachwagon. That was nearer, and it was open, while the larger establishments on Main Street might well be closed at this hour.

"M'yes, indeed, that will be better," he said aloud, and turned around.

His foot was on the top step of the stairs leading down into the variety store when a truck, backfiring in the street behind him, caused him to stop and look over his shoulder.

Then he froze there with his hand on the wooden railing.

The truck was a familiar, red-and-white striped Quarl's Quality Oil truck.

And the driver who was racing the engine so violently was a blonde girl.

In a fur coat!

The blonde girl, unless Leonidas was very much mistaken!

He swung quickly around, but the striped truck roared off with another burst of ear-shattering backfires, and disappeared up the street.

"Oh!" Leonidas said wistfully. "Oh, if I had a car! A bicycle! A scooter—"

The Navy beachwagon caught his eye.

A moment later he was in it, driving off in pursuit of the truck.

"I regret this action!" he said with deep sincerity aloud to himself. "I definitely regret it! I could wish that this vehicle came to me through the courtesy of someone other than the United States Government!"

Of course, people were sometimes given rides in jeeps as a reward for buying bonds. One could justify oneself, in one's own mind, Leonidas reflected, by thinking that the brief use of a government beach-wagon was only due and proper recompense for Haseltine's not inconsiderable tax contribution.

But the fact remained that virtually no one else would be inclined to view his act of thievery from the same charitable point of view.

Three blocks further along, he caught sight of the truck's taillights, drove close enough to reassure himself that it was indeed the Quarl truck, and then slowed down and stayed behind it.

However inefficient she might be in the matter of making actual deliveries of oil, Leonidas thought, the girl was unquestionably a good driver. The difficult hairpin turn at the corner of Eucalyptus and Hazelwood took a bit of doing even in an ordinary passenger car, and the girl manipulated the long truck around it with deft and skillful efficiency.

She couldn't, he told himself, be delivering oil now, at this time. She must be on her way home. And even if she were a hardier type, and not the lily of the field Dave had made her out, she must be yearning for home and bed and a good night's rest after her somewhat

185

garbled day tending babies and letting out skunks and generally romping around his cellar.

The truck roared slowly on, and Leonidas followed it with growing impatience. While he wanted to see the girl and find out what part she might have played in the events of the evening, he also wanted to get to see Meiklejohn before the man retired and had to be ruthlessly jerked from his slumbers.

Several miles beyond, in the Daltonville section, the striped truck swooped suddenly up a side street, and then slowed down.

A small hooded spotlight, apparently focused from within the cab of the truck, was swung onto the door numbers of several houses, and then the truck turned up a wide driveway to the left.

Almost at once, the brake lights flashed on, and the truck was backed rapidly out.

A car, shooting down the drive in front of it, swerved as it hit the street, caromed, and headed straight toward Leonidas and the Navy beachwagon.

Leonidas grabbed at the wheel and twisted it with all his might just as the driver of the car seemed to regain control.

But it passed by the beachwagon with not much more than a sixteenth of an inch to spare.

It was one of those near misses, Leonidas thought weakly as he leaned back against the leather seat, that left the palms of your hands damp, and gave you a feeling of incredible limpness. If some passer-by were

186

to mistake him for a used dish towel, it wouldn't surprise him in the least!

As if he were in a daze, he watched the truck turn back up the driveway again.

For a lily of the field, Leonidas decided, that blonde girl possessed amazing stamina! Not only had she also just missed a collision with that car, but she had been forced, in addition, to retreat down the driveway from it as it came speeding toward her.

"For my part," he murmured, "I couldn't blow a horn. And yet she can pull that truck—dear me, I wonder if Dave did not perhaps err in his estimate of Miss Suzanne Quarl!"

He had to force himself to reach out and open the door. As he stepped out, the gremlins from the bread wagon returned for a painful, fleeting moment to torture his eyeballs. He leaned against the beachwagon until his head cleared, and then walked along the sidewalk toward the driveway up which the truck had disappeared.

It would appear that Miss Quarl was still delivering oil. She certainly couldn't live here. While it was a perfectly reputable section—the teller of his bank lived here, and so had several of Meredith's junior masters—it was in no way associated in Leonidas's mind with mink coats and square-cut emerald bracelets.

He paused as something flashed at him from the lawn.

It was a sign, a name sign with studs that caught car

187

headlights and glowed in their beam. Apparently he had passed it at just the right angle to have it reflect back the street light.

Leonidas retraced his steps to catch the exact angle again.

Then he stood stock still.

While he ordinarily put a certain amount of faith in signs, he could not bring himself to believe the sign that was gently glowing at him now.

Unquestionably, he told himself, it was the work of those gremlins who had been plaguing his eyeballs. He had gremlin trouble, that was all.

But the sign continued to glow the same name at him.

"No!" Leonidas said firmly aloud. "It's not possible. Things don't happen this way. Not even the excellent Haseltine could tie together the long arm of circumstance and the long tentacles of fate and get that sign to read 'John Meiklejohn!' "

A car drove up the street behind him. Even its dimmed headlights caught the sign, which for a second flashed brightly.

Leonidas sighed.

"Oh, very well!" he said. "Very well. It *does* say 'John Meiklejohn,' then!"

As he walked on toward the driveway, something began to tingle suddenly in the base of Leonidas's spine.

It was all very well for him to have contemplated calling on John Meiklejohn. He had a perfectly logical

188

and justifiable excuse. He hoped to find out more about the Haymaker accounts.

But why was Miss Suzanne Quarl calling on him?

"Ostensibly," he murmured, "to deliver oil! But I wonder. M'yes, indeed, I wonder!"

After all, in at least three instances that day, Miss Quarl had called on people ostensibly to deliver oil, and had done nothing of the sort!

It occurred to him that an oil truck was an excellent vehicle for anyone to go around in, if anyone was bent on any activity of a slightly shady nature. An oil truck, these days, was something in the nature of a cross between a Magic Carpet and an Open Sesame. You drove where you pleased. No one questioned you. You yelled 'Oil!' and people urged you hospitably to come in and have a bottle of beer. Maids, like Elspeth Agry's maid, let you in without question. Young mothers unhesitatingly trusted you with their babes in arms. You had, in fact, what amounted to a carte blanche.

Certainly, Leonidas thought, ten minutes past eleven at night was an odd time to be delivering oil, under any circumstances.

And why to John Meiklejohn, of all people?

Was it just possible that Haymaker's blonde young ward, whose tastes so obviously ran toward the more expensive things in life, might have some interest in the Haymaker accounts, too?

Leonidas, avoiding the scrunchy gravel of the driveway in favor of the damp and quieter grass, pondered

189

the question as he walked up toward the square white frame house.

The oil truck was parked by the kitchen door. Its hose had not been pulled out, but a shaft of light showing from the foot of the cellar windows indicated that Miss Quarl had at least progressed that far.

Leonidas went to the nearest window, knelt down, and peered through the scant inch of glass left uncovered by the shade.

Miss Quarl was just coming down the cellar stairs that apparently led from the first floor.

She was beautiful. There was no getting away from that, Leonidas thought. Even in a drab gray denim coverall, well splashed with oil, she was one of the most beautiful creatures he ever remembered having seen. Lieutenant Haseltine himself had never met up with anyone quite so ravishing. Not even on the radio.

Leonidas watched as the girl hurried over to a broken chair, picked up her mink coat, and started for the cellar door.

Then she stopped.

The gesture of picking up her coat suggested that she was on the point of leaving, and Leonidas himself immediately thought of the uncoiled hose out on the oil truck in the drive.

Wasn't it her intention to deliver any oil here, either, he wondered?

He found himself unable to diagnose what she might be thinking from the expression on her face. It was a complex sort of expression that somehow insinuated bewilderment and indecision and confusion, topped off with a touch of panic and a lot of plain unvarnished worry.

With a funny, impatient little movement, the girl dropped the coat on the floor, turned, and ran quickly up the stairs again.

Leonidas got up from the damp ground, walked to the cellar door, opened it, and silently mounted the stairs after her.

On tiptoe, he went from a kitchen into a dining room, and then into a hall.

The girl was standing back to him in the doorway of a room further up the hall. Her hands were gripping the lintels, and she was leaning forward slightly.

Suddenly she darted into the room.

Noiselessly, hardly daring to breathe, Leonidas tiptoed up the hall.

He almost gave away his presence when he caught sight of the room.

He had never witnessed a more thorough shambles. Loose, torn papers littered the chairs, carpeted the floor, and snowed under the desk top.

In the corner a steel file had been opened, its drawers pulled out, and their contents poured out on the floor to make a young mountain of torn papers. The torn pages of a ledger made a smaller mound at the base of a bridge lamp.

There was only one thing in the room that was not

blanketed with torn papers, and that was the davenport by the fireplace.

And on it was the trussed-up figure of a man.

CHAPTER 8

Leonidas put on his pince-nez, and looked from the figure on the davenport to the blonde girl, who was kneeling on the floor, staring blankly at one of the torn papers.

Had she had sufficient time, Leonidas asked himself, from her entering the driveway until he saw her coming down the cellar steps, to have achieved this fine, destructive litter?

Automatically, he shook his head.

He'd spent perhaps four minutes clearing up the gremlins and perhaps three minutes more considering that studded sign out on the lawn. Seven minutes were hardly enough for her to effect such—he sought for a word—such a farrago. It would take him, personally, several times seven minutes to perform as neat and complete a truss-up job as that which had been done on the man lying on the davenport.

Of course, she was a girl of stamina, and women in a frenzy were supposedly capable of creating terrific destruction. Women presumably trussed things well, too. But Leonidas seriously doubted if Miss Quarl had ever had much experience trussing poultry in a kitchen.

He thought suddenly of the car speeding out of the driveway.

The driver of that car, he decided, was far more inclined to be the person responsible for all this mess. The reckless haste of his departure, his headlong spurt toward the oncoming oil truck, his careening swerve on to the street—Leonidas twirled his pince-nez, and nodded. That was very possibly the solution.

"M'yes," he didn't realize that he had spoken aloud. "M'yes, I think so!"

The girl swung around and stared at him.

"My God—Shakespeare! Are you *real?* Are you— come, come, Suzanne!" she added severely, apparently to herself, "you ought to be used to this sort of thing by now. Your Day! Look, are you real?"

"M'yes," Leonidas said. "Er—I do hope you got the number of that car."

"Car? *Car?* What car?"

"The car," Leonidas said patiently, "that forced you to back down and out of the driveway when you came."

"Oh, *that* idiot! I barely noticed him," the girl said. "After some of the drivers I've met up with today, he was comparatively sensible. At least he had his lights on and I saw him coming. The woman who slammed out at me from that Daltondale drive didn't, but mercifully a cop saw the whole thing. Look, what should we *do?*"

"We should undo," Leonidas said, and drew out his pocketknife.

"Look, Shakespeare," she said as they ploughed through the papers across the room to the davenport, "this may sound odd, but—well, believe it or not, I came upstairs for oil coupons. It said to."

"What said to?"

"A note on the cellar door." The girl started to unknot the man's gag. "When I found him, I was petrified. I knew I ought to call for someone, but—oh, dear, it's an awfully long story. Too long to go into now. I was going to run away, so I wouldn't get involved with the police or a lot of publicity and all. Then I came back, and well—all of this sounds so absurd, but I saw my name on one of those papers, and I was reading the page when you came. I'm sure you don't believe a word of it, and I don't blame you for not believing me, either, but—"

"I believe you," Leonidas said.

"No!"

"M'yes. Why not?"

"Shakespeare, you revive my faith in human nature," the girl said, "and let me tell you, it's taken a perfectly frightful pounding today! No one's believed me since seven o'clock this morning. Way back there. I think," she added, "I've finally got this damned knot coming— there! All right?"

She lifted the handkerchief gag off and revealed the man's round, bland, rosy face.

"Can I get you a glass of water or something?" she asked.

"No, indeed, Miss Quarl—thank you so much!" There was something birdlike in the man's voice. He almost, Leonidas thought as he sawed away, chirped. "My one hope was that the oil really would get here as it was promised, and that the driver might wander this far to hunt up his coupons. Otherwise I should have been here until Katy came tomorrow morning. My wife and daughter are away. I'm very grateful to you and Mr. Witherall. I don't suppose either of you has any inkling of who did this?"

"Regretfully, no."

Leonidas cut the last rope around his ankles, and the little man sat up and surveyed the room's litter with incredible calm. Clearly its condition distressed him, but when he spoke, he sounded entirely unruffled.

"I do hope Katy can clear this up before my wife returns. She's so tidy." He straightened out the plaid collar of his dark-blue smoking jacket and patted his tie into place. "Really, Miss Quarl, this was very kind of you!"

Suzanne smiled at him. "You know my name," she said, "but I'm afraid I don't know yours—I only looked at the number on the slip."

"I'm John Meiklejohn. I've seen you at the store a number of times when you've been calling on Mr. Haymaker. I take care of all the accounts, you know. And I'm afraid," he said sadly, "some of yours are down there on the floor this minute. And Mr. Witherall—of course I've known Mr. Witherall by sight for a long time. We're very happy to have you associated with us, Mr. Witherall. And how was your first day in business, Miss Quarl?"

She shuddered.

"First days are always a little trying," Meiklejohn said sympathetically. "I can still remember my first day as change boy to old Mr. R. H. I made five mistakes and cried most of the night. I trust you enjoyed your first directors' meeting, Mr. Witherall? I know Mr. Haymaker was very pleased with you, because he made rather a point of telling me so."

"Did he, indeed?" Leonidas was conscious of a certain glow of pride. "You bring me directly to the point, Mr. Meiklejohn, and to the reason for my coming here. I wonder if you'd be willing to answer some questions for me?"

Meiklejohn expressed himself as being only too happy to serve Mr. Witherall in any way possible.

"I'm always answering directors' questions, you know," he added. "It's a part of my job. Sometimes Mr. Haymaker calls me from bed to clarify some situation for him."

"Look, if you'll give me the coupons," Suzanne said, "I'll put in your oil and get along."

"I know you're tired," Leonidas said, "but would you wait, Miss Quarl? I've a few things to ask you, too."

"What about?" she asked quickly.

"Oil. Mr. Meiklejohn, can you tell from this mess what papers of yours someone might have been after, and what might have been taken?"

Meiklejohn looked around the room and smiled wearily.

"Six months from now, I might be able to hazard a guess," he said.

"This afternoon, or some time after the directors' meeting, did Haymaker ask you for some accounts?"

"Yes, he told me of your question in the meeting," Meiklejohn said, "and I took him in a few figures. I wasn't sure just how extensive a report he wished to make to you."

"You didn't find anything wrong?"

"In my figures? Oh, no," Meiklejohn said. "I don't wish to sound boastful, Mr. Witherall, but I have not made any mistakes since that first day as change boy."

"Did you guess," Leonidas asked, "that Haymaker found something wrong?"

"He didn't say so." A cloud seemed to flit over Meiklejohn's rosy face. "But frankly, I felt that something worried him. I know Mr. Haymaker quite well, and I know when he is upset."

"He didn't mention anything to you?"

Meiklejohn shook his head. "I knew that he would tell me eventually. It's his way, you know, to think things over very carefully."

"I see," Leonidas said. "I see. Now, Miss Quarl, d'you

mind my asking if Haymaker approved of your entry into the world of commerce?"

Suzanne smiled. "You mean my being a lady oil man? Yes, he did. But I had to fight him tooth and nail every step of the way. Probably Mr. Meiklejohn knows all about my scenes with R. H."

Mr. Meiklejohn raised his eyes and looked expressively at the ceiling.

"We've had quite a time with Miss Quarl," he said.

Suzanne giggled. "Tell me, now what finally moved him to say yes? Was it my threatening to join the Waacs, or run a drill press?"

"I think we got the idea that you intended to do *some*thing," Meiklejohn said, "and Mr. Haymaker decided it was easier to keep you here under his wing, where he could look after you."

"I *had* to do something," Suzanne said. "And it was my chance, with dad away. He's never let me do anything, ever, except sell tickets to hospital benefits, and when he found out I was working in the wards, he cut off my allowance. But I think R. H. was right when he said I couldn't guess what I was getting in to. He said I'd run into a lot—and haven't I just!"

"Are you going to continue?"

There was, Leonidas thought, something faintly suspicious in Meiklejohn's eager tone.

"After R. H. said I couldn't last week? I am delivering oil," Suzanne said, "if I have to deliver it from a stretcher!"

"Tell me," Leonidas said, "why didn't you leave oil at the place where you tended the baby, or at the place where you found the skunks?"

"Would *you* stop to leave oil in a place that was simply crawling with skunks?" Suzanne retorted. "As for that other place in Pomfret, I just forgot."

"Er—what about my house?"

"*Your* house?"

"Exactly. My house. Witherall. Forty Birch Hill Road."

"Oh," Suzanne said. "Oh. Why, I never went there! Look, what's all this, anyway? How did you know about the skunks, and the Pomfret baby? Has R. H. Haymaker had someone keeping tabs on me all the time? Oh, I suspected it! I suspected it! I'm going straight to him, and—"

"Wait, please," Leonidas said. "I have a lot to tell you, and Meiklejohn too. But first, Miss Quarl, I want you to tell me a few things. Believe me, it's important. Now, about—"

"It certainly *is* important!" Suzanne said. "If he *dared* butt in and check up on me, when he promised he wouldn't! I'll admit he was right when he said I'd find it harder than I thought. It *is* hard work. You have to make out your schedule by neighborhoods, so you don't waste gas and tires, and then someone isn't home, or someone's in the bathtub—you can't imagine the number of people in Dalton who are *always* taking baths! Or talking over the phone. It gets you all mixed up and slowed down. And everyone always expected you yesterday, or last week. Or else they expect you to-morrow, or next week. You're never on time. R. H. was right when he said I'd learn a lot, too. I certainly have. But I think it was mean of him to have me trailed! I suspected it. And I only wish I could have caught his spy!"

"What," Leonidas said, "did this—er—spy look like?"

"Oh, he was a huge creature in a turtle-neck sweater!"

Leonidas, watching Meiklejohn closely, saw the lit-tle man's eyebrows go up.

"So you spotted Turk!" he said. "Of course, Meikle-john, you knew that Haymaker had—er—assigned Turk to look after her?"

"Oh, yes," Meiklejohn fell into the trap. Then he looked at Leonidas. "How did *you* know about that, Mr. Witherall?"

"You told me," Leonidas said blandly, "just as Miss Quarl is going to tell me why she was hunting mink coats in my cellar. It's simply for the purposes of the record, I assure you," he added. "You can hunt mink coats in my cellar any time your heart desires. De-lighted to have you. Er—run in any time at all!"

"You," Suzanne said slowly, "you were the—oh. So that's why your voice sounded familiar! *You*—well, I certainly can't brush off *that* business lightly, can I?"

"It is my impression," Leonidas said, "that valuable time will be saved if you—er—break down, as the saying goes, and come clean."

Suzanne sighed. "It's all the fault of R. H.'s beastly spy—what did you say his name was, Turk? Well, around noon, it began to occur to me that either everyone in the world had turned into a fellow in a turtleneck sweater, or else I was seeing an awful lot of that one lad. During the afternoon, he haunted me. But he never got near enough for me to speak to him. It rather frightened me. I couldn't guess what he was up to. Well, this evening I finally got to this house on Birch Hill Road. Your house, Shakespeare. And someone yelled down for me to have a bottle of beer, and I was so tired, I did."

"Next time," Leonidas said, "you must bring it upstairs. Er—go on."

"Well, I sat down and took off my coat and drank your beer, and just as I was finishing, I saw this creature pass by the door. I decided I'd had about enough of being haunted by him, so I ran out and called to him. And he ran, and I ran. And he ran quicker. I thought I'd lost him," Suzanne said, "and then he went tearing by in a truck. And I was just sore enough to climb into my truck and tear after him."

"Leaving," Leonidas said, "your coat on my cellar floor!"

"Yes. Well, I lost him—but by then I was clear downtown, and I suddenly remembered I had an appointment to have my hair done. I'd made it for five-thirty. In my innocence," Suzanne said with a slight touch of bitterness, "I thought I'd be through by five. I thought everyone always got through work at five. I thought there was a law, or something. Of course it was after six, then, but I tooted over to Henri's anyway, and had my hair done. I needed someone to fawn over me and call me mademoiselle at that point. My spirits were at a very low ebb."

"And you were at the hairdresser's," Leonidas said, "during that blackout and alert?"

"Yes—and did anyone ever find out the reason for that?" Suzanne asked curiously. "Was it just another mistake?"

"Peculiarly enough," Meiklejohn said, "this time it was not a mistake. Not one of the ordinary mistakes, that is. My warden was telling me about it a while ago. It appears that someone gave the proper code word, and headquarters thought it was all quite genuine until someone pointed out that neither the Pomfret nor Carnavon sirens had sounded, and that the turnpike lights hadn't been turned out. They're not controlled locally, you know. My warden said everyone was still confused about it."

"Henri was so unnerved," Suzanne said, "he virtually let me burn to a crisp under the drier. Well, when I came out—visibly refreshed, I might add, in spite of a charred ear—I remembered that my coat was up in a cellar on Birch Hill Road. So I took the truck and went back up there to get it. I looked on my list for the house number, and it was One-forty. So—"

"But my house is Number Forty!" Leonidas interrupted.

"I know, I know, but I," Suzanne said, "learn things the hard way. I went to One-forty, and it dawned on me that it didn't look a bit like the house I'd been to. It wasn't sleek and modern, it was a perfect ark. In fact, it *wasn't* the house I'd been to! On the other hand, it *was* the house where I was supposed to have left two hundred gallons of oil. Now d'you begin to understand the situation, Shakespeare?"

"M'yes," Leonidas said, "I think I begin to. You came originally to Forty instead of One-forty, and had —er—pleasantly aroused me with the prospect of getting oil—now that I think of it," he added, "I didn't expect you until next week. I was grimly anticipating an unhappy little period of huddling around the cannel coal in the grate."

"Had you run *out?*" Meiklejohn sounded shocked.

"I follow," Leonidas said, "what is doubtless a most unpatriotic method. Instead of being very chilly all the time, I prefer to be comfortable part of the time, and freeze during the oilless interim. To me, partial warmth is rather like a partially good egg. To continue, Miss Quarl, you discovered that whereas you were supposed to have left oil at Haverstraw's, at One-forty, you had actually gone to Forty."

"Yes, and you'd been so sweet, urging me to have

some beer—after having other people harry me with dogs and skunks, I appreciated that friendly gesture. Anyway, it seemed terribly scurvy to let you down. But you weren't supposed to have the oil," Suzanne said, "and One-forty was. And I'd had just enough experience with people who expected oil and hadn't got it that I didn't want to bandy words with you. So I left the truck up at the corner and went to your house on foot. Just as I started, I saw a prowl car drive up the street, and a minute or two later, I heard the cops running around. I gathered, from what I could hear, that they were hunting for a prowler."

"Er—they were," Leonidas said. "I shouldn't be at all surprised to find that they still are."

"Well, I didn't think anything about them," Suzanne said. "After all, I wasn't any prowler. I went along on to your house and went into the cellar, and hardly before I got through the door, I heard these cops pounding after *me!*" She paused and drew a long breath. "Look, can you understand how all day long I've tried to keep out of any trouble, so R. H. wouldn't have anything to crow about? And there I was in that cellar, where I hadn't any particular right to be. And there were those cops, hunting a prowler. And all of a sudden I had this simply frightful vision of me trying to explain to those cops that I was the oil woman, only I hadn't left any oil, and my truck was up at the corner, and that I'd just dropped back for my mink coat, which I'd left when I rushed off from drinking a

205

bottle of beer to chase a man in a turtle-neck sweater who'd been haunting me all day, only I went and got my hair done instead—well, you see what I mean!"

"My, my!" Meiklejohn said gently. "My, *my!* I really don't think you'd better tell Mr. Haymaker about this, Miss Quarl, if it can possibly be avoided. I'm sure Mr. Haymaker wouldn't approve at all!"

"D'you think I wasn't thinking about that?" Suzanne demanded. "I saw myself shivering in the dock— do they have docks in Dalton, I wonder? Anyway, I could just see R. H., with his spats and cane and black Homburg, bailing me out in his best Gentleman- of-the-Old-School manner. I'll have to admit I didn't particularly distinguish myself today as an oil woman, but I was frankly damned if I was going to get mixed up with the cops, and have R. H. nip off my career in the bud! So I huddled there in the cellar. I could hear the cops padding around outside. And someone was banging at the front door, and yelling, and ringing the bell, but nobody answered—and still, I *knew* there was someone home, because I could hear 'em moving about upstairs! I didn't know what I'd got into!"

"Tch, tch, tch!" Meiklejohn clucked his tongue. "And all this happened at your house, Mr. Witherall? Your house?"

"I fear," Leonidas admitted, "that it does not sound in keeping with the dignity of a Haymaker director, does it? Do go on, Miss Quarl!"

"It's a funny thing," Suzanne said, "but I feel better

just telling someone about this! Well, my only desire was to get my coat and get out. I didn't dare put on a light. So I groped around, and groped, and groped, and groped. But I couldn't find the coat. And I was *so* afraid I'd bump into something that would tip over and bang! Once I tripped on a cardboard carton full of flattened tins, and I was sure then that I was done for. To me, it sounded like a clap of thunder, but mercifully no one else seemed to hear it. I kept groping—I could *see* the legs of those cops standing out by the back door, and I could hear these noises from upstairs. Like people walking around. Really, it was just like coming into the middle of a movie and trying to figure out what'd gone on before. I nearly went *mad!*"

"It sounds like a movie," Meiklejohn said interestedly. "Can you account for any of it, Mr. Witherall?"

"M'yes," Leonidas said. "I can, at least, hazard a guess. It's my impression that after Miss Quarl chased Turk downtown, he lost her. Without doubt, he must have had a duplicate of her list, although whether he himself secured it in some underhand manner, or whether Haymaker may have secured it for him through some—er—connivance, I could not, of course, venture to say. Turk, therefore, must have gone back to the right number, One-forty, and thereupon he became Haverstraw's prowler, an incident by which the good citizens of Birch Hill Road will undeniably date things, like the time the old ice house burned down. M'yes, that must be the way of it. Turk went to the Haverstraw's. Then, fleeing from the police, he ducked into my cellar—"

"*Your* cellar?" Suzanne interrupted. "You mean, where *I* was? Oh, he couldn't have ducked in there. *I* was the only person in your cellar until the people from upstairs came down. A man and a woman. *You* and a woman, that is."

"I rather think it will turn out," Leonidas said, "that Turk reached my cellar before you arrived, and was there all the time."

"*He* was there—oh, he couldn't have been, Shakespeare! I never heard him! What makes you think he could have been there, anyway?"

"I saw him leave," Leonidas told her. "M'yes, Turk certainly was there, and because he very likely had his orders not to let you know that he was keeping tabs on you, he made no effort to apprise you of his presence. On the contrariwise, I dare say he was straining every sinew to keep out of your way. You know, it makes rather a lovely picture—the beautiful blonde fearfully groping for her mink coat, the prowler desperately trying to—er—become one with the cellar wall, Dunphy and O'Malley on the back stairs, Compton pounding on the front door, Pink and I creeping around with Lady Baltimore and Uncle George's Dahlia Cup!"

Suzanne cocked her head to one side and stared at him. Meiklejohn, too, Leonidas noted, was eyeing him strangely.

"I don't understand a word of it," Suzanne said,

"but if I'd suspected that anything that sounded like what you just said was going on, I—oh, I don't know what I'd have done! I was a *pulp* by the time you and that woman came down the stairs. I had to dig my nails into my hands to keep quiet. I hoped and prayed you'd go right out without ever guessing I was there. And then that woman went and fell on my coat!"

"My, my," Meiklejohn said, "how trying, after you'd groped and groped, to have someone else stumble on it!"

"Trying," Suzanne said, "isn't quite the proper word. You see, *I* didn't know it was Shakespeare, here! I didn't know *who* the people could be. They were so stealthy and—and surreptitious, I thought they were burglars. I *aged!* I could positively feel my hair turning white! I never was so frightened in my life. Finally it struck me that you wouldn't be any more anxious to get involved with the cops than I was. And after what I'd been through, I was simply determined to get my coat. And then I looked up suddenly at the cellar window and realized that the cops' legs weren't there any more. So I spoke up—and got the coat. But if you'd called my bluff, I'd have collapsed right then and there!"

"Pink guessed as much," Leonidas said. "Er—what did you do then?"

"I dashed to the oil truck just as fast as my little legs could carry me," Suzanne said, "and beat it! I wouldn't have delivered any oil to One-forty at that point if icicles had been hanging from their living room ceiling! I went back to the yard, intending to put up the truck and stagger home—and found that the new girl who had Route Three had got into a fight in West Dalton, and got a black eye, and gone home crying without even be*gin*ning to make her deliveries. And some of 'em had to be made, so I went to work on 'em. That's what I've been doing ever since. That's why I'm here."

"It seems," Leonidas said appreciatively, "to have been the sort of day you might possibly sell to a newspaper syndicate. Tell me just one more thing—er—*why*—er—why *did* you—er—choose to wear a mink coat on such a job?"

"Why," Suzanne said simply, "I have just two decent cloth coats to my name, and they've got to do for the duration. You can't *get* wool, you know. Only three per cent mouse fur, six per cent rat hair, nine per cent old pasteboard, and the rest milk. I'm certainly not going to wear out my good cloth coats messing around in the *oil* business!"

"I see. Er—just using up the old mink. Er—m'yes." Leonidas could see the twinkle in Meiklejohn's eyes. "M'yes. Very thrifty and prudent of you, I'm sure. Dear me, yes! Have you at any time since leaving my cellar caught sight of Turk?"

"I'm not sure. I wasn't particularly watching for him," Suzanne said, "and anyway, I was so worn out, I probably wouldn't have noticed—wait a minute, though! Now I think of it, while I was waiting at that traffic light—why, of *course* that was Turk! Over in Pomfret. I'd gone back," she added parenthetically, "to that place where I minded the baby and forgot the oil. I'm sure that was Turk on Main Street. With a girl. A cute girl with red hair."

"You have," Leonidas said with relief, "removed a great responsibility from my mind. M'yes, it all works out. Jinx fled from the Lady Volunteers, after finishing her chop suey, meatless, and was somehow saved by Turk."

"You know what I'm beginning to suspect?" Suzanne inquired. "I'm beginning to suspect that your day makes mine look like an old shoe, Bill Shakespeare!" she giggled suddenly. "Except I'm willing to wager you didn't have to buy thirty-two double chocolate sodas for the United States Navy!"

"Er—what?"

"Oh, coming back from Pomfret," Suzanne said, "I had a slight brush with the Navy. They were hunting a Navy beachwagon someone had stolen—did you say something, Shakespeare?"

"It's just a tickle in my throat," Leonidas said. "I must remember to get some red stuff from the drugstore for it—d'you mean that someone actually had stolen a Navy beachwagon?"

"Yes, and the Navy was pretty sore about it, too," Suzanne said. "When they hailed me, I just thought they were being fresh, and went on. And when they found out I didn't intend to stop, they all but fired a

211

shot across my bow. Then when I did stop, and they found I was a woman, I practically couldn't get rid of them even though I kept telling them I hadn't seen their old beachwagon anywhere. The sight of a blonde apparently excited them anyway, but a blonde oil woman was almost more than they could bear. I finally bore them off to a Howard Johnson's and bought them off with chocolate sodas. Four apiece."

"I wonder," Leonidas said thoughtfully, "if perhaps it wouldn't be wise for me to purchase a few gallons of ice cream and a bit of chocolate sauce, just in case. Dear me!"

"May I ask," Meiklejohn said, "what this is all about, Mr. Witherall? I have no desire to pry, but really, I find myself very curious. Very."

"It's going to be very sad and unpleasant news, Mr. Meiklejohn," Leonidas said. "I deeply regret having to be the one to tell you. I only hope you will understand the reason for my conduct."

Meiklejohn's face never changed during Leonidas's recital, but Leonidas knew that he might as well have been stabbing the little man himself with Pink Lately's great-great-grandfather's samurai sword. Suzanne's blue eyes opened wider and wider.

"Oh," she said when he finished, "oh, how perfectly frightful! I don't know what *I* can do, Shakespeare, but I'm going to help you. Whether you like it or not. At least I might be able to guard you from Compton, if he tracks you down again!"

Meiklejohn's lips were tightly compressed, but he still spoke in the same calm, unruffled tone as he got up from the davenport.

"If you'll just wait," he said, "until I get my hat, I'll go along with you, Mr. Witherall. Obviously Mr. Haymaker realized that something was very wrong with those figures I gave him—oh, if only I had spoken up and asked him, when I saw that look on his face! A hat and a scarf, and I'll be ready to accompany you."

"All this—" Leonidas pointed toward the litter of papers. "Can you possibly guess what might have been taken?"

"The accounts I keep home here," Meiklejohn said, "are rather a miscellany, Mr. Witherall. That file in the corner contained only lodge and club accounts, and my own household accounts, and the accounts of the various clubs my wife belongs to. Everyone has a habit of making my wife a treasurer. I've sometimes wondered," he added reflectively, "if they realize that she can neither add nor subtract, and has never learned the multiplication table. The only thing that pertains to our problem is the ledger I brought home from the store in my briefcase tonight."

"Is that it, by the base of the bridge lamp?" Leonidas asked.

Meiklejohn nodded. "It contained the figures I gave Mr. Haymaker. Frankly, I was curious to make some comparisons and see if I could guess what had upset him. He, of course, could tell at a glance. I should have

213

looked at them earlier in the evening, but several friends dropped in, and then our warden came in to ask if I'd be willing to take over his duties tomorrow night."

Leonidas picked up the ledger and looked at it carefully.

"Ah, yes," he said, "quite a gap has been torn out here. And again here. And here." He bent over and scrutinized the fragments of paper at the foot of the lamp. "But these bits on the floor seem to have come from other ledgers. Quite different ink, and different lining. I wonder, now, if perhaps your assailant did not tear his heart out, so to speak, purely for the effect! I'm inclined to think that he wanted only certain pages from this ledger, and that he bore those away with him. M'yes, I think so. Have you any idea who it was, Meiklejohn? Can you think of no clue to his identity?"

"No, Mr. Witherall. None whatever. Obviously he entered by the cellar door, which I had purposely left open for the oil man. I was sitting here at my desk, making some notations—preparatory to getting to work on that ledger. Then something hit me. That's all I know."

"M'yes, I've had some experience with the technique," Leonidas said. "The quick, hard biff—er—do your eyeballs hurt?"

"They did," Meiklejohn said. "When I came to, I heard papers being torn. You know, Mr. Witherall, unless you have spent a number of years working with figures, you cannot conceive of the agony of being
214

forced to listen to the sound of papers being torn, when you know instinctively that they are papers covered with figures over which you have long labored. My eye-balls hurt, but that sound hurt me more. Now," he added, "I assume you'll want to go to the store at once?"

"Er—the store? You refer to Haymaker's?" Leonidas inquired.

"Oh, yes. I'm sure we want to go there at once, Mr. Witherall. Because there would have been no particular use in knocking me out and stealing those papers from that ledger, you know, as long as the duplicate ledger was in the store. I rather fear that someone may already have tampered with that—if such is the case, then we may be very sure that Mr. Haymaker was killed before he could expose some irregularity. If the ledger is there, intact," Meiklejohn said grimly, "a few hours' work will enable me to tell you in what department the irregularity occurred. I could not of course tell you who was responsible, but the field would be narrowed down."

"Mr. Meiklejohn, you are without doubt going to be a valuable addition to this affair," Leonidas said sincerely. "My mind had not even remotely considered duplicate ledgers."

"Oh, but you don't work with figures," Meiklejohn said. "And I wonder, Mr. Witherall, if all those wrong-number phone calls—this person with an oddly muffled voice kept wanting to speak to some Eddie—weren't

215

made by someone checking up to see if I was at home! I'll get my hat and scarf."

"He's such a dear little man," Suzanne said softly after Meiklejohn left the room. "He reminds me of one of dad's Dickens plates. And he feels so terribly about R. H., doesn't he? He's being so stoical and so brave, and he just yearns to cry his eyes out. And did you notice the glint in his eye? If he ever finds the person, he's going to tear him apart with his bare hands! He—"

She broke off as Meiklejohn, with a bright tartan scarf tied around his neck, came back to the doorway.

"I'm ready." He put on the derby he'd been holding in his hand. "Shall we go?"

"What about the oil?" Suzanne asked.

Leonidas smiled. "I fear," he said, "this is going to turn out to be another household where you had to leave without delivering your wares. But *do* run down cellar and get your mink coat, please!"

Outside on the lawn, a few minutes later, Suzanne turned to Leonidas.

"What are we going to do about the transportation problem, Shakespeare? My truck accommodates one, unless you want to do an uncomfortable amount of sandwiching. And it's not a very speedy vehicle."

Leonidas looked hesitantly up the street toward the parked beachwagon.

"Er—perhaps you have an available car, Meiklejohn?"

"I'm afraid mine's jacked up in the garage for the winter, Mr. Witherall."

Leonidas sighed.

"My offering is a beachwagon," he said, "which, I admit with considerable regret, is the property of the Navy Department."

"Shakespeare!" Suzanne said. "You never told us about that! Did you—were *you* the one who swiped that over in Pomfret?"

"We did not swipe it," Leonidas said hastily, "although I can easily see where we might have—er—given that impression. Dave Haymaker jumped into it, thinking it was his own, and since that Pomfret cop was so close on our heels, we did not pause to correct our error after we had become aware of it."

"Dave Haymaker—that stick? That utter *stick?*" Suzanne said, in unbelieving tones. "*He* swiped a beachwagon with cops chasing him? Oh, he never did! He never did anything in his life that wasn't absolutely correct. He's a Haymaker to the bone."

Leonidas looked at her quizzically.

"If you had seen—or even heard him being a Lion over at the swop," he said, "you would not long cling to that strange opinion. Shall we take the beachwagon, or crowd into the truck?"

"I'm for the beachwagon," Suzanne said. "I'm frankly tired of trucks—Shakespeare, who drove that here? The beachwagon, I mean? Did you?"

217

"M'yes," Leonidas said. "I hated to do it. It went against the—er—grain. But I required something in which to pursue you."

"Talk to me about syndicating *my* day!" Suzanne said. "You could sell yours to Hollywood. It's a natural for Lieutenant Haseltine. Come on, let's take the beachwagon. It'll take a third the time, and besides, they're only hunting over in Pomfret."

"Er—what's your opinion, Meiklejohn?"

"It certainly would seem much quicker, Mr. Witherall. And far more comfortable, don't you think, for Miss Quarl?"

Suzanne hooked her arm through his.

"Call me Suzanne," she said. "Come along, Shakespeare! I hosey to drive."

A quarter of an hour later, she drew the beachwagon up by the curb at the rear door of R. H. Haymaker's.

"So far, so good," she said as they got out.

Standing on tiptoe, Meiklejohn reached up and rang a bell high over the door's iron grille.

After several minutes of fruitless ringing, he stepped back and drew a bunch of keys from the pocket of his smoking jacket.

"I thought I'd better bring these along," he said, "just in case—ah, here it is!"

He selected one, deftly undid the catch in the grille, and then unlocked the door.

"Er—shouldn't there perhaps be a night watchman?" Leonidas inquired as they entered the still, pallid gloom of the store.

"There is one, but he's probably over in the annex and didn't hear us. We've been cut down to one, which I considered rather dangerous," Meiklejohn explained, "but as Mr. Haymaker philosophically pointed out, we have so very little left that's particularly worth stealing, it really hardly matters. It was the silks and perfumes we used to worry about most—this way."

Their footsteps echoed hollowly as he led them along the long empty aisles flanked by cloth-covered counters.

"I never saw anything so simply ghostly!" Suzanne whispered to Leonidas. "It frightens me! How funny it all looks with everything swathed in covers! And how deathly quiet—oh, I beg your pardon, Shakespeare, I didn't mean to bump you!"

"You didn't," Leonidas told her. "It was a dummy."

"Eeek! I don't like it!"

But she brightened considerably when Meiklejohn stopped before the elevators.

"Can I please—oh, but they're all dark!" she sounded disappointed. "Aren't they going?"

With a smile, Meiklejohn pulled back a door, snapped on a light, and stood aside to let them pass in.

"Can I *please* run it?" Suzanne demanded. "Please? I've always wanted to run an elevator!"

"D'you think perhaps it's wise?" Leonidas said

219

blandly. "I mean, after all, you've had a very trying day, and it's—"

"The trouble with you," Suzanne said shrewdly, "is that you want to run it yourself, don't you? May I, Mr. Meiklejohn?"

"I'm sure Mr. Haymaker never would have permitted—" Meiklejohn stopped short. "Why, I suppose you may, if Mr. Witherall doesn't object. Will you promise to be very careful?"

"Careful? Of course I'll be careful! It certainly can't be any harder," Suzanne said, "than driving an oil truck! What do you push?"

Six minutes later, she let her two slightly shaken passengers out on the seventh floor.

"Er—thank you," Leonidas said politely. "I might sum that up as one of the most exciting flights I've ever made, and I include the Clipper trip during the course of which we returned nine times to Lisbon!"

"Well," Suzanne said defensively, "if you'd only *told* me about that safety-catch button thing in the first place, I'm sure I wouldn't have jammed so—you know, it's nowhere near as *hard* as driving the oil truck, but it's certainly *dif*ferent! Anyway, it didn't upset Mr. Meiklejohn. Where do we go now?"

"This way. Of course," Meiklejohn said, "my fears about the ledger we want may be quite unfounded. The ledger should be in the safe. Ordinarily I see to their being put there, myself. But today, with all the excitement on the ground floor, I quite neglected to.

Miss MacIntosh is very reliable, but we were all rather upset, and she just possibly may have overlooked it."

As they followed him along a corridor, Leonidas pointed out a doorway to Suzanne.

"That," he said, "is the directors' room, where I raised this issue of accounts—"

"I'm so sorry, Mr. Witherall," Meiklejohn said apologetically, "but that is the manager's office. The directors' room is along the hall on the right, ahead of us. I'll show you when we—here. This is it."

He stopped suddenly.

"Er—is anything the matter?" Leonidas asked.

"Mr. Witherall, I'm almost positive I heard a noise in there!"

"Noise? What—"

"Listen!" Suzanne said. "Sssh! I heard it then, too! Listen!"

The next time, Leonidas also heard the sound, and diagnosed it as that of a chair being scraped or dragged across the floor.

"You don't suppose that the night watchman—"

Meiklejohn didn't bother to finish his whispered question.

The same thought had also occurred to Leonidas, who had never quite been able to dismiss the watchman from his mind since their entrance into the store.

Reaching out, Leonidas grasped hold of the knob, and pushed open the door.

The room was dark, and he fumbled along the wall

by the side of the door until his fingers closed over the button of the electric light switch.

The room was empty!

"Quick!" Suzanne said. "Hurry over to that door, Shakespeare! I'm sure someone went through that door when the lights went on!"

She darted across the room, and Meiklejohn followed her.

"Quick, Mr. Witherall! I thought I saw someone, too!"

Leonidas hurried after them, but almost as he passed through the doorway, he heard Suzanne's voice raised in disappointment.

"This other door's locked!"

"Look out!" Leonidas said warningly, and turned around.

But he was not quick enough.

The door through which they had entered was slammed, and a lock clicked.

CHAPTER 9

"MEIKLEJOHN," Leonidas said, "d'you know where the light—ah, thank you. Suzanne, you're privileged to behold a sight rarely offered to the feminine portion of Dalton. You're going to have a fine, long, uninterrupted view of the directors' washroom."

"You mean we're locked *in? Here?*"

"M'yes, we appear to be. And while the—er—management," Leonidas said, "has thoughtfully provided soap, towels, combs in little paper cases, and even bay rum, they did not think to provide us with anything in the nature of a good, useful tool with which to open either of these locked doors."

"Would a screwdriver help?" Suzanne asked.

"It would," Leonidas said, "certainly contribute to our morale, even if it didn't literally help."

Suzanne reached into the pocket of her mink coat.

"This do?"

She held out a long and efficient-looking screwdriver.

Leonidas put on his pince-nez and looked at her with honest admiration.

"The millennium," he said, "has arrived. At last I have seen a crisis where a woman did not bring forth a nail file and expect one to move mountains with it. What a tremendous help you would be, Suzanne, to a man like Lieutenant Haseltine! M'yes, indeed. How does it happen that you have this—er—instrument with you?"

"Oh, I did a little tire changing tonight," Suzanne said. "Way back there a few hours ago, before I met up with you boys. D'you take back your nasty crack about my elevator running?"

"Please," Leonidas said, "consider it unsaid!"

"Mr. Witherall!" Meiklejohn said suddenly.

"M'yes?"

"We walked into a trap!"

"M'yes." Secretly, Leonidas felt that Meiklejohn was a little late in catching on. "M'yes, we walked into a trap."

"Why did he bother?"

"Er—I beg your pardon?"

"I said, why did he bother?" Meiklejohn repeated. "Of course you realize, Mr. Witherall, that if we had passed by and if he had not made that little scraping noise, we never would have known anyone was here, at all! Now, he certainly *knew* we were in the building, the instant he heard the elevator. And he *must* have heard the elevator. He couldn't have helped hearing it! Miss Quarl—uh—Suzanne really—uh—"

224

"Go on and say it," Suzanne said. "I pushed it around."

"Well, he certainly heard us coming!" Meiklejohn said. "He had no need to stay here. He could have gone down on the freight elevator, or if he didn't dare chance the noise, he had three flights of stairs at his disposal. Had I been in his shoes and heard the elevator starting up, I'd have been downstairs twice over before the elevator finally reached the seventh floor!"

"I said it once, and I say it again—Meiklejohn, you are a definite addition to this affair!" Leonidas twirled his pince-nez. "M'yes. If he had any reason to suspect we were headed for the accounting department, and if for some unfathomable reason he could not leave this floor, he had only to hide in some room on the other side of the elevator bank. Not on this side. But he deliberately ensconced himself in the directors' room, and deliberately enticed us into it, and then in here—hm!"

"I don't see why you two are worrying so," Suzanne said. "He enticed us, and we bit! That's what it amounts to. Look, how's for—"

"Why we worry," Leonidas explained, "is that he went to such pains to trap us when he could have slipped out like a little mouse without our being a whit the wiser. I wonder, now!" he looked thoughtfully at the mirror above the washbasin. "M'yes, I wonder!"

"I think," Meiklejohn looked at the mirror too, "that

225

he wanted to know who we were pretty badly, don't you, Mr. Witherall?"

Leonidas permitted himself a grin.

"If he listened to the progress of that elevator, I'm sure he yearned to know! It would have been obvious to him that we couldn't have been burglars. But if we sounded as raffish as that elevator sounded, he must have thought we'd just escaped from the club bar, across the street. M'yes, indeed, he had a fine look at us! I really must give the fellow credit. That was exceedingly ingenious."

And Haseltine, he mentally added, would use the device at the earliest opportunity!

"What do you mean, he *saw* us?" Suzanne demanded. "How did he see us? *We* never saw *him!* I didn't actually *see* a person coming through this door as much as I *felt* that someone went through it. How did he *see* us?"

Leonidas pointed to the mirror over the washbasin.

"I opened the door, snapped on the light, and the three of us were reflected in here. He took a good look, darted out and snapped the lock, and then darted around and locked the other door."

"Well," Suzanne said with a shrug, "so he knows us—how's for going into action with my screwdriver?"

"I said," Leonidas told her, "even if it couldn't accomplish much, it was nice for our morale. That door is solid mahogany, and beautifully made. The rear door is—oak, would you say, Meiklejohn? M'yes, I

226

think oak, treated to match the other. It, also, is beautifully made and beautifully hung."

"You mean you can't do anything with the screwdriver? How are we going to get *out*?"

"Stone walls do not a prison make," Leonidas said, "and all that sort of thing. How smart of him to pick a place without windows! If he'd only locked us in the directors' room, we'd have been out in a trice!"

"The directors' room has no phones, Mr. Witherall!" Meiklejohn said.

"M'yes, but we had only to pull up the shades," Leonidas returned, "and every warden and civilian-defense-minded member of the club would have been at our throats before you could say 'Douglas MacArthur.' Most of the card-room habitués spend their evenings with an eye to the alcove·window, snooping for dimout violators."

"Isn't my screwdriver any good at *all*?" Suzanne persisted.

"We will consider its potentialities," Leonidas said, "after we have run through the possibilities of Meiklejohn's keys. D'you have them handy? Ah, thank you."

One key of the lot very nearly did fit.

"If we had a file," Meiklejohn said tentatively, "I might—"

Suzanne reached into her pocket and drew out a small leather case.

"There!" she opened it to disclose two steel nail files, a pair of nail scissors, and orange sticks.

"What the well-dressed oil woman carries," Leonidas murmured. "Oh, come, come, Suzanne, it's not kind of you to jump on my poor tired feet! Would either of those files work out, I wonder, Meiklejohn?"

"Try the scissors!" Suzanne said with irony. "Who knows, maybe one of the orange sticks would work! While you boy locksmiths pick around, I'm going to sit down on the floor and take a nap. If anyone walks through with sandwiches and coffee, wake me up. Or almond bars. I could do with a good almond bar, all lousy with vitamins that put pep and vigor—Shakespeare!"

"What is it?"

She pointed toward the bootblack stand in the corner.

"Look!"

"M'yes, I'm looking," Leonidas said patiently. "What is it?"

"Underneath, on the floor, next to the can of Dutch Cleanser and the brush—oh, you can't see 'em standing up! Keys! Keys on a string! Get 'em, quick!"

"I must make a note," Meiklejohn said as Leonidas unlocked the door half a minute later, "to send Martha a turkey at Thanksgiving."

"Who's Martha?" Suzanne asked.

"The cleaning woman. She's a very inefficient cleaning woman, and very absent-minded. Sometimes she cleans the sixth floor and forgets us entirely. She also loses keys by the gross. Of course, she claims that she never really loses them, she merely misplaces them. Up to this minute, I have never felt that she was a particularly valuable employee—is the door to the corridor locked? No matter, Mr. Witherall. One of mine fits that."

Once in the corridor, Meiklejohn made a beeline for the accounting department.

When Leonidas and Suzanne caught up with him, he was standing in the doorway, surveying the large rectangular room.

"Things look all right," he said. "The safe hasn't been touched. I'll open it, and see if the ledger we want is inside."

The safe contained many ledgers; but Meiklejohn, looking them over swiftly, shook his head.

"It's not there! Maybe Miss MacIntosh—I wish I knew if she'd put it anywhere! We *could* go through all the files and drawers, of course—"

Leonidas pointed to a phone. "Why not call her?"

"There's no one at the switchboard," Meiklejohn said. "But Mr. Haymaker's office has his private line. I'll go call her from there."

He looked puzzled when he returned.

"It's really amazing," he said in response to Leonidas's question. "I don't understand it at all. Miss MacIntosh says she had it on her desk earlier in the afternoon, but when she came back from helping out at the stocking sale, it was gone. She thought *I* took it!"

"It's really even more amazing," Leonidas said pen-

229

sively, "to think that if someone filched it earlier this afternoon, they should return for it now! Why didn't this person put it in his briefcase and march out with it, even as you marched out with yours, Meiklejohn?"

"Perhaps someone hid it away, Mr. Witherall, thinking it might be safer to wait a while before taking it from the store. Perhaps someone meant to take it tomorrow, and then, in a moment of panic, decided to come back here tonight and remove it from its hiding place. Perhaps—"

"Oh, perhaps," Suzanne interrupted impatiently, "someone was going somewhere where someone didn't want to be bothered with lugging a briefcase. Or a ledger. I don't like to carp at you boys, but all this perhaps-ing and someone-sing is getting me down!"

Leonidas put on his pince-nez and looked at her thoughtfully.

"You also," he said, "are proving extraordinarily helpful! Meiklejohn, listen. Haymaker goes to the club, which he leaves alone. It is bruited about that he intends to call on me. Perhaps he does, but I think—not that it matters tremendously—that he started for his own home first. Somewhere en route he is joined by someone whom he trusts so little, at least by the time he ultimately reaches my house, that he causes his cherished Homburg to be left on my lawn as a sort of danger signal for Turk, who he assumes is following him shortly."

"Was the hat actually *in* plain sight when Dave found it?" Meiklejohn asked.

"No, it was in the corner by my hedge. I think it was more clearly visible, but that the wind blew it," Leonidas said, "to the hedge. It's my impression that if R. H. Haymaker firmly told someone to let his hat blow away, and not to retrieve it, that person would not dare to do so, however much he might feel that the hat was a signal. Now, I think this person who joined Haymaker was waiting for him to walk home. I think he waited near Mrs. Lately's, where he filched that samurai sword. Now, if this person who was waiting suspected that Haymaker suspected *him*, he would hardly burden himself with any incriminating ledgers. Or briefcases stuffed with obvious ledgers. Of course he would leave that ledger here!"

Meiklejohn nodded.

"Very likely when he took the duplicate from Miss MacIntosh's desk, he also hunted for the original, but when I went down to the first floor, I automatically put it in my desk and locked the drawer. That gave him the added task of getting the ledger away from me to-night. I suppose," he added, "it wouldn't have mattered if I'd studied the figures before he took it. After he took it, I had no proof."

"After leaving your house with it," Leonidas said, "he came here—I wonder what caused the delay? Six minutes, at the rate he was going when he left your street, would have brought him here. Six minutes more should have sufficed for him to get his hidden ledger and depart! I wonder how he still happened to be here when we arrived?"

"He got a flat on the way,'" Suzanne said. "That's what usually delays people these days. It's what delayed Quarl's Quality Oil deliveries this evening. If you give him a flat, Shakespeare, the timing's perfect."

"An extraordinarily helpful girl! So he had a flat," Leonidas said. "Then, when he heard us, he decided to take a look at us. A wise and ingenious man."

"Where do you suppose he is now, Shakespeare?" Suzanne asked.

"Establishing an alibi. At least, that's what I, personally, would have been doing at intervals all evening. Meiklejohn, let us hunt around for some trace of your night watchman. It is my firm feeling that the poor fellow has been sharply biffed and doubtless thrust into some convenient hamper."

"I still can't begin to understand any part of that episode!" Meiklejohn said. "Nothing like that ever happened in our Lost and Found before, Mr. Witherall! Not in the fifty-two years I've been associated with the firm! Unless it was in the elevators in the Christmas rush, no one was ever biffed at Haymaker's, *ever!*"

"Ah, well," Leonidas said, "we're beginning to piece together some of this. Perhaps the rest will come to us, in time. Perhaps, out of the blue, inspiration will strike —er—did you say something, Suzanne?"

"I said," she told him, "it *better!*"

232

"Don't scoff, Suzanne! We've pieced together rather a lot!"

"I'll grant you a very smart piece job, Shakespeare. But what I'd like to know is, Whodunnit?"

"For the time being," Leonidas said, "I wish you would—er—freeze that sixty-four-dollar question. Now, do let us hunt up that watchman!"

They found him, after a brisk hunt over the seventh floor, in a broom closet near a staircase.

He blinked up at Meiklejohn as they untied him.

"Don't ask me, Mr. Meiklejohn!" he said. "All I know is, I thought I heard a noise out on the landing, and then something hit me. Oh, my eyeballs! My eyeballs feel like they was on fire! You won't have to get anybody else, though, Mr. Meiklejohn. I'll be all right just as soon as my eyeballs stop!"

"I think," Meiklejohn said, "I'd better phone your relief—what do you think, Mr. Witherall?"

"It's just those gremlins," Leonidas said. "They pass. But perhaps, in case our friend takes it into his head to return, you'd best summon an—er—auxiliary."

After the substitute watchman had been called, Meiklejohn guided Leonidas and Suzanne back to the elevator.

"No, Shakespeare!" she pushed him away from the controls. "Let me. I've had experience, now. I really got the feel of it. Please let me!"

She was crowing with pride when the elevator glided to a smooth stop at the first floor.

"There! A perfect three-point landing! If I'd been elevating all my life, I couldn't have done any better —what's the matter back there, Shakespeare? You struck dumb?"

"These advertisements." Leonidas pointed to the gaudy placards hung on the elevator's grillwork. "I read them earlier, on my way up to the sixth floor. Now, I understood from what Jinx said that sometimes you had unannounced sales, Meiklejohn. It says here, 'Sudden Special: Rayon House Coats, Zipper Front.' Er— but there's no mention of that sudden stocking sale!"

"Oh, that sale!" Meiklejohn said wearily. "I heard about it, but I didn't realize till they took all my staff away to help that something really out of the ordinary was going on. I rang for the elevator ten full minutes, and then walked down—did you know, Mr. Witherall, that three women fainted? The elevator girls gave them first aid."

"So that's why I waited!" Leonidas said. "Jinx forgot to tell me about that! What was it, a Sudden Special? I ask you, because Jinx said Haymaker was very irritated when he found the sale in progress. She said she thought he hadn't been told about it."

Meiklejohn shook his head.

"Nobody was told about it! They were still trying to find out who was to blame, when I went home. Major Beeding was terribly upset. I saw him marching around. It seemed that someone phoned orders to the stock room, and the stock was brought down, and the sale began—and what a bedlam it turned out to be! It was rather like our mysterious Alert," he added. "It was unquestionably a mistake, but it was a mistake in very good order—what's the matter, Mr. Witherall, is it that tickle in your throat again?"

"It is the tickle in my throat to end all tickles in my throat!" Leonidas said. "Meiklejohn, I am a dull and stupid clod!"

"You mustn't say that, Mr. Witherall! Mr. Hay-maker said you were one of the brightest men he'd met in a long time!"

"I am a dolt!" Leonidas said. "It has taken me since I came to in that wagonful of French bread to grasp this—this so exquisitely simple connection! Of *course* there was a stocking sale! It was to clear the sixth floor, Meiklejohn!"

"Do you *feel* all right, Mr. Witherall? Would you like a glass of water, perhaps?"

"I never," Leonidas said truthfully, "felt any better in my life! Don't you see, Meiklejohn, it was *deliberate* confusion! Someone sat down and pondered. What, he asked himself, would cause the greatest confusion? In bell-like tones, the answer rang back: a stocking sale!"

"Of course," Meiklejohn said, "the *real* trouble was that those stockings were—well, not exactly being hoarded, but laid aside for Christmas. But once they were put on the counters, they went like wildfire. And it was our holiday stock!"

"Better and better," Leonidas said. "Brilliant plan-

235

ning, brilliant planning! He caused a wonderful state of confusion! He cleared the sixth floor! He cleared your floor! He put the elevator service into a state of acute paralysis! People run around every which way. They leave ledgers on their desks. Oh, masterly! M'yes, indeed, masterly!"

"Wouldn't you like to sit *down*, Mr. Witherall?" Meiklejohn asked anxiously.

"Now who," Leonidas said, "was expected on the sixth floor? What was expected? What was it cleared of all witnesses for? Think, both of you! What had someone planned to do, what was to take place on the sixth floor, that Pink Lately and I so innocently burst in to?"

"I always carry this little tin of aspirin around," Meiklejohn said in a distressed voice. "Really for my wife—she has headaches. Now if you'd just take one of these, Mr. Witherall, I'll go get some water from the drinking fountain, and I'm sure that will make you feel better in *no* time! There's nothing like an aspirin—"

"Shakespeare," Suzanne said suddenly, "I'm catching on. Our bright boy has dirty work to do on the sixth floor. He clears it by throwing a silk-stocking sale that throws everyone into a frenzy. You and Mrs. Lately barge in and louse up his plans. Bam—into the hampers! Is that it, approximately?"

"No dog," Leonidas said. "No dog!"

"Oh, come now, Shakespeare!" Suzanne said. "Don't

get me to thinking you need aspirin, too! What do you mean, no dog?"

"Major Beeding!" Leonidas said.

"I *thought* of suggesting that we call him in to help!" Meiklejohn said. "He's a very imaginative man, although you might not think so to look at him. He always has ideas. Mr. Haymaker always said he had a very deceptive exterior. D'you think we'd better ask him to help us, Mr. Witherall?"

"Er—that was not," Leonidas said slowly, "precisely what I had in mind. Er—no."

To himself, he was thinking that Beeding was around. Beeding was all over Birch Hill Road. And Oakhill. Beeding wanted to be a director of the bank. Beeding was at that meeting. Beeding heard him ask about accounts. Beeding was a man of action.

And Beeding didn't have a dog!

Suzanne leaned back on the elevator's little jump seat.

"What I keep wanting," she said, "is clues. I love clues. Don't you suppose, Shakespeare, that with all my wandering about the streets of Dalton and vicinity, I must have seen something that was a clue, even if I didn't recognize it as a clue at the time?"

"Did you, in your peregrinations," Leonidas said, "happen to see anyone removing a sword from a porch? Pink Lately left that samurai sword out on her porch so that it might be viewed by a potential swopper. When she returned home, someone had removed it

237

from beside the potted fir. But perhaps Olde Forge Road was the street you missed, today."

"Olde Forge Road? A potted fir? Shakespeare, I saw—" she broke off abruptly. "Look, first let's make sure I'm not working myself up for nothing. This was on Olde Forge Road, on the corner, around—oh, time had got to mean nothing to me then, but it was somewhere between half past four and five. Maybe later, but not much."

"Go on," Leonidas said in a voice of infinite calm. "If you can go on, Suzanne, please do!"

"There isn't much to go on *to!* I saw a man take something from the porch of a big, rambling house near the corner of Olde Forge Road, that's all. I thought it was a cane, or a stick. I don't think I'd have remembered him at all if you hadn't mentioned the potted fir. I noticed it when I came back, after turning around."

"Where was the man?"

Suzanne shook her head.

"I don't remember seeing him, then. I don't know why I have the impression that he drove off in a car. If I saw the car, I don't remember it. Perhaps I *heard* it drive off—oh, Shakespeare, I know you're disappointed I can tell you so little! Isn't it frightful, to have seen him, and not to have noticed any more than that? I could describe the potted fir beautifully, but not the man. Perhaps," she added, "I'll know him if I see him again. And then, of course, there's Turk!"

"That's true," Leonidas said. "If Turk was trailing you at the time, he may have spotted the fellow—Suzanne, think back to that car coming down Meiklejohn's driveway at you. Did you notice the driver at all? Did you notice anything about the car? It passed so very close to you when it swerved on to the street!"

"It passed so very close to your beachwagon," Suzanne retorted, "I thought for a second he wasn't going to make it—but did *you* notice him? Or the car?"

"Touché," Leonidas said. "Touché."

"There was only one thing about that car," Suzanne said, "that I can remember. No, two. The engine had a funny roar. It sounded like a big car. A powerful car. And I seem to remember that the headlights were close together. Not in the fenders, but more in front of the radiator, sort of. You know, the way they used to be before streamlining. Heaven knows that isn't much to remember, but it's more than you managed to notice, anyway!"

Leonidas took the first move he'd made to step out of the elevator since Suzanne had so expertly landed it at the first floor.

"Action, at long last?" she inquired.

"If you can term it that. I think we'll go to the swop and collect Pink and Dave—"

"That *stick!*" Suzanne said scornfully. "But will the swop still be going on?"

"M'yes, I hope so. It seems to me that the handbill advertising it made some prophecy about its winding

239

up with a dance. Pink's car is out of gas," Leonidas said, "and Dave's beachwagon is over in Pomfret, so I'm trusting that they will have stayed put. We'll pick them up, and then I think we'll make rather a strenuous effort to locate Turk, and see if he by any chance happened to notice the man on Olde Forge Road this afternoon."

At the store's rear door, Suzanne paused and surveyed the beachwagon's tires.

"I don't know why," she said, "but I somehow expected that the Navy would have been sunk. In books, the villain always slashes tires so no one can pursue him—d'you suppose he didn't dare slash the Navy?"

"I suppose he rightly felt there was no necessity for any slashing," Leonidas replied. "After all, he had us quite effectively immobilized up there in the directors' washroom. If you'll drive us over to Lyceum Hall, Suzanne, please? Er—whether or not we find Pink and Dave still there," he added as he made room for Meiklejohn on the front seat, "I think perhaps we'd best abandon the Navy somewhere in that area, and transfer to some vehicle in which we may feel—er—more secure. Like a safe, commonplace cab."

Several blocks from the store, Suzanne slowed down.

"What in the world are you muttering about, Shakespeare? It sounds as if you kept saying 'No dog!' over and over again!"

"Not 'No dog,'" Leonidas answered absently. "'No dog. Hat.'"

"I still have that little tin of aspirin right here in my coat pocket," Meiklejohn said hurriedly. "Are you sure that you wouldn't like to have one, Mr. Witherall, right now?"

"Thank you, no," Leonidas said. "I'm quite all right, I assure you. It's simply that there couldn't have been a dog. Not so much because a dog was not visible as because he didn't dig up my tulip bulbs. Every other dog in the neighborhood has. No, no dog. He just wanted to establish himself as being there. No dog at all. He was also hunting for the hat."

"My boy!" Meiklejohn said. "My, my, you really worry me, Mr. Witherall! Don't you think that perhaps we should go to Major Beeding's, and ask him to assist us? After all, you've had a very strenuous day, what with the directors' meeting, and that hamper, and everything that's happened since. There's no reason why you shouldn't feel a little hys—I mean, overtired. Shall we just *not* go to the swop, perhaps, but drive instead to Major Beeding's?"

"Later, possibly," Leonidas said, "we may find it necessary to call on the Major. But not now, Meiklejohn, not now!"

To himself, he kept thinking what an ingenious fellow the Major was! To have marched around whistling for a dog, in a neighborhood where people were always marching around whistling for dogs! And if he met someone who knew he personally possessed no dog, he had only to say that he was whistling for some-

one else's animal. Beeding hadn't even bothered to
alibi for the dog when he talked to Henry Compton by
Hassett's street light, earlier. What was it the fellow
had said when—eliminating any mention of Jinx—he
had explained his part in the prowler incident? Something about walking along Birch Hill Road, whistling
and minding his own business!

"Major Beeding's really clever," Meiklejohn said.
"I'm sure he could help. He *thinks* of things!"

"Major Beeding is an exceedingly ingenious indi-
vidual. I agree with you wholeheartedly," Leonidas said
with perfect truth. "I concur with no reservations
whatsoever. Er—he *thinks* of things! M'yes, indeed,
Major Beeding most certainly and assuredly thinks of
more things than—"

"How near," Suzanne interrupted, "do you want to
get to the hall, Shakespeare? Shall we be completely
brazen, and park the Navy smack out in front of the
main entrance?"

"I don't feel," Leonidas said, "that it would be wise
for us to be *quite* so flamboyant. There's a little side
street with a variety store, where Dave parked it earlier.
I think it's the next corner—yes. To the right. It's a
nice quiet block. Er—beach it here, anywhere."

Suzanne expertly sliced the beachwagon between
two yellow-painted parking markers.

Practically before she turned off the ignition, Dave
Haymaker rushed up to the car and wrenched open
the front door.

242

"Bill Shakespeare! Oh. For Pete's sakes, where did he pick *you* up?"

"Hello," Suzanne said unemotionally. "I thought you'd be in the Army with everyone else."

"So did I," Dave returned. "Hullo, Meiklejohn." He surveyed the latter's smoking jacket and tartan scarf. "You look as if they'd wrenched you away from a quiet evening with a good book! Bill, Pink Lately's nearly gone mad, worrying about you! Can I depend on you to stay put while I go collect her? We've been wandering around, hoping you'd come back, and trying to catch sight of you—oh, here she is. She must have seen you."

Pink pulled open the other door.

"Shakespeare, are you all *right*? Oh, you found the Quarl girl—and dear Mr. Meiklejohn! You haven't changed a bit since I saw you last—how long ago could that possibly be, I wonder?"

"Thirty years," Meiklejohn said precisely, and then looked as if he wished he hadn't said it.

"You had charge of counting noses at the reception, didn't you, and seeing if we needed the extra cake?" Pink said reminiscently. "I remember that it was your job to rush out and get it if we ran out, because someone or other decided if we put *all* the little white boxes out at once, people would be tempted to stuff their pockets full. I remember those little boxes as if it were only yesterday. They had the loveliest satin bows —Bill Shakespeare, where have you been?"

"Get in, and I'll tell—wait, Pink. Er—have you seen any Navy about?"

"Only Admiral Coe-Chester, but he went long ago. He found his cousin—Gidding's wife, you know. And there were some sailors dancing over at the hall, but they don't count, I'm sure."

"Then," Leonidas said, "if the coast is quite clear, you and Dave get in, and I shall attempt to—er—re-capitulate. I—"

He stopped suddenly, whipped on his pince-nez, and stared unbelievingly at the white cardboard box which Pink was so tenderly depositing on the floor by the beachwagon's back seat.

"Pink," he said, "*what* have you got there? Is that —certainly my eyes are deceiving me! Is that—*can* it be Lady Baltimore?"

"Yes," Pink said simply. "Isn't it perfectly amazing, the way things work out?"

"Amazing! But, Pink, I swopped that over in Pomfret for the lion's head!"

"The little boy said he was from Pomfret," Pink returned. "He was a dear youngster with sandy hair and a lot of freckles, and he simply fell in love with that old music box I'd swopped your Dahlia Cup for. He begged me to swop, and he was so sweet, I said yes—I really wasn't terribly wedded to the music box, anyway. So he trotted away with it, and when he brought me back *his* swop, of all things, it was Lady Baltimore!"

"Er—how does she look?" Leonidas inquired.

"Well, she's aged," Pink said critically, "but she's intact. Of course I always *had* to make hardy cakes for the Lately boys to take to picnics and all, but I'm inclined to think that this is just about the hardiest cake I ever made. What's happened, Bill? What have you been doing? Where'd you go? Where'd you pick up these two? Have you found out anything?"

"First," Leonidas said, "permit me to render proper thanks for your faint. It was both timely and artistic, and I feel that without it, our—er—adventure would have terminated in a most abrupt fashion."

"Oh, it was nothing! I love to faint," Pink said. "To pretend to, I mean. When all the Lately boys got rambunctious at once, sometimes the only way I could bring them back to their senses was with a good faint. But didn't you think Dave was splendid—wasn't that lion business wonderful? He says it just came to him."

"Both of you were masterly. But Suzanne has been masterly, too," Leonidas said, "and so has Meiklejohn. Now, listen."

Halfway through his narrative, he noted that Dave was eyeing Suzanne with something akin to respect.

"So," he concluded a few minutes later, "there you are. No dog. Hat."

"Oh!" Meiklejohn said, "now I begin to understand, Mr. Witherall, and I—truly, I apologize for offering you that aspirin. But really," he sounded as if his calm had at last begun to be slightly shattered, "it can't be Major Beeding!"

245

"It has to be Major Beeding. It can't be anyone other than Major Beeding," Leonidas said. "To begin with, he has access to the store. He was at the directors' meeting. He could easily have ordered that stocking sale to be held, himself, and then have denied knowing anything whatsoever about it. After all, the whole thing was dependent on one simple little telephone call to the stock room, you told me!"

"But I saw Major Beeding at the sale, Mr. Witherall! He looked terribly upset!"

"If I had been the person responsible for the sale," Leonidas returned, "I, too, would have been there, marching around and looking upset as anything. It would have been no trick to have bounced down to the sale long enough to have people see you, and to impress on everyone your extreme perturbation. Now, Major Beeding was jealous of me because I, through no fault of mine, became director of the bank, a position he coveted. In the directors' meeting today, I brought up the topic of accounts. I think we may safely assume that Major Beeding has been manipulating figures to cover up a serious shortage—he is in a position where he could do that, is he not, Meiklejohn?"

"Yes, Mr. Witherall, but—"

"After the directors' meeting," Leonidas continued, "Haymaker made a sudden and unexpected call for figures in order to furnish me with the information which I didn't particularly want, and of which I feel certain I could have made neither head nor tail. When, by the way, I term his action 'unexpected,' I mean I'm assuming that he ordinarily would not have called for those figures today—would he, Meiklejohn?"

"Not till Friday, Mr. Witherall."

"One glance at the figures proved to Haymaker that something was radically wrong. I gather, Meiklejohn, that after Haymaker called you, you promptly called other people for current figures?"

Meiklejohn nodded.

"Now," Leonidas said, "Beeding had no chance to take any covering steps during the brief interval between the close of the directors' meeting, and the time Haymaker called for the figures. Er—am I right, Meiklejohn?"

"As a matter of fact," Meiklejohn said slowly, "Mr. Haymaker sent the Major to Boston on an errand, directly after the meeting. Something to do with a leather buyer, as I recall. His secretary told me when I called his office for the figures."

"Ah!" Leonidas said, "that settles that satisfactorily! Now, Beeding later causes this sale and its accompanying confusion, during the course of which he—er—pinches the ledger from Miss MacIntosh's desk. He filches the vital pages of the other ledger from Meiklejohn tonight. Then—"

"But what about his biffing me and putting me into that laundry hamper?" Pink interrupted plaintively. "What about his biffing you and putting you into the bread thing? What did he have against *us*, anyway?

247

Against *me!* I mean, he certainly couldn't have put on that silk-stocking sale just to biff us, and all, could he?"

"For some sinister purpose, at whose nature I will not hazard a guess," Leonidas said, "Beeding cleared the sixth floor by the sale. You and I were—er—flies in the ointment. He therefore disposed of us. He took a chance, but apparently whatever risk he ran seemed worth it to him. Later he left the store and went to the corner of Olde Forge Road, near your house, Pink. He was waiting for Haymaker to walk home—now I wonder, did he perhaps pick up that samurai sword on impulse, and then decide to drive off and meet Haymaker en route? I rather think that was the case. M'yes."

"Say, Shakespeare," Dave said, "providing he picked uncle up, either in a car or on foot, wouldn't someone have seen 'em around your house?"

"I doubt it," Leonidas said. "The Haverstraws are my nearest neighbors, and the intervening trees almost entirely obstruct their view of my house. Being a little deaf, they're rarely moved to look out and investigate sounds—as, for example, the sound of cars coming or going. Besides, I rather feel that the murder was committed during that odd Alert, when all good citizens were presumably off the streets and away from windows."

"There's quite a time gap there," Dave said thoughtfully, "from uncle's leaving the club this afternoon to that Alert this evening."

Leonidas nodded.

"M'yes. That is why I feel that Beeding, after taking the sword from Pink's, drove away and intercepted Haymaker. Perhaps Beeding took him to his own house, down the street. Or perhaps they drove around—while the latter may seem unlikely, I dare say one does not compute gasoline wastage when one is contemplating a murder. Let us assume, at all events, that he picks Haymaker up, that Haymaker murmurs something about accounts—"

"Hey, I've got it!" Dave interrupted. "Beeding takes him to his house—Beeding's, I mean. I know they didn't go to uncle's, and I don't think they did any driving around. Uncle hates to be driven by anybody but Turk. At Beeding's, Beeding tries to talk uncle into thinking he's all wet, or that if there's any shortage, it's the fault of two other guys. *That's* where the time went, and that's why I couldn't find uncle anywhere. What d'you think of that, Shakespeare?"

"You are as efficient in hitting a nail's head," Leonidas told him, "as you were in explaining a lion's head. M'yes, indeed!"

"Beeding had uncle at his house," Dave went on, "talking his ear off to save his skin—that sounds strange, but you know what I mean, anyway. Perhaps he nearly succeeded. Perhaps uncle says something like okay, but why did Witherall bring up the subject of accounts, maybe Witherall knows something. Or maybe he says he wants to talk to Witherall before he commits him-

self. Uncle was always wanting to talk to someone before committing himself, wasn't he, Meiklejohn?"

"Yes, Mr. Dave, it was one of his favorite phrases,"
Meiklejohn said. "Of course, he never really *did* talk
with anyone. He said so to gain time."

"Well, say that they left Beeding's just before the
Alert," Dave said, "and after the sirens went, they kept
on walking. Probably they were nearer your house then,
Shakespeare, than Beeding's—d'you approve of all this,
or does it sound crazy?"

"I don't think it's crazy," Pink said before Leonidas
had a chance to speak, "but it bothers me. *I* should
think it would've been awfully dangerous and suspicious for Beeding to have had Ross at his house at
all, if he had any intention of killing him!"

"Not at all," Dave said. "Uncle is alive when he
leaves. He walks off on his own two feet. Say, Shakespeare, is Beeding a—"

"M'yes," Leonidas said, "he is a warden. He is what
we refer to in this organization of ours as a floater. He
has no set post. M'yes, Dave, I think you're making
progress. Say that just before the pair reaches my house,
the wind blows off Haymaker's hat. Perhaps I was not
entirely right in thinking he permitted it to stay on
the lawn as a signal to Turk. The street lights were off
then, and it's quite possible that he might not have
been able to locate it."

"There's still the chance uncle didn't *want* to locate
it," Dave said. "I don't suppose we'll ever know the
250

truth of the matter, but I'll always like to think he let it stay there for Turk to see."

"They must have arrived," Leonidas said, "only a few seconds after I rushed off on my bicycle. Probably about the time I was blowing my whistle at the Haverstraws."

"How could they have got *into* your house, Mr. Witherall?" Meiklejohn asked curiously.

"I wondered about that earlier," Leonidas said with a smile. "Then, on our way here from the store just now, I remembered the key collection. The metal drive, you know. Beeding made the neighborhood collection only yesterday. I gave him all the odd keys and the duplicates I didn't need. Some of the latter bore tags which I neglected to remove since they, too, were metal. In short, Major Beeding had keys."

"When you first suggested Beeding as a suspect," Dave said, "I thought you were crazy. I never liked the man, but I couldn't think of him as a murderer. But brother, how this all fits together!"

"*I* don't think so!" Pink said. "Not one single bit. I mean, I think it's Beeding, but it doesn't fit."

"Why, of course it does!" Dave told her. "Beeding grabbed up those keys of Bill Shakespeare's before he left his house with uncle—just in case Bill hadn't managed to get out of the hamper, and wasn't home!"

"But," Pink protested, "suppose that Bill *was* home? What *then*, I'd like to know?"

"Well," Dave said hesitantly, "well—oh, well, I sup-

251

pose if you mean to kill someone, any place will do. If Bill *wasn't* home, he was going to kill uncle in Bill's house. If Bill *was* home, I suppose any part of Bill's grounds would have served his purpose just as well!"

"But what about that sword?" Pink demanded. "Beeding would have had to carry that with him! And Ross Haymaker certainly wouldn't be fool enough to march around with a man he suspected, if the man was carrying a sword! How could Beeding have explained that sword to Ross?"

"Oh, how do you explain *any*thing away?" Dave said. "You invent. Probably, just as they left the house, Beeding picked the sword out of his car and said casually that he really must return the nice sword Witherall was kind enough to lend him for the fancy-dress ball, or the play, or something like that."

"But if Bill was home," Pink said firmly, "then Beeding would look pretty silly, returning Bill's nice sword that Bill never laid eyes on before!"

"He could have tossed it in the bushes, or left it in Bill's hall—oh, I don't know!" Dave said. "I give up. Shakespeare, you take over. *You* explain it!"

"It would all be so simple," Leonidas said, "if we could only prove that it was Beeding who was responsible for causing that mysterious Alert. Knowing I'm a warden, he'd know I wouldn't be home. He'd purposely take my door keys, and he could carry practically anything he might say he wanted to return to me, and know that I'd not be there to—er—gum up the—"

252

"Bill Shakespeare!"

Pink spoke so urgently that Leonidas automatically looked around to see if Henry Compton had again managed to track him down.

"Er—what's the matter?"

"Bill, brother told me! That is, he as *good* as told me, but I never stopped to think what he meant! He was telling Gidding about that unexplained Alert, while they were bringing me to, and he said *no* one could understand it. He said he could understand it least of all, because he was the head of all the code signals, or something like that, in this quadrant, or sector, or whatever they call it! And he said that absolutely *no* one could have given that code signal this evening but the proper persons, and the proper persons claim they never did!"

"Er—that's very interesting," Leonidas said, "but I'm afraid I fail to see—"

"Oh, wait, wait! He went on to tell Gidding what fine code signals they were, and he said—*this* is the important part, Bill! He said that Major Beeding had seen them and Major Beeding said they were perfectly *splendid* code signals, and he'd never seen anything more efficiently arranged in the Army—Bill, don't you see? Beeding saw that code book! Beeding knew the word to give to cause that Alert!"

"Well," Dave said, "there you have it, Bill! That fills in those gaps! Beeding himself called and gave the signal just before he and uncle left. And before they

253

got to your house, the sirens were going. Now we've only got to get him!"

"Er—yes," Leonidas said. "M'yes. That's all."

His irony went over Dave's head.

"The boy's bright, Bill! If he was seen going to your house with uncle, and if anyone questioned him, he'd only to say he left uncle there and rushed out to be a warden. And if he floats around, you couldn't pin him down."

"You couldn't," Leonidas said, "but I'm sure Beeding went to great pains to be seen later during the Alert. I'm sure that after he killed Haymaker, he rushed out and wardened like mad. I know that he handed in his report at once, because Henry Compton congratulated him warmly tonight, in my hearing, on being such a fine, co-operative warden. Compton wished that more of his wardens, including me, were like Beeding."

"How lucky the man's been!" Suzanne said.

"His luck," Leonidas returned, "is largely a matter of ingenuity. Major Beeding is very, very ingenious. Haverstraw had a prowler. At once, Beeding established himself as a prowler hunter. He helped the police. When I tripped him, he made it seem as though he had personally been attacked by the prowler, and he helped the police to hunt with even greater vigor. That prowler made an excellent second line of defense, and Beeding realized it and took full advantage of it."

"What d'you mean?" Pink said.

"I was the first line. Beeding expected that when I returned from post A-1, and found Haymaker, I would at once call the police. He could guess that they would ply me with questions. Having set Haymaker's watch back to four-thirty, he knew I was in a bit of a hole—er—perhaps I should say, a bit of a hamper. He could guess that for the next few days, I would be subjected to considerable hue and cry and publicity. A number of boards might hurriedly stop wanting me on them—thus leaving space for him. The chances of my being labeled a suspect were very good, at least till brighter souls than Dunphy and O'Malley took over. And our local police are sometimes very loath to let brighter souls, like the state police, take over. But when and if people got through fussing about with me, they still would have the mysterious prowler to fuss about. To Beeding, he must have seemed God-sent."

"What about the dog, Mr. Witherall?" Meikeljohn asked. "The dog that wasn't?"

"He was Beeding's excuse to march around and keep tabs on my house, and me," Leonidas said. "He knew I'd been at my post. He must have wondered why I hadn't returned and found Haymaker, at once. He went out to see, with his dog. Probably he thought that the police summoned by Haverstraw were coming to my house, and it must have amazed him when they didn't. If he'd seen me, doubtless he'd have come and called, to force discovery of the body."

"It's going to be rather difficult, isn't it?" Meikle-john said. "We know practically everything, we've figured out the rest, and we haven't a shred of proof. Because he *has* established himself as a warden, and as hunting prowlers. *I* can't prove he came to my house. I never saw him. We can't prove he was at the store. We didn't see him."

"And he's in well with the cops," Pink added. "And with my brother, who probably saw him wardening. Brother would have apoplexy if anyone suggested that Beeding was a murderer! And, Bill, he established him-self as being at the swop, too! He dropped in early in the evening, and he came back again just before I left a while ago!"

"Doubtless," Leonidas said, "he went there directly upon leaving the store. M'yes. Now, I wonder why he left the—"

"I still almost can't believe it, though!" Meiklejohn said. "A man whom Mr. Haymaker trusted!"

"Ah, but you told me, yourself," Leonidas pointed out, "that Haymaker said that Beeding's appearance was deceptive! He appears to be hearty and tweedy, a man of action rather than a man of brains. But Hay-maker realized that he *did* have brains. That he was a man of ideas, and imagination."

"That's just what uncle told me, too," Dave said, "when I complained about the fellow. Uncle certainly was right! Well, we've got the motive, Shakespeare. He did it to keep uncle from exposing him—but what

about that sixth-floor business? D'you suppose he originally planned his murder there, but got crossed up
when uncle left?"

Leonidas shook his head.

"I don't know, Dave. At this point, I find myself
wondering why he left—"

"No dog," Pink said, "is nothing to convict anyone
on! And that's about all we've got. Dear me, I can't
see how we can get him, now that we've *got* him! We
haven't anything to confront him with! We can't confront him with no dog! We—"

"That car that's starting up!" Suzanne said suddenly.
"Look, Bill! Listen—hear that engine? See those lights?
Bill, *that* is *the* car, right over there! *See* those lights,
near together?"

A roadster passed them, and sped away up the street.

"Beeding's." Leonidas spoke almost casually. "I
recognize those pipe things sticking out. Now, I wonder why he left the Army! Whom do I know in the
Army? I wonder if—"

"Bill, you're certainly not going to sit here like a
bump on a log," Pink said, "wondering why he left the
Army! Go after him! Start up, Suzanne—go *after* him!"

"Don't bother, Suzanne," Leonidas said. "Er—why,
Pink? As you just said, what could we do after we got
him?"

"Well, we've got to *do* something!" Pink said defensively. "We can't just sit here, saying what a nice
bright, ingenious murderer he is!"

"Neither," Leonidas said, "can we at this point rush after him—particularly in this vehicle—and tell him that we know him for an evil man, a biffer, an embezzler, and a murderer!"

"All I know is," Pink said, "we've certainly got to *act!* We've got to *make* him confess! We've got to make him *admit* he killed Ross Haymaker!"

"If we go," Leonidas said, "and waggle our fingers in his face, and tell him firmly he must confess to Haymaker's murder, I'm very sure he'll march to the phone and call the police—but he won't confess! Don't lose sight of the fact that this murder is not a matter of common knowledge. That we have not made it such. That we—"

"Hold it, Bill!" Dave said. "Hold it! Can we—no. We can't. We're encircled."

Leonidas looked toward the sidewalk .

Admiral Coe-Chester was standing there.

And closing in on the beachwagon was what looked like most of the Navy.

CHAPTER 10

LEONIDAS quickly opened the door and stepped out.

"Er—good evening, sir," he said.

"D'evening," Coe-Chester returned.

And waited.

Leonidas drew a deep breath.

"I regret, sir," he said, "the necessity for—er—appropriating this vehicle. Regretfully, I had no opportunity to apprise you of the fact at the time."

"That so?"

Coe-Chester, Leonidas thought, looked like a composite picture of all the admirals in the world. Like a freshly scrubbed and very patient bulldog who was just barely able to hold himself in check.

"M'yes," Leonidas said. "Time was of the—er—essence."

Coe-Chester nodded toward the group in the beach-wagon.

"Car pool?" he inquired.

"These people," Leonidas was beginning to feel a little desperate, "have been assisting me this evening in a—er—"

"Oh, whyn't you say so!" Coe-Chester smiled. "Didn't understand you were working on my problem, Witherall! If you'd only spoken up this noon and said you wanted a car, been only too glad to lend you one. Thought of it, anyway, matter of fact. Getting anywhere?"

Leonidas drew another long breath. Coe-Chester thought he was working for him. Coe-Chester should be told the truth. But if he were!

"Er—we have managed, sir," he said, "to make certain discoveries."

That, he told himself, was nothing but the truth!

"Good!" Coe-Chester said. "Very anxious to get the matter settled, you know. Very. Think you'll settle it tonight?"

"Well, sir," Leonidas said, "that is on the laps of the gods. While I would not care to make any prophecies, I can—er—"

He paused, not quite knowing how to finish his sentence.

And Coe-Chester's next words made him wish violently that he had never started it!

"I get it. You think you will! Good! Good work, Witherall! I think I'll come along with you, if you don't mind."

"Oh, of course!" Leonidas said. "M'yes, indeed! Delighted to have you, sir. Of course, it may take us most of the night, but I'm sure you won't mind the inconvenience of it at all!"

He was gambling on Coe-Chester's dislike of any inconvenience, and lost.

"Need me with you, anyway. Need some authority. Harrison, go cancel those orders about the beachwagon —never mind. I'd better phone, myself. You wait right here for me, Witherall. Got to phone—"

He broke off as an enormous scarlet van drew up beside the beachwagon amid a tremendous squealing of brakes.

While Leonidas was digesting the fact that it was a Haymaker van, Jinx jumped out of the front seat and ran toward him.

"Hey, Shakespeare! We hunted all over—" her eyes caught the gold braid on Coe-Chester's sleeve, and she abruptly stopped.

"Miss—er—Jinx," Leonidas said, "Admiral Coe-Chester. Miss Jinx is still another member of my—er— car pool."

"Hm." Coe-Chester. looked at her appreciatively. "Been around, Witherall, haven't you? Wait here. I'll be back in a few minutes."

He marched off his men, who looked a little thwarted. They had, Leonidas noted, taken a far greater interest in the proceedings after the arrival of Jinx.

"Gee, I never saw anything like *him!*" Jinx said. "Like a Christmas tree—gee, Shakespeare, we been hunting you the hell and gone! Those two Lady Volunteers almost grabbed me in that drugstore, and I ducked

261

out and ran away, and gee, if Turk didn't see me running, and yell! He was in the van, here. So I got in, and just then he saw this girl in an oil truck he's been having to chase for Mr. Haymaker, so we left—and when we finally got back, we couldn't find you at the swop, or anywhere. You see, besides hunting you, we had to keep after this girl, only we've lost her again. That's what Turk's been doing all day!"

"So," Leonidas said, "I found out. I have the girl, right here in the beachwagon—"

"Hey, Turk!" Jinx said. "Turk, *he's* got her!"

The young fellow in the turtle-neck sweater who swung down from the truck was nearly large enough, Leonidas thought, to be an entire Dalton Demon team all by himself.

"Chum," he said to Leonidas, "you got that blonde? The Quarl girl?"

Leonidas pointed toward Suzanne.

"Chum," Turk said in a pleading voice, "is she through? Is she going *home?* The boss said I had to follow her till she went home!"

"Has Jinx told you," Leonidas asked, "about Mr. Haymaker?"

"Chum, she told me about the boss, and that's why I want that blonde to get home! I'm going to help you, see?"

"Listen, Turk," Leonidas said, "did you follow Miss Quarl to Olde Forge Road this afternoon? You did?

Good. D'you remember seeing Major Beeding's car over there?"

"I seen his car," Turk said. "Him, too. I waved, but he pretended like he didn't see me. Jinx told me about the hampers and all, too. It was me."

"Er—what was you?"

"After we left Olde Forge Road, see, the blonde stops to get some sandwiches. So I duck downtown, see, to talk to the boss. I know he wants to hear what's been going on, see, and, chum, I had plenty to tell him!"

"He used the freight elevator," Jinx said. "That's why I didn't see him. He went up in that, and Mr. Haymaker'd gone, so he walked down to the sixth floor to get a sandwich himself—"

"And when I come out of the restaurant," Turk chimed in, "I see these two hampers—one's the bread, and one's the laundry, see? And Mary Miller in the restaurant says will I shove 'em along to the freight elevators, so I do. I don't know you're in 'em, chum. I don't know *any*body's in 'em! I just shoved 'em along, that's all I did! Say, you found out *who* the guy is?"

"M'yes."

"You let me at him, chum!"

Leonidas looked at him, and then looked speculatively at the scarlet van.

"Bill!" Pink called out. "Bill! come here! Bill, Dave

263

says he heard Admiral Coe-Chester say he was coming with us! Bill, we can't have that! Bill!"

"Turk," Leonidas said suddenly, "drive that van—oh, eight or ten blocks away from here. In the direction of Birch Hill. We'll follow."

"We going to get the guy, chum?"

"We," Leonidas said, "are going to make a stab at it! Go along with Turk, Jinx."

He turned back to the beachwagon.

"Bill!" Pink said. "You must *do* something about that man! We can't—"

"Suzanne," Leonidas said, "follow the Haymaker van. I know we can't, Pink. We have a little matter of Cannae to attend to."

"What's that, Mr. Witherall?" Meiklejohn said, as the beachwagon started off.

"Cannae." Leonidas spelled it. "C-a-n-n-a-e."

"Oh, I know that," Pink said. "That's what Lieutenant Haseltine always thinks of. For pages and pages, he gets buffeted by fate—more buffets and more fate than you'd ever imagine possible—and then he thinks of Cannae, and solves everything."

"I'm afraid I still don't understand," Meiklejohn said.

"Cannae," Leonidas said, "is the historic battle between the Romans and the Carthaginians, fought in Apulia in the year 216 B. C., in which the small, weak army of Hannibal cut the incomparable forces of

264

eighty-five thousand proud Roman legionnaires to pieces—"

"Shreds," Dave corrected. "Haseltine always says shreds."

"To shreds. In that," Leonidas continued, "by means of an ingenious strategical concentration, it caught the enemy from the flank with cavalry, and surrounded him. Clausewitz and Schlieffen of the Prussian General Staff elaborated the idea of Cannae into a general theoretical doctrine, and then compressed the doctrine into an exact strategical system. That, in brief, is Cannae!"

"And if you actually wrote Haseltine," Dave said, "you couldn't reel that off any better!"

"Are you," Meiklejohn still sounded puzzled, "referring to the blitzkrieg?"

"Basically," Leonidas said, "but without latter-day elaborations. It does not necessarily involve—er—getting there firstest with the mostest men, but getting there firstest. Has the van stopped, Suzanne? Call out and tell those two to come back here."

"You sound," Dave remarked, "as if you were suddenly very sure of yourself, and of all this mess, too, Shakespeare!"

"M'yes," Leonidas said. "Er—somewhat to my own bewilderment, I rather think that I am. While I entertained no doubt concerning Beeding's guilt, the sixth-floor problem has been prickling me to a greater degree than the gremlins prickled my eyeballs this

265

afternoon. And Coe-Chester's problem has been prickling me even more painfully than either. Coe-Chester took it for granted just now that I was solving his problem for him. It has subsequently occurred to me that very possibly I am. That, without in the least being aware of it, I have been solving his problem all along!"

"Bill, what are you talking about!" Pink said.

"The sixth floor. It was the umbrella," Leonidas told her.

"The *what?*"

"Umbrella. An umbrella is a very handy instrument in which to secrete certain things," Leonidas said. "Not as impressive as a briefcase, to be sure, but quite as effective for the transportation of small objects, and not a bit inclined to arouse suspicion in the breast of the beholder. Do any of you have a pencil and paper? I've got to make out this schedule rather accurately, and it will have to be written down."

"Schedule? What for? What d'you mean, umbrella? What's it got to do with Admiral Coe-Chester? *Or* the sixth floor?" Pink demanded.

"We were after umbrellas," Leonidas said. "We announced the fact. At least, you did, and I concurred. Beeding was expecting someone after an umbrella, but he very definitely did not expect us. M'yes, I'm inclined to think he was slightly nervous. I also think that he spotted us—and me in particular—when we left the elevator. After all, that washroom incident proves he's quite adept at spotting. M'yes."

"Bill! Talk sense!" Pink said. "What—"

"And I'm very sure," Leonidas went on, "that some-one must have passed on to him the apparently cur-rent rumor that I in some way am involved with the government. Possibly, as Henry Compton suggested, in the secret service. M'yes, indeed!"

"Bill, *are* you?" Pink asked excitedly.

"No. Does anyone have a pencil and paper?"

"Here's a pencil, Mr. Witherall." Meiklejohn gave it to him.

"Er—thank you." Leonidas considered it a personal triumph that the little man was not attempting to thrust aspirin at him again. "D'you have any paper?"

"Just this small pocket account book, Mr. Witherall. Will it do?"

"Splendidly, thank you—get in, Jinx. Crowd in, Turk. Er—meet Miss Quarl, by the way. I believe you know her by sight—oh, tell him to come back, Jinx! Suzanne isn't going to bite him! She understands every-thing, now. Before I begin, do any of you know any generals?"

"This a game, chum?" Turk inquired.

"Er—no," Leonidas said. "I rather want a flesh-and-blood general, preferably one in the immediate vicinity. All the generals of my acquaintance are scattered over the face of the wide world."

"If you'll settle for a colonel," Dave said, "I know one on this very block."

"D'you know him well enough to wake him up,"

Leonidas inquired, "and drag him from his bed?"

"Well, he's a cousin of my mother's," Dave said, "and he gave me a rocking horse when I was three— yes, I think I know him well enough to roust him out of his downy cot."

"Then run along and—er—roust," Leonidas said. "See if you can possibly find out from him—or have him find out from one of his colleagues—why Major Beeding left the Army. While it's not going to affect our plans any, I'd like to know the real reason for his having left the service. After contemplating his actions tonight, I'm very sure he's not in any way physically disabled. Indeed, I'd be willing to testify in court that Major Beeding was definitely in—er—the pink."

"He sure is, chum," Turk said. "I got him to sub on the Demons last week's game. He's like an ox."

"What are we going to *do?*" Pink asked as Dave opened the door and got out.

"We know so much more than Beeding has any right to suspect we know," Leonidas said, "that we are going to—er—confound him with our knowledge. We may just possibly bring it off and extract a confession from him. At all events, we are going to try. Go along, Dave. If you can't get anywhere within ten minutes, give it up and come back. M'yes, we're going to try."

"*How* can we make him confess?" Meiklejohn asked. "My, my, Mr. Witherall, you're not planning any— uh—"

"No, Meiklejohn, we're not going to—er—jab red-

hot needles under his fingernails, or anything like that,"
Leonidas said. "Run along, Dave. Now, has anyone a
flashlight?"

Suzanne produced one from the pocket of her mink
coat.

"Thank you," Leonidas said. "Will you hold it,
Meiklejohn, please? Now, all of you be very quiet while
I attempt to work this problem out in the very best
Haseltine manner!"

Before ten minutes passed, Dave returned.

"I knew when I left that it was a fool's errand," he
said. "I *knew* George wouldn't know!"

"And—er—didn't he?" Leonidas looked up from the
notebook.

"He didn't know anything definite, Shakespeare, but
he'd heard a dandy rumor, and I think it's the sort of
thing you probably were guessing at. George says it's
pure, unadulterated gossip, and he heard it from usually unreliable sources, and then it was only whispered
behind a couple of locked doors."

"It certainly sounds promising!" Pink said skep-
tically. "What was it?"

"Something about building contracts," Dave said.
"Back in the early days of rush camp building. George
doesn't know if it was lumber, or plumbing, or just
pay-roll padding. He has absolutely no proof, and
there never was a speck of publicity about it—George
says there was a period when people were terribly
touchy about having that sort of thing screamed to the
skies. Politics and all. George thinks if Beeding was

269

messed up in some deal, he might have done a bit of bargaining to keep it quiet, too. You know, promised to give it all back, and to tell a lot more if only they'd let him quietly resign, and all. George says on the other hand, Beeding just may have had a bad heart, or a bum lung, or something."

Turk snorted.

"Chum," he said, "I'm telling you that guy is an ox! Nothing wrong with *him!*"

"I concur," Leonidas said. "I think we will assume that account juggling is nothing new in Beeding's life! Now, let's run through this—"

He broke off as a beachwagon drew up alongside them, and Admiral Coe-Chester jumped out.

"Oh, dear!" Pink said. "Oh, dear, oh, dear! And all those sailors, too! Oh—"

"Matter, Witherall?" Coe-Chester demanded as he opened the door. "Couldn't you *wait?*"

"At that time," Leonidas said, "it—er—appeared unwise to remain in that particular spot."

"If you think I'm going to let you get away again," Coe-Chester said, "you're mistaken, Witherall! Way I've trailed you around tonight! Junk parades—"

"Er—*what?*"

"Junk parades," Coe-Chester said firmly. "Been hunting you before that, of course, but you weren't ever home. Junk parades, bond speeches, lions' heads—I tell you, Witherall, if you're planning any more flitting, I'm going to flit with you! Makes me nervous to watch you. Feel safer being *with* you!"

Leonidas put on his pince-nez and stared thoughtfully at the admiral.

"Er—tell me, Roderick," he said at last, "er—could you bear to take orders? I have no time for explaining now."

"Been taking orders all my life!" Coe-Chester retorted. "Don't see why you ask a damn fool thing like that!"

"Turk," Leonidas said, "move over and make room for the admiral. Sit down on the floor, Roderick, while I do a bit more paper work."

"Operations schedule?" Coe-Chester inquired in professional tones.

"M'yes, I've got to write in a part for you," Leonidas said. "Er—could I possibly make use of your—er—forces?"

"Why not?"

"They can drive Meiklejohn back to the store for his errand," Leonidas said, "and that will give Suzanne time—m'yes. Turk and Dave and I could have managed adequately at my house, but I feared we'd have to resort to burnt cork or the Dalton Demons to achieve any success at Beeding's. He knows us. We'll use your men for that, too. M'yes. They can be very helpful. I'm very glad you tracked us down, Roderick."

"What do I do?" Coe-Chester demanded.

"While your part is very largely decorative," Leon-

271

idas said, "in the sense that you are to impress, rather than to act, I think perhaps you'd also better serve as Chief of Operations. You'll supervise the timing, which is quite tricky. Oh, and I'll need a sailor for Henry Compton, too."

"What d'you mean, you'll need a sailor for brother?" Pink demanded.

"If Compton's still hovering around my doorstep," Leonidas said, "he'll have to be immobilized—"

"Don't know about that," Coe-Chester interrupted. "Compton's a civilian, isn't he? Got to be careful about civilians. Can't go around immobilizing them, you know!"

"Roderick," Leonidas said firmly, "if Henry Compton is on my doorstep, one of your men is going to immobilize him, and that's all there is to it! D'you want this problem solved, or don't you?"

"Sorry," Coe-Chester said meekly. "Forgot."

"Don't," Leonidas said, "let it happen again, Roderick! Now, if Compton's not at my house, we'll post a sailor on *his* doorstep. This was another problem that was worrying me, you know. I hated to waste Dave on such a comparatively minor thing. This sailor will stand guard at Compton's door, and if Compton comes out, the sailor will inform him that owing to—er—maneuvers, his grounds are temporarily a military area, and to go right back inside, at once! We cannot afford to take the chance of having Henry S. C. Compton gum this up! Now—"

He wrote busily for several moments in Meikle-john's notebook.

"Now!" he said, "Now, if you'll call over your men, Roderick! Open the door so they can hear, Suzanne. Ready? This is what you are all going to do, and none of you can fail me. There can't be any slip-ups. Is that clearly understood?"

Fifteen minutes later, the scarlet Haymaker van set off, followed by the two beachwagons.

Still later, just as the tower clock of the Dalton Congregational Church struck three times, Jinx tripped out from behind a bush on Birch Hill Road, went to Beeding's front door, and rang the bell.

"Mis-ter Bee-ding!" she called out. "Mis-ter Bee-ding! Oh, Mr. *Bee*-ding!"

Beeding's head appeared at an upstairs window.

"Oh, Mis-ter Bee-ding!" Jinx shrilled.

"Who is it? What's the matter?"

"It's Jinx, Mr. Beeding. Gee, I hate to disturb you, Mr. Beeding, but can I talk with you?"

"What's the matter?" Beeding demanded.

"Have you seen my sister, Mr. Beeding? She came to tell you why I couldn't go to the morale class on account of my mother had to go to the hospital and I had to go with her, Mr. Beeding! They say they've got to operate, and now my sister's never come home —was she here, Mr. Beeding? Gee, I'm so afraid some-thing's happened to her, and I called the cops to see if there'd been an accident, and they said there'd been a prowler up here—gee, Mr. Beeding, I'm nearly crazy!"

"Wait a minute," Beeding said. "I'll be down."

In the bushes, Admiral Coe-Chester nodded approvingly.

"Good girl," he said. "She's got him down, and it took her no time at all. Bet he'll ask her in. You'll have to be ready to jump, Pink. Because you'll have to be near the door when she comes out—"

"Shush," Pink said. "Here he is. Listen!"

"Oh, Mr. Beeding!" Jinx said, "I sent my sister Evelyn up to tell you why I couldn't go to morale class, on account of I hated so to miss it and I didn't want to get any demerits, and it was only because of mother. Mother had to go to the hospital, and they say they've got to operate, and gee, now I can't find Evelyn, and nobody's seen her noplace—gee, Mr. Beeding, was she *here*, huh?"

"Why," Beeding said hesitantly, "I didn't—wait, now, Jinx, maybe I *did* just catch sight of her! Does she look like you?"

"Yes," Jinx said, "and she has red hair, and she was dressed like me. Gee, what d'you suppose's happened, Mr. Beeding? The cops said there'd been a prowler but they knew he wasn't around here any place now, and they said they didn't know what *they* could do, and for me just to wait and see if she didn't turn up, because she might be anywhere—gee, Mr. Beeding, I

274

don't know what to do, but if you think you seen her, maybe you'll help me hunt for her, huh?"

Her final "huh" was so poignant that Coe-Chester sniffed in sympathy.

"Why, you poor kid!" Beeding said. "Sure. I'll help you have a look around. Come in while I get dressed, and then we'll go take a look around. I'm almost sure she can't be up here, because the police combed—"

Jinx went in, and the door closed.

"Hah!" Coe-Chester said. "Got him up, got him dressed, got him inspired to go out. Wonder how they're coming along at Bill's house?"

"Wonder if Meiklejohn's got back from the store," Pink said. "Oh, look—you can see Beeding up there in his bedroom! See? He's rushing like mad."

"Watch carefully, now!" Coe-Chester said. "Think you better get started, Pink. Stand behind those evergreens till you see the door open—remember, *you've* got to get him away from the house!"

When Jinx and Beeding stepped out, Pink was in front of the flagstone walk.

She turned her flashlight toward the front door.

"Oh, Mr. Beeding, what luck—oh! I didn't *realize* you weren't *alone!*"

She half turned away, as if the sight of Beeding emerging from his house with a girl at that hour both startled and shocked her.

"I'm just helping this poor child look for her sister,"

275

Beeding said. "She just came and told me she'd lost
her sister, and I was going to help her—what I mean
is, her sister was here earlier, at least I think she was,
and she hasn't come home. The sister, I mean—"

"Really, Major Beeding, you don't have to explain
anything to me!" Pink said. "I understand."

"Is anything the matter, Mrs. Lately, that you're
here at this hour?" Beeding sounded as if he felt very
uncomfortable. "Nothing's wrong, I hope?"

"It's only my key ring," Pink said. "I was going to
ask you to help me hunt for it, but of course, if you're
already busy hunting someone's sister, I'm sure you
don't want to be bothered. I dare say I'll find it, myself."

"Key ring? You've lost a key ring? Here?" Beeding
said.

"My beachwagon," Pink said unhappily, "ran out
of gas. Way down on Chestnut near Maple. Brother
said he'd take me home from the swop, but he forgot, and I've had to walk every step of the way. With
this cake, too."

"Cake?"

"In this box here, under my arm. I swopped it,"
Pink said. "And it's the *most* uncomfortable thing to
carry! Anyway, I just stopped to shift it, and get a
handkerchief, and when I put my hand in my coat
pocket, I realized my key ring, with the beachwagon's
keys and my house keys and all—it's gone! And worst
of all, my diamond ring, too!"

"On a *key* ring?" Beeding was beginning to sound thoroughly confused.

"I put it on the key ring when I washed my hands at the swop," Pink said, "and then forgot to take it off. I remember now that I heard a little clink—that must have been when the ring fell out. Oh, I hate to lose that ring, and the keys, and the diamond! Someone might give the keys to the key drive, but they'll never return that diamond ring, ever! But I'm sure you're not interested in my troubles, Major Beeding. Don't let me keep you from—what was it, hunting a sister?"

"Gee," Jinx said, "that's too bad—losing a *diamond!* Gee, hadn't we better help her, huh?"

Coe-Chester grinned to himself. In Beeding's boots, he thought, he'd be torn between being a gentleman and helping Pink, and dashing off to prove that he *was* hunting a lost sister.

"That's sweet of you, dear," Pink said. "I couldn't have lost it beyond here, because it was right here I realized the key ring was gone. But if you've lost a sister, please don't bother!"

"I've lost her, all right," Jinx said, "but gee, a *diamond!* Let's us help her, Mr. Beeding!"

"I really think it was down nearer the foot of the hill," Pink said. "Near that old boulder. If you had a flashlight, you could take one side of the road, and I could take the other. But I don't wish to *delay* you—"

"Come on," Beeding said briefly.

277

Coe-Chester watched the trio straggle off down the hill. When they reached the foot, he stepped out into the middle of Birch Hill Road and blinked his own flashlight in the direction of Leonidas's house.

A moment later the scarlet Haymaker van rolled down the street. Leonidas jumped out.

"All right?"

"Proceeding on schedule," Coe-Chester said. "Jinx fixed the front door catch while he was dressing, I'm pretty sure. You ought to be able to go right in. Meiklejohn back?"

"M'yes. Go down and oversee Suzanne, will you, Roderick? He's got to be kept away at least ten minutes."

"Right."

Coe-Chester, carefully keeping on the grass, hurried down the hill and arrived within earshot just in time to hear Beeding decide that they'd better give up.

"My advice," Beeding said, "would be for you to wait till daybreak, Mrs. Lately. No one's likely to spot it before then. And I promised this child I'd take a look around the woods for her sister."

"Oh, yes," Pink said. "Yes, of course. The sister. By the way, how did you lose her?"

"Gee," Jinx said, "the time I been having! You see it's my night for morale class, but—"

While she ran once more through her routine, she took a few steps toward a giant boulder at the side of the road, and Pink casually followed her, occasion-
278

ally interjecting exclamations of sorrow and surprise.

"So," Jinx concluded, "that's how I lost my sister. I don't—say, listen, did you hear something then?"

"Hear *what?*" Beeding, who had been impatiently shuffling around, walked over to them. "Jinx, we should be getting—"

"But listen, Mr. Beeding! It was like a woman's voice I heard!"

Beeding listened.

"By George!" he said. "I heard it then, and it certainly *does* sound like a woman's voice! Give me that flash. I'll go into the woods and see!"

The next time the voice was heard, it came from a different part of the woods altogether, and Coe-Chester was filled with admiration at Suzanne's agility.

Then, at the sound of something falling, he stiffened.

The girl had tripped!

And Witherall had said that under no circumstances should Beeding be permitted to catch a glimpse of Suzanne's face!

Could he, Coe-Chester wondered, possibly manage to get between Beeding and the girl? He could try, he told himself stoutly, and slipped into the woods.

"Oh, Major Beeding!" he heard Pink's voice ring out. "Major Beeding, look out for the brook! Look out for—oh, dear!"

Coe-Chester stopped as he heard a splash, followed by several paragraphs of unprintable language.

"Well, goodness *me!*" Pink said. "I *told* you to look out for that brook, Major Beeding! Why weren't you more careful? I *knew* that brook was there—it always *has* been! I tried to save you—I put out my hand to *grab* you before you got to it!"

"Dammit, you pushed me in!" Beeding said furiously. "You *pushed* me!"

"Well, really, Major Beeding! All I can say is, you have a strange sense of gratitude!" Pink sounded highly indignant. "And I shall certainly tell my brother that his dear good friend the major *cer*tainly uses some *very* unpleasant language when—"

"Well," Beeding interrupted hurriedly, "maybe you *did* mean to help me, Mrs. Lately, but it certainly *felt* more as if you were giving me a push! Now I've lost all sense of the direction of that sound—I'm sure it was a woman, and I think that crash and thud was her falling!"

"If it was a woman," Pink said, "she's gone, I'm sure. I can't hear a thing, now."

"Where's that light?" Beeding demanded. "Where'd it go? Who's got it? Who took my light? Did you take my light, Mrs. Lately?"

"Really, Major Beeding, I don't know why you think *I'd* take your light!" Pink was the acme of injured innocence. "*You* had it yourself when you fell into the brook."

"Well, where is it now? I'm sure that was a woman, and I'm going to take my light and go after her—if

I can find the light! Help me find it! Jinx, come help hunt for that light."

Minutes passed in futile search, while Beeding got angrier and angrier. Just as Coe-Chester was glancing at the radium dial of his watch, Pink spoke up.

"I can understand my wanting to find my key ring, and this girl's wanting to find her sister, but really, Major Beeding, I think it's silly of you to persist in trying to find a little old flashlight at *this* time of the morning—do you *know* how late it's getting to be? And you all soaking, dripping wet! *I* think you'd better go back home and change your clothes!"

"Gee, I think so, too," Jinx said. "You're shivering, Mr. Beeding, and that's a bad sign!"

"I want to find out if that was a woman!"

"Gee," Jinx said, "it must have been a deer, or something. I haven't heard a sound since you fell into the brook!"

"Deer or woman, I'm sure she's gone." Pink spoke with certainty, knowing that the time table called for Suzanne's departure from the scene at least six minutes before. While her own unscheduled gesture of pushing Beeding into the brook had eliminated the game of tag that Leonidas had planned, it and the flashlight had taken up the time very nicely. "Come along, Major Beeding, we—"

Coe-Chester slipped away and hurried back up the hill.

The scarlet Haymaker van had disappeared. Beeding had never seen it, heard it, or guessed that it had called at his house. Things had worked out, Coe-Chester thought, very well indeed. There'd been no need to utilize Plan B, where the van's presence would have been explained to Beeding by Seamen Fraddy and Soloman, one wearing Turk's turtle-neck sweater, and the other Dave Haymaker's coat. Bill had made up a very good story for them, too, all about a broken-down van, and delivering a rug that was plainly marked as a gift.

Coe-Chester waited till Beeding, flanked by Jinx and Pink, started up the flagstone walk.

"What you need is a toddy," Pink was saying, "and even if you don't think so, I'm going to make one for you!"

The front door opened.

Coe-Chester waved at Fraddy and Soloman, back in uniform, and beamed as he walked rapidly toward Beeding's back door. He liked to have things go off well.

"A hot toddy," Pink said as they entered the hall, "is—what's the matter, Major Beeding?"

"There's a light on in my library! *I* didn't leave a light on in the library, I know I didn't!"

He walked toward the doorway.

Pink and Jinx remained in the hall. They knew the sight that was going to greet him in the library.

He was going to find Haymaker there, with the samurai sword. And his black Homburg hat beside him.

282

Pink could hear his sharp intake of breath.

Then footsteps sounded on the stairs behind him, and Beeding swung around to see Meiklejohn, with a ledger under his arm, slowly descending.

Without a word, Meiklejohn passed by him and went into the library, and at once Leonidas entered the library from the living room. With him was Dave Haymaker, who carried a sheaf of papers in his hand.

Pink was watching Beeding's back. The man had begun to shiver uncontrollably.

Then the hall door beside Beeding opened, and Coe-Chester marched in. He was carrying an umbrella.

Beeding, his teeth chattering, swung on his heels and started to dash for the front door.

Then he stopped.

Turk, with two sailors, stood there and looked at him.

Leonidas came out into the hallway.

"Ah, Major Beeding," he said. "This way, please. We'd like you to sit down at your desk and write us a full confession—"

Beeding's mouth worked, but no words came.

"Dave has some papers," Leonidas waved toward the first chapter of a new Haseltine which Dave was clutching, "which his uncle sent him this afternoon. They—er—concern you."

"But—but he said he hadn't mentioned it to a soul!"

"Did he indeed!" Leonidas said. "Had you forgot-

ten what a cautious man he was? And Meiklejohn
has accounts handy, in case you want to refresh your
mind. He—"

"But—but there were only two ledgers that mattered!"

"Er—three." Leonidas pointed to the ledger he had
retrieved from his own attic. "Meiklejohn leaves
nothing to chance. And Admiral Coe-Chester has the
codes that were in the umbrella, and—"

"Trouble with you, Bill," Coe-Chester said gruffly,
"you're soft. You, Beeding, go in there and write that
confession!"

Beeding's eyes traveled from the admiral to Leonidas, then to the floor, and then to Dave, with the
sheaf of papers, and to Meiklejohn, with the ledger.

"You going to?" Coe-Chester barked. "Or'm I going to have to call in the boys? Stop that shivering,
and answer me!"

"Y-yes!"

"Dammit," Coe-Chester said, "when you talk to me,
say *sir!*"

"What I don't understand," Pink said later over at
Leonidas's house, "is about the codes and the umbrella, and all. Only first tell me, did Beeding confess
to everything, and did it all happen the way we
thought?"

"It did, and he did." Leonidas frowned. "It's my
impression that instead of sending the elevator girls

to a morale class, he should have gone himself. He was apparently completely shattered—and I think your pushing him into the brook had something to do with it. You see, Pink, Coe-Chester told me at lunch today that some codes had been stolen from Meredith's—not codes in current use, but new codes, as yet unused. Their theft would have caused no damage, but a lot of work would have gone for nothing."

"How'd Beeding ever get the codes from there?"

"The Meredith pool is open to a select group of Dalton men twice a week," Leonidas said. "After they'd been swimming last night, the codes were reported stolen. Someone had carelessly left an office unlocked. I knew all the men on the list, and had vouched for them, so Coe-Chester asked me to think over the names and see if I could round him up some suspects."

"How'd you guess Beeding? And *why* were they in that umbrella on the sixth floor's Lost and Found?" Pink said. "That was why you sent Meiklejohn back to the store, wasn't it, for the umbrella?"

"M'yes. Beeding stole the codes," Leonidas said. "He intended to sell them, and use the money to cover his shortages at Haymaker's, which were apparently getting out of hand."

"But if the codes were still in the umbrella when Meiklejohn brought it back just now," Pink said, "then Beeding never sold them after all!"

"Exactly. He'd cleared the sixth floor this afternoon. He was waiting for a man to come give him money, for which he would hand over the umbrella with the codes in it. After all," Leonidas said, "that is not the sort of deal one transacts by mail."

"But the man never *came?*"

"He never came. Beeding did not get the money to cover his shortages. He couldn't make restitution, as he'd planned. That is why Haymaker was killed."

"Of all places, why'd he leave the codes and the umbrella there at the store?"

"Why not? No one, certainly, would look for them there, and no one would claim that particular umbrella—" Leonidas got up to answer the door chimes, and ushered Coe-Chester back into the living room. "Everything all right over at Beeding's now?"

"Fool cops think I got him all by myself! Must say, Bill, I'm glad to get the codes back intact. He only broke the outer seal. Hated to think of 'em going to waste. Nice night's work. Lunch tomorrow? Join us, Pink?"

"Love to—look, I'm still confused," Pink said. "If Beeding went to all that work to clear the sixth floor, he expected the man to come and buy 'em. Why didn't he?"

"All the fault of young Gordon," Coe-Chester said. "Impetuous boy. He's the one left the door unlocked last night. All broken up about it. He saw this fellow get off the train this morning, and nabbed him. Knew his face from some of our pictures. Nabbed him right away. Never stopped to figure he ought to wait and follow—see our trouble then? We had the fellow who was going to buy the codes—"

"How'd you know he was?" Pink interrupted.

"Habit of his. We knew the bird and wanted him, anyway. We had him, see, but we didn't know who took 'em. Found out, thanks to Bill—I still think Beeding was mixed up with this fellow before, Bill, when he was in the Army. He wouldn't say so now, but I think he will before we're through with him. Well, got to get the boys home. See you tomorrow!"

"I wonder," Pink said when Leonidas came back from the door, "if Suzanne *ever* waked up at all while Dave and Meiklejohn were taking her home? She was so tired—I hear another car out there. See if it's Dave with your coupe. He's got to take me home."

Leonidas peered out the window.

"It's a beachwagon—why, it's Jinx getting out! And there's Turk with the van!"

Pink followed him to the front door.

"It's mine!" she said. "Jinx, isn't that *my* beachwagon?"

"Yes, Mrs. Lately. Turk heard you talk about it, and I knew where it was, so we got it for you."

"But it was locked!"

"Oh, that doesn't matter to Turk!"

"And out of gas!" Pink said.

"You got some now, courtesy of Haymaker's," Jinx said. "Good night!"

Pink and Leonidas watched the van depart.

287

"And to think I thought Dalton was dull! Bill, give me Lady Baltimore. I'm going home. To think if I hadn't baked that cake in the hope of getting a pound of coffee, and left that sword on the porch while I rushed downtown to get walnuts for the frosting, and got caught in the rain—Shakespeare, what did you just take from the pocket of your coat?"

"The fat lady's pound of coffee. I swopped the lion's head for it. Here. Now, give *me* Lady Baltimore! What a saga that cake could write. 'My Night in Dalton,' by a Lady of Quality, or—"

"Bill, look who's coming up the street! He barely waited for daylight!"

"Your brother? My report," Leonidas said, "is ready! See, on the table? I've stamped it with that 'File for Record' stamp, and under 'Incidents,' I wrote 'None'—look out, Pink, I must give it to him and try to make amends. Ah, Compton, your report! *So* careless of me not—"

Compton snatched the report, glared, and marched away.

"Dear me, I fear he's still annoyed. 'File for Record'—that has a certain ring, hasn't it? 'File for Record'—m'yes, I think that would make a nice title for Haseltine."

"I know a better one," Pink said, "if anyone could write tonight! 'Taken—' "

" 'For a Beeding,' " Leonidas said. "M'yes, I thought of that, too!"